PRIMA

This is a work of fiction. Similarities to real people, places, or events are entirely coincidental.

PRIMA

First edition. July 11, 2025.

ISBN: 978-1964094052

Written by John Pulver.

For Diana

Chapter 1

The ocean at the Concha Pointe pier is blue and beautiful, with gentle waves. That is how I remember it. Unless I cannot sleep—then, my memory is of a violent ocean, twisted green and black, hurtling itself into white spume on the barnacled pier pilings. In fragments of my dreams, it is only gray. Perhaps my shifting memories aren't odd. The ocean, like a person, can be many things.

On my twentieth birthday, my parents took me to my favorite restaurant, The Pelican's Roost, which sits at the entrance of the pier. From our balcony seats, I watched the sanderlings scooting at the water's edge. Seagulls made piercing calls as they battled for scraps. Farther out, pelicans glided above the water.

As we sat there waiting to order, a surprising thing happened when my father's phone rang.

Here we go again, I thought. *He'll be taking the call and rushing off without even having dinner with us.*

Instead, I was astonished when he unclipped the phone from his belt and turned it off.

He said, "That'll take care of that. No more interruptions."

I had never seen him *not* answer his phone, or at least not look at who was calling before ignoring it. I pinched the underside of my thigh to make sure I wasn't dreaming.

As he placed his phone on the table, I looked at my mother. She arched her eyebrows high. Lifting them was no small feat considering all the fillers and Botox treatments she'd had on her forehead.

Rather than sit there with my mouth hanging open, I said, "Wow, Dad, don't you have important calls you might miss?"

"Maybe, but the only thing that matters right now is enjoying our meal for your birthday, Prima."

"Oh, right, of course. This is great," I said, stumbling for words. "I wish Garrett could have come. He really wanted to be here, but people can't live without having their pizzas delivered, apparently. His boss wouldn't let him off."

My father nodded and said, "Hmm. That's too bad, but just the three of us is nice."

"Maybe if you have time this weekend, he could come over. He wants to talk with you about something."

"That would be fine. I'm not planning on working this weekend."

My mother couldn't contain herself any longer.

"You're not going to be working?" she said, nearly choking on her words. "Don't you mean you're not going into the office?"

As long as I could remember, my father was always working. He was a fertility specialist MD who owned a group practice that served the aging affluent; people who had waited to have babies until the odds of conception were against them. It seemed that even when he supposedly wasn't working, he was taking calls or shuffling into his home office to take care of details that popped into his mind. At best, he was always preoccupied.

In the past few weeks, he'd been more distracted than usual. Kind of edgy and irritable.

My mother and I had a hand signal that we used to warn each other about his mood. When he wasn't looking, we'd cup our hands in a C-shape, which stood for cranky. We'd been making the "C" a lot lately.

Suddenly, today his mood had shifted.

My father didn't answer her. He simply looked out the window at the sky, and then down at his phone. I feared he might turn it on again if my mother started badgering him. I wanted him in a good mood for my birthday—and for when Garrett came over to see him.

"Robert," my mother said. "Since when are you not working?"

I had to do something. I slipped the ring in my pocket onto my finger.

To distract her, I blurted out louder than I intended, "I have a surprise."

It felt like every head in the restaurant turned in my direction.

My cheeks turned red—I don't like being the center of attention. I took my hand out of my pocket and held it above the table. My mother grabbed my wrist and pulled my hand toward her to take a closer look.

"What a beautiful diamond," she said appraisingly. "It has hints of blue. French cut, I believe, not your typical brilliant round." My mother knew her diamonds. As an afterthought, she said, "This is an engagement ring."

When she released my hand, I moved my hand over to my father. I doubted if he could tell one diamond from another.

"I assume that is why Garrett wants to see me? He must have delivered thousands of pizzas to buy it."

"Nope, it's old. It belonged to his grandmother. Daddy, when you see him, you have to act surprised. He's kind of traditional. I promised him I'd keep it a secret until after he spoke with you."

"I don't think that will be a problem," he said.

"You have to act surprised too, Mom."

Reluctantly, I slipped the ring off and returned it to my pocket.

"Don't you think you're a little young?" my mother asked.

"No," I said, bracing for an argument. When it didn't come, I added, "Besides, we're not planning on getting married right away. Not until he finishes his bachelor's. Now that he'll be transferring to Stanford, he's afraid I might meet someone while he's away. He said the ring is an insurance policy."

My father laughed. My mother didn't.

My father dipped his chin and peered at my mother from beneath pinched eyebrows.

"Did you know about this?" he asked. "Not that I'm surprised. They've been going together for over a year."

When my mother shook her head, he turned to me and said, "And how do I know he's good enough for my little girl?"

"He's going to be an investment banker. He's going to be rich. He's like you, Daddy. He's a straight A student, very mature, and he has plans to have his Master's by the year 2000. Sometimes I think he's *ten* years older than I am, not just one. He's even got a full scholarship. Actually, he got one B, but the teacher was unfair."

I started to rattle on about him. I could have talked about Garrett endlessly, but the waiter came to our table, which cut short my chattering.

The waiter's name was Delphineaus. My mother always called him Del. He was from Costa Rica and it seemed that each time we saw him he became more feminine. He was passing and his latest transformation was breasts that jiggled under his puffy shirt. He took my mother's hand when he greeted her.

"You look absolutely radiant today. Just stunning. Your husband is a lucky man."

My mother might have blushed—it was hard to tell beneath her tan. Unlike me, she loves attention. She is the eternal seeker of the fountain of youth. Nothing much rattles her, except signs of aging. If my father weren't present, she'd have been swapping plastic surgeon stories with Del.

When my father isn't with us, Del calls my mom and me "sisters," which never fails to delight her.

Del extended his hand with formality and shook my father's while telling him, "Dr. Otomo, it is such a pleasure to have you join us. We wish we saw you more often."

If my father found him odd, he didn't remark, but it was hard to tell with my father. He was a very contained man. I did notice that he slipped his hand under the table after the handshake, where I imagine he wiped it.

I was glad I'd slipped my ring back in my pocket by the time Del came to our table. Thankfully, my mom didn't mention the big news to him. He'd have made a big fuss about it. I also felt a flash of relief that Garrett wasn't with us for dinner. He isn't tolerant of people he thinks of as different.

That's okay, I told myself because I planned on changing him for the better. Nobody's perfect. If we agreed on everything, it would be pretty dull.

While Del chatted with my parents, I watched the waves down on the beach, although I couldn't hear them through the windows or over the chatter and clatter of voices and dishes. My parents told me that, when I was little, I was afraid of the water. Once they finally got me in it, however, it was hard to get me out.

The surf was getting larger, but it was uneven and closing out this late in the day. Only two surfers in wetsuits were still in the water. People are often surprised at how cold the water is in Southern California, due to the Alaskan current. Their boards were too long for the beach break. I couldn't see their faces from this far away, but from their gestures they looked like they were having fun messing around and not minding that they weren't catching any real rides in the darkening water beside the pier.

When Del took our order, I pointed at the menu to indicate my choice of salmon. My mother told Del to bring a Cabernet Sauvignon for her and me.

Let me be honest here. Her ordering wine for me was a surprise. My parents were overprotective. Besides, I'm a teetotaler like my dad because I'm super sensitive to the effects of alcohol. Though, this time, I was glad she ordered it, because with my birthday and my big news, it might relax me.

He turned to me and said, "I'm sorry, I'll have to ask you for identification. It's ridiculous, I know, but twenty-one is the legal drinking age in California."

I felt uncomfortable and avoided looking at him.

"What?" my mother protested, "My sister and I are the same age. You didn't ask for my ID."

Without missing a beat, he said, "I've checked your identification before. It's hard to believe you're over twenty-one, but as far as I can tell your driver's license looks authentic." He winked at my mother.

"Sorry, I forgot my I.D.," I managed to say.

"Rules are terrible things sometimes," he said, and slapped his pen on his notepad. "I won't be able to serve you any alcohol."

I shrugged. Then another thing happened at dinner that was unusual: my father ordered wine. My mother's eyebrows arched again.

As Del was about to leave our table, Dad said, "Bring my daughter a cranberry juice in a wine glass, if you would, please."

I was about to object to the combination of salmon and cranberry juice, but noticed a little smile on my father's face. Sure enough, when the drinks were delivered, he switched ours.

By the time we finished dinner, I'd had two glasses of wine.

I felt loopy. I pretended to enjoy the taste, but I'm not sure I like the way it makes my head feel, either. It's weird, like things are happening around me faster than I can process them.

Maybe I inherited my father's aversion to alcohol, but I was proud that he was treating me like an adult.

I'm going to like being twenty.

Chapter 2

After dinner, we strolled out on the pier. I lagged back, fidgeting, moving my head from side to side, feeling the effects of the wine. My brain moved slower than my head. I watched the two silly surfers who were still in the water. When I looked up, I saw my parents standing by the railing on the right side of the pier, the side where the sun drops into the water. There were clouds in the sky and, at that moment, the sun filtered through them so that my parents were partially silhouetted, with the red-orange canvas of clouds behind them. My father shook the railing with both hands. Safety conscious as he was, I guessed he was testing its strength to make sure it was okay to lean against.

My mother turned and rested her back against the railing, her eyes on my father, not the sunset. The ends of her blonde hair were lifting in the breeze, looking like they were on fire. She was only a few years my father's junior, but looked much younger.

In contrast to her various European ancestry—Midwestern mutt, as she called it—my Japanese father had black hair, dark eyes, and naturally golden skin. I had inherited his black hair and brown eyes, though mine were not as dark as his, and the light skin of my mother. However, unlike my perennially tan mother, my alabaster skin only burned, except for the strange exceptions of my face and hands.

My father stood beside her with one hip pressed against the railing. With only a view of his profile, I couldn't tell if his eyes were on my mother or the sunset.

They were a striking couple. They could have been on a poster for a romantic movie.

I carry that image of them in my mind as if it were a photograph.

My mother reached up and stroked my father's temple. Her hand looked unsteady. I think she'd had at least one more glass of wine than I had. She brushed her fingers over his forehead, his ever-rising forehead that didn't bother him at all, but offended her in her ongoing war against aging. Though, this time, her gesture looked tender, not critical. Her war extended to him—she was forever feeding him vitamins and trying new hair topicals to stop his hairline from receding. He'd take the vitamins for a week or two to placate her. Soon, the bottles of shampoo and conditioners would sit untouched, collecting dust; the contents of the sprays would congeal and gum up the nozzles. If the caps were loose, the liquids would evaporate. I think sometimes he'd purposely left them uncapped to give the impression that he used them, because in most things, he was meticulous.

My father pulled my mother toward him and gave her a long kiss. I flushed with embarrassment. I knew public affection embarrassed him, and, if I'm honest, I felt the same. No one likes to see their parents acting like infatuated teenagers.

"I'm getting chilly," I called out to them. "Can't we go back to the car?"

Before walking back, my father put his arm around me. He gestured toward the sky. The undersides of the clouds were changing to an electrified pink. It was a striking sunset.

"Sometimes," he said, "The sky looks like something spilled out of a test tube."

"I'm glad you decided to pursue medicine instead of poetry," my mother told him.

"I could have been a poet," he protested. "Science has its own poetry."

My mother said, "I guess it does," and looked over at me.

"My friend, Mysti, is a poet" I said, not knowing what else to say. Thinking back now, I was immature for my age.

We walked back to the parking lot on the pier. My father's new Mercedes was the first sports utility vehicle we'd owned. I thought of it, and all the various brands and models of SUVs, as the mutated spawn of Jeep. The pragmatic rectangular shape of its progenitor was now hidden under arched lines, chrome trim and a black diamond, metallic paint. It was luxurious.

My father bought it only a couple of weeks ago. At the dealership, he'd made a fuss about the details of its safety features. My mother and I hoped buying it would lift his dark mood, but it hadn't seemed to affect him much. Only a few days ago, even before the new license plates arrived, someone stole all the air bags out of it. That hadn't helped. Whatever was bothering him I didn't know, and my mother didn't seem to know either. At least if she did, she didn't confide in me.

I was thrilled that on my birthday, he seemed happy again.

I sat behind my mother in the car. I was the last to close my door. I gave it a strong pull because the interior was nearly airtight. It made a soft woofing sound like the bark Wolfears, my dog, does in his sleep. I rubbed my fingertips over the firm leather seat and inhaled the lingering new car smell. From the driver's controls, my father locked the doors and rolled all the windows down a couple of inches. Then he reached back and checked that my seat belt was snug.

So much for his realizing I'm an adult, I thought.

He backed out of the parking space and, as we were driving along the parking lane, I felt the need for fresh air and pressed down on the window button. It didn't respond.

"Dad, my window doesn't work. Did you accidently hit the child safety lock for the back doors?"

The slow clip-clop of the pier planks under our wheels was the only answer. Even with the comfort suspension, we were gently jostled on the uneven surface. My mother cleared her throat to get his attention. He ignored her too. He was probably distracted, back to thinking about work again.

As he drove toward the far edge of the pier parking, my mother said, "Dear, the exit is the other way."

He didn't pay attention to her, and she held her hand up by the side of her head forming the letter C, signaling that she thought our respite from his dark mood was over. If they were going to start arguing, I didn't want to ruin the perfect image of them by the railing. I put on my headphones.

A boy and girl walked slowly in front of the car with their arms wrapped around each other. The sight of them made me think of Garrett, who wouldn't approve of their clothes. The boy was wearing a tight, black AC/DC road tour T-shirt and baggy jeans, barely hanging on his butt. The girl's pants were squeeze-tight with pre-faded spots. If Garrett looked at her, he'd feel the point of my elbow in his ribs.

The couple stopped directly in front of our car. The boy gave a shampoo commercial toss of his hair, draped his arms over the girl's shoulders and they looked into each other's eyes. Their heads begin swaying side to side in unison as if entering a private, hypnotic world.

My father began clenching and unclenching his fingers on the steering wheel. When the boy bent down to kiss the girl, my father's patience ended. His left hand gripped tightly on the steering wheel while he slammed the heel of his right hand on the horn.

The young lovers jumped out of the car's path. The guy bared his teeth at us like an angry chimpanzee. With one hand he hitched up his pants, with the other, he gestured at us with his middle finger. The girl stared at us wide-eyed and open-mouthed with her head thrust forward.

I couldn't stop laughing. I didn't know if my laughter was from the sight of their reaction or embarrassment. I recognized them from back in high school.

Even though they were out of the way, my father continued pressing his hand on the horn.

He drove forward. When he came to the dividing curb at the end of the parking area, he didn't turn, but drove straight towards it. The wooden divider proved no obstacle for our high clearance vehicle.

I pulled off my headphones.

My mother said, "What are you doing? Are you feeling all right?"

We were in the pedestrian area, driving toward the end of the pier.

Chapter 3

We stopped. The length of the pier stretched before us. My father released the horn. Neither my mother nor I spoke, not wanting to break the quiet that held us in the moment. It was like we were balancing between our normal world and one of a warped reality. It was only seconds, but it seemed as if time stopped.

My mind wandered. Sometimes, I have disassociated thoughts, random, non sequiturs. I don't know why my mind does what it does. For some reason, I thought about how it felt on top of the high dive platform moments before a dive. People on the pier surrounding us were staring like they were witnessing a bizarre stunt. Some of their mouths hung open like spectators peering up at a dive meet.

I imagined I was making the meet's final dive—my score to decide our team's victory or defeat. Frozen. I was frozen. Never have I known fear at the platform's edge, only exhilaration. Yet there I was paralyzed with fear.

I flashed back from my imagined comparison to the moment. Only my eyes moved.

My father was rigid. His hands were gripping the steering wheel so tightly that they were shaking. Undoubtedly, he was staring straight ahead. Maybe he was as confused as I was, uncertain as to what had just happened. I worried that he'd just had a stroke.

And then his foot jammed down on the gas pedal.

His shoulders pressed back against the seat, his head thrust against the headrest. The pitch of the engine wound louder and higher. Beneath us, the tires spun, unable to gain traction on the wood planks. The car's back end swayed. It felt as if the tires were digging us down through the pier. Through the crack in the window came the smells of burning rubber, exhaust, and scorched wood.

My eyes stung.

He jerked his foot off the pedal and the car skipped forward a few feet. The pitch of the whining engine lowered. The tires stopped spinning. He pressed his foot down, gently this time. We began moving forward.

"Have you lost your mind?" my mother said, in a voice that was surprisingly calm.

My father's only response was to press down on the gas pedal. We picked up speed. People shrieked. Some waved their arms spasmodically as they scrambled out of the way. Soon they were flinging themselves against either side of the pier to avoid being struck.

I could no longer hear the screaming voices of the people on the pier, and realized it was because I myself was screaming hysterically.

"Stop, stop, stop," I joined my mother in her pleading shrieks.

Our chanting pulled me back from the maelstrom of madness of whatever was happening.

My mother started pounding her fists on my father's shoulder and arm. One of his hands was on the horn again. It was difficult for him to steer on the uneven surface of pier with my mother flailing on him. The car started to wobble as if he might lose control.

He stopped accelerating, but we were already moving fast. He didn't brake.

My mother lunged for the steering wheel. Her left hand snagged his face, and her diamond ring tore a gash in his cheek. Both of his hands were back on the steering wheel now. She tried to pry them off, but his grip was too strong for her to break.

A line of blood smeared his cheek, making it look as if his face were painted with grotesque clown makeup. Blood flowed down his neck and began soaking his shirt collar. Small details kept me from being consumed by horror.

Even without the blare of the horn, people scattered before us like bowling pins leaping out of the way before a strike. Amazingly, we'd not hit anyone.

My survival instinct suddenly kicked in. Time moved in slow motion. I started to undo the seat belt and stopped, realizing I needed it on unless I could escape before we reached the end of the pier. I frantically pulled on the door handle. It was locked and useless. I clawed at the door lock knob. It too was disabled from the child safety lock. I looked around, desperately groping about, looking for something, anything.

There was nothing to be found. The car was even freshly vacuumed.

I reached my hands into the small open space at the top of the window and hooked my fingers over the edge of the glass. With all my strength and the weight of my body, I pulled down. The glass neither broke nor budged. My fingers cramped from the effort. I lifted them off the glass and let my hands fall loosely, uselessly, in my lap.

A woman grabbed a child from a stroller, whisking him up with such force that the two of them nearly toppled over the edge of the railing. The empty stroller was clipped by our bumper and sent spinning. It ricocheted off the railing and bounced back against the side of the car with a loud bang.

Two fishermen in our path dropped their tackle boxes. One of them held out his fishing rod in front of him, as if it were a weapon that could protect him. The car was moving too fast to stop. There was nowhere to swerve without hitting other people. In the instant before he was struck, his companion pulled him away.

Other frightened people were pressed against the railing. A little girl covered her ears with her hands. Someone threw a bucket of fish offal. It clattered onto the hood, splattering its contents in a smear across the windshield.

I screamed at my mother to turn off the ignition key. Panicked beyond hearing, she was now flailing her arms uselessly against the dashboard. Her voice rose into ever higher pitched screams.

She ran out of breath and stopped her terrified shrieking. Her hands clasped her face as we neared the pier's end.

My father, back in complete control, began accelerating again.

I lunged for the key, forgetting the seat belt. It locked, stopping me far short. Even if I had reached it, we were moving too fast for it to make any difference. With my right hand, I reached up and grasped the grab handle above the door.

We sailed through the wood railings at the pier's end as easily as if they were made of toothpicks.

My body strained against the seat belt and shoulder strap. The pulsating rattle of the pier slats ceased.

Whether intentionally or by luck, my father had hit the vertical four-by-four post directly dead center. Because of that, the car did not twist or roll as we made an arc through the air. The rear of the car felt as if it lifted as we started to fall. I thought we might flip over and land upside down when we hit the water.

Chapter 4

The view through the windshield was a blur of choppy, green ocean water. My stomach rose into my throat. There was a whooshing sound from the air through the cracks of the windows. We didn't somersault, we arrowed toward the water. Before we hit, I closed my eyes.

The car pierced the water.

It felt like hitting concrete—the wind was knocked out of me. My lungs stopped working; it felt as if my ribs were crushed.

The engine noise stopped, and snapping and popping noises filled my ears. An image of shark teeth crushing a fiberglass surfboard flooded my mind—probably the crackling of the electrical system shorting out. As the car plunged deeper, my eyes popped open, so wide that it felt as if my eyeballs would pop out. I learned what wide-eyed terror meant. With small, gasping breaths, I was able to suck in some of the precious air still inside the car.

Water sprayed through the window crack and spurted onto my mother's head. I braced my feet against her seat, expecting we would hit the bottom, but we popped back up to the surface like a cork, seemingly suspended, motionless, as if being held by the wind. Again, I thought we might flip onto our back, but we landed upright and floated briefly, slanting nose down.

My feet slid off her seat into wet, cold water on the floor. It was flowing in from the vents and leaking through the cracks. For the moment, the air in the rear compartment was keeping us from submerging.

If the air bags weren't stolen last week, they might have deployed and helped us stay afloat.

Outside the car, sea water sloshed against us. I could feel the front of the car sinking. With still-stiff fingers, I managed to unclip my seat belt. My mother had stopped screaming.

I would have screamed if I could have.

I remember the salesman at the car dealership had shown us the tire jack under the rear bench seat. If I could get to it, maybe I could use it to break a window.

I slid off from where I was sitting and squeezed my butt partway into the gap between the front seats. I pulled on the bench, lifting it toward me, but I was in the way and couldn't open the seat far enough. I reached around under it, but I couldn't even touch the jack without pushing the seat down and trapping my arm. From crouching down, my butt was now wet from the rising water. I twisted and sat back down, thinking about crawling into the back compartment for a few more moments of air.

I heard sobbing. My father was cradling my mother's head on his lap. She was limp and unconscious. Blood covered her forehead. Evidently, she'd unfastened her seat belt before impact. Maybe the blood was from his cheek; from where she'd caught him with her ring. I couldn't tell.

His fingers were rhythmically stroking her hair. Tears flowed down his face and mixed with the blood on his face. The mix dripped off his chin into my mother's tangled hair. He seemed oblivious that we were sinking.

"Daddy, you are supposed to protect us," I hissed between short breaths.

He ignored me.

I beat my fists on his shoulder. He turned toward me. His eyes widened and his lips quivered as if attempting a smile. His hand slapped at the window switches. With the electronics fried, it was a futile gesture. What happened to my brilliant father? I'll never know if he was trying to open the windows or make certain they were locked, because at that moment the car lurched sideways. His hand flew up and smacked his face. He reached toward me.

I recoiled, curling into a tight ball with my knees tucked up to my chin, to avoid the touch from whoever this man was in the front seat. I couldn't look at him.

There was a popping sound, and water burst through the dashboard.

I rolled my back onto the seat and thrust my feet toward the window with all the strength in me.

The window shattered. The glass cut my ankles and calves, but my feet were outside above the water. I flipped over onto my stomach and pushed my body crab-like backwards through the opening. By the time my torso was free, the front of the car was dangerously low in the water.

The swell pushed me away from the car. I swam back to it and managed to reach in through the broken window and hold onto the grab handle. I pulled off my sandals to be able to tread water more easily in the chilly water.

"Push mother out to me."

He ignored me, lost in whatever reality he now occupied.

"*Daddy*," I screamed.

I repeated it over and over at the top of my lungs as water rose inside the car and it sunk lower in the sloshing ocean. My hand slipped from the grab handle, but I managed to hook my fingers on the window casing. Finally, my screaming jarred him. He looked over at me and mouthed three words. Bullets would have been less painful.

In the next instant, the car lurched forward and began sliding beneath the surface. I lost my grip, but the suction began pulling me toward the ocean floor. I inhaled a gulp of air before being dragged under. Kicking my feet and clawing the water with my hands, I fought toward the surface, but my efforts were useless. It was as if I were trying to swim up a waterfall.

Realizing I needed to conserve my strength, I stopped fighting and went limp with the flow.

Though the salt water stung my eyes, I managed to keep them open as we descended. The water was becoming dark green in the fading light, and as I went farther down, it lost all color. I became surrounded by murky, sand-churned water. I felt a painful pressure in my ears from the depth. I couldn't pop them without pinching my nose and my arms were trailing uselessly above me like blades of kelp. I began to think my head might explode.

As we went deeper and the strength of the suction diminished, I was able to reach my nose. I pinched my nostrils, keeping my lips tightly sealed, and blew until the pressure popped. The relief was immense.

The car stopped. It had hit the bottom. I crumpled into it and bounced off, losing all contact with it.

The descent had been quick enough that I still had a reserve of air, so I groped around in the dark water trying to find the car until I became disoriented. When I could no longer ignore the need to breathe, I discovered I no longer knew the direction of the surface. Guessing wrong, I swam directly into the sand on the bottom. Twisting around, I gathered my legs under me and pushed off toward the faint light above. As I did, I wondered if I could hold my breath long enough to reach the surface.

The water was even colder below and my muscles weren't responding as normally. Though I was trying to move quickly, the water seemed thick and my arms and legs heavy. My clothing also added resistance and slowed my progress. I wondered if the wine was affecting me.

The cold was numbing me. Desperately trying to hold my breath, I forced myself to swim upward, knowing at any moment I'd involuntarily suck in a lungful of water.

Suddenly the pier lights turned on, illuminating the water above. Only a few more kicks and strokes, I told myself, while trying to control my coordination.

I felt as if my lungs would burst. Even though I was close to the surface, my vision began to darken and tunnel; I felt consciousness starting to float away.

When I was almost there, my muscles stopped working.

My lungs expelled their spent air in a large burst of bubbles, and I involuntarily gulped salt water.

This can't be happening. This isn't real.

Chapter 5

I broke the surface and found myself in a sea of broken glass. That is how it looked beneath the pier lights. I retched up salt water and my dinner. In short gasps, I inhaled air, oxygen, sweet everything. As I caught my breath, I managed to take off my shoes. When I tried to dive to reach my parents, I found my arms were made of spaghetti. My legs were as useless as kelp stalks swaying in the current. I heard a helicopter and looked up. A wave smacked my head. The world began spinning.

The next thing I remember was being pushed toward shore on a lifeguard's rescue board. When we slid onto the sand, paramedics lifted me. We started up the beach with one of them supporting me on each side. Wet sand squished between my toes. My rubber legs pretended they were walking.

I made a noise that might have been a word and turned back toward the water. I managed to swing one arm up and point toward the end of the pier. The paramedic beside me shook his head.

"I'm sorry," he said. "There's nothing you can do."

I uttered another noise. It wasn't a word, only an animal cry. My parents were dead. I became dead weight. They lowered me onto the sand. Two more paramedics joined us with a stretcher. The four of them carried me on it to the beach parking lot beside the pier where two ambulances were parked. A crowd of onlookers had gathered. Several police were keeping them back. Instead of putting me directly inside one of the ambulances, they took me between them.

As if they'd choreographed it, two of them held up sheets around me for privacy, while another one helped me stand. My teeth chattered and my body shivered, but I didn't feel cold.

"I'm okay," I said.

"Even supergirls are vulnerable to hypothermia," he said and gave me a smile.

I attempted to pull off my top, but my numb fingers didn't seem to be working. He used scissors to deftly cut off my remaining clothing while somehow keeping his eyes averted, not that he'd want to look at a half-drowned rat. When I was free from my clothing, they wrapped the sheets around me and placed me on a gurney. After strapping my torso, thighs and ankles, they loaded me headfirst into one of the ambulances.

A blanket was added on top of the sheets. With a single whoop of the siren, the ambulance made a path through the crowd and we were on our way. We rolled down Pacific Coast Highway, the asphalt ribbon that hugs the California coast, not driving fast, which reassured me there was nothing critical about my condition, not that I cared at the moment. We even stopped at the occasional red light.

They'd not turned on the siren since the parking lot. I felt thankful for that.

For some reason, the thought of the siren screaming would be embarrassing. I'd had more than enough attention. I found it a silly and strange thing to be concerned about, but better than thinking about the impossible that had just happened.

Lying on my back, I saw PCH from a new perspective. Mountains rose on one side like a vain fortress against the timeless onslaught of the sea. On the ocean side, with the twilight gone, the sky was now a dark shroud. My view became fragmented by the jolting glare of streetlamps as we came to more populated areas.

When we turned off PCH, the faces of buildings appeared behind the streetlights. Lit windows became the glowing eyes of ghouls. The buildings leaned forward, voyeurs gawking at me as I lay shivering beneath the bleached blanket and sheets. I realized that I was cold. I imagined the blanket and sheets tumbling around in an industrial drier stripping away memories of all the people whom they'd covered. My imagination of their tumbling in hot air didn't make them feel warmer. My teeth chattered. When I clenched them, my jaw shook and my skull vibrated.

One of the EMTs was thin with a high forehead. He looked familiar, perhaps someone I'd seen jogging on the beach. He had his hand placed on my forearm. Maybe it was there to comfort me, maybe he'd just rested it there because it was a convenient spot. When he noticed my looking at him, he lifted it. I reached across with my other hand and pressed his hand back down on my arm. He smiled at me. I parted my lips to smile back, but my lips only clung to my clacking teeth. The only part of my face that worked was my eyes. I blinked several times. He gave my arm a squeeze and looked out the back of the ambulance. My attempt at a smile must have looked grotesque.

It suddenly struck me that we were headed to a hospital. Odd as it may sound with my father being a doctor, I'd never been inside a hospital as a patient. I had an irrational fear of them.

Throughout my childhood, my father had repeatedly admonished me not to allow any medical procedures without his consent, and that if I were ever in need of medical treatment, they were to call him first. No exceptions. I had special needs, he'd said, and he knew how to best take care of me. What my special needs were, he'd never articulated.

When I'd asked, he and my mother would simply say, "You're special."

I believed them. Logic told me that they were being overprotective of their only child, but now, such was the result of his reminders that it sparked in me a reaction of panic. My breathing accelerated, causing staccato catches in my throat as I sucked in air. Not only was I going to a hospital, but they couldn't call him.

How could this be happening to me, a special person? Maybe I wasn't special after all.

The paramedic's eyes knitted in concern at my sudden change in breathing.

"Don't worry, we'll get you warmed up soon," he said, and squeezed my arm again. "We're almost there. They have warm blankets waiting."

I had traveled on the Pacific Coast Highway countless times. Now it would never be the same. The security of my world had vanished. Maybe the world is entirely chaos and anything the resembles order is merely an illusion.

I didn't want to speak, so I looked away from him. Somehow it seemed that if I spoke it would all be real and not some kind of mad dream where everything goes wrong and you can't wake up. I reached down to feel the one solid thing that would help me hang on.

It was gone. My engagement ring was inside the pocket of my pants, floating in the ocean.

"We've got to turn around," I blurted.

From the expression on his face, he must have assumed that I didn't know the fate of my parents and wanted to return for them.

"The most important thing . . . right now, umm, is making sure you're okay."

"I'm fine," I said. "If you can't take me back, just stop and let me out. Please."

"I'm sorry . . . we can't do that."

"Driver," I called out. "Stop the ambulance."

The driver ignored my request. Strapped as I was, there was nothing I could do other than scream.

Somehow, I managed not to scream and stared at the headliner of the ambulance. I focused on my breathing until the ambulance pulled under a concrete overhang of Saint Pilar's Hospital. Its solid gray expanse was punctuated with lights that looked like the smaller menacing cousins of the streetlamps we'd past. The blue-white light from them made me think of the light from alien spaceships that sucked up human beings for experimentation. Nothing real, of course, undoubtedly an image from something I'd read or seen in a movie. I wished aliens were real.

They could take me away.

Chapter 6

The paramedics wheeled me through the emergency side entrance of Saint Pilar's that was reserved for ambulance patients. I inhaled and was smacked by the smell that is unique to hospitals, causing me to shudder from something other than being chilled.

We stopped rolling. I heard a television laugh track. Turning my head, I saw we were in a hallway beside the main waiting room. It was full of people, some in obvious pain. One man lay on the floor, hands clutched over his stomach. He thrust his head from side to side. I felt guilty to be lying on my back instead of standing or sitting uncomfortably in one of the waiting room chairs. I was special again and would have traded my mental pain for a physical one.

My eyes drifted to an aquarium against the far wall. Algae was overtaking it. Two large goldfish were swimming through the misty green water, somehow looking both bored and anxious. Occasionally, they would shoot to the surface to look for food or take gulps of air. At least they weren't coughing or moaning like the waiting patients.

A child noticed the aquarium, too, and toddled over to it. She slapped her hand on the glass. startling the fish who darted through the green water, banging into the sides. The child laughed. A sharp groan from the man lying on the floor caught her attention. She lost interest in the fish.

I tugged on the sleeve of one of the paramedics, and said, "I'm okay. These people need help more than I do. Some of them should take priority."

"That's not the way it works," he said.

He placed his hand on the side rail. The gold of his wedding band popped against his skin and dark blue uniform. Before I could protest again, a triage nurse joined us and spoke with the paramedics. She nodded and glanced at me. I obviously had no say in the matter.

We started rolling again. The foot of the gurney rammed the metal plated double doors. With a clang, they swung open.

The main ER room seemed surprisingly calm considering the crowd in the waiting room. I stared at the ceiling, closing my eyes each time we went under a light. They took me to a room with four beds, two on each side separated from one another by blue curtains the color of a lifeless sky. My bed turned out to be the one at the end on the right. They wheeled the gurney next to the bed and deftly lifted me onto it. A nurse raised the head of the bed so I could sit up. He positioned what looked like a freestanding, chrome coat rack next to the bed. I noticed his blue-green scrubs looked brighter than the curtains and freshly pressed. I guessed that he'd just come on duty. He left and a female nurse came with a hospital gown and helped me into it.

She asked me if I was comfortable and pushed a damp strand of hair on my forehead to the side of my face. The hair plastered to my cheek and ear took a bit more effort to free.

"I'll be back soon with the doctor," she said.

The ambulance guys came in and hovered around my bed with concerned expressions. Other than the one who'd sat next to me, I'd not really paid attention to them before. They were sharp-looking in their navy-blue uniforms, guys not much older than I. Two of the three had mustaches, neatly trimmed. One of their radio's crackled. They looked disappointed that they had to leave for another call.

"Thanks for everything, "I said. "Don't you need your sheets back?"

"We'll get them later," one said.

Another said, "We've got plenty."

"Thanks, again," I said.

Though I was sure I looked like a half-drowned rat, I gave them the best smile I could manage. The one who'd ridden beside me in the ambulance was the last to leave.

"See you on the beach," I told him.

From his curious expression, he had no idea what I was talking about. Maybe he wasn't anyone I'd seen jogging. Then again, I didn't look like I did when I ran.

Like mine, the front curtain of the bed across from me was pulled open. The woman lying there didn't speak English. Her husband was translating to the doctor and nurse at her bed. She'd been admitted with heart palpitations and difficulty breathing. The doctor's diagnosis was that she'd had a panic attack. The husband couldn't believe that she was under any stress and was arguing with the doctor.

The man said, "She is a housewife. She just stays home with the kids. She doesn't work."

The doctor briefly looked in my direction when he stepped away. The nurse closed the woman's curtain and left without glancing at me.

I felt alone and hollow. I was still cold. At least my teeth no longer chattered. The one thing I did know was that I didn't want to be there. I might be a bit bruised, but at least physically there was nothing seriously wrong with me.

A plastic bag with the remains of my clothing hung on the wall. I could see water collecting in the bottom of it. I had no purse, no pants, only a scissored top, bra and underwear. I could hardly slip away unnoticed in a hospital gown or dressed in the soggy remnants of my clothing.

Nestled among the equipment behind me was a phone on the wall. From its location, it didn't look like it was meant for patients.

I swung my feet over the edge of the bed and managed to reach across and grab it. I pressed the switch hook, suspecting it might only be connected internally, but I got a dial tone. Luckily, I knew the number for Garrett's pizza shop. As expected, he was out on a delivery. I told one of his coworkers that I had an emergency and he needed to come to Saint Pilar's and bring me clothes.

"Yeah, okay," the guy said, as if all his calls came from girlfriends wanting their clothes.

Just as I hung up, the doctor who'd been at the bed across from me came in with the male nurse. In contrast to the trim rescue workers, the young doctor looked far from fit. His white lab coat had a dark smudge on the shoulder and hung open, exposing his considerable belly that pressed against his scrub top.

While he questioned me, the nurse put a cuff around my arm to take my blood pressure. I gestured over the diagonal line on my torso where the shoulder strap restrained me when we hit the water. He poked at my ribs without asking first. I didn't care for his bedside manner.

My ribs, breast and shoulder were tender and I winched under his touch.

"You'll hurt a lot more later," he said in his delightful manner. "We'll take some x-rays."

"Can I go home then?" I asked.

He didn't answer me. For a moment he looked like he might smile. Then gave me a patronized look and grunted.

When the nurse removed the blood pressure cuff, I grimaced from the ripping sound.

I asked again, "Really, when can I leave?"

"We need to keep you for observation," he said.

"I want to go home," I told him.

The doctor ordered the nurse to give me saline drip and a drug I didn't recognize. Then, he made an attempt at bedside warmth.

"I think you're a very lucky young lady."

I asked him, "What are you giving me?"

"Just something to keep you hydrated and to help you stay calm."

A professional smile flickered on his lips before he left.

Warm blankets were brought to me. They felt marvelous, like they'd just been taken out of a dryer. Then, the nurse put a needle in the back of my hand and hung a bag with an IV drip on the clothes rack beside my bed.

"I'll be checking on you," he said.

Each time I heard footsteps approaching, I hoped it would be Garrett coming to rescue me. With the hazy warmth from the blankets and whatever drug was in the IV bag, I drifted off to sleep against my will.

Chapter 7

When I opened my eyes, I saw Jesus hanging on his cross on the wall opposite my bed. He was between a television and a round clock whose hands read three thirty-seven. The minute hand quivered as if impatient. I was alone and it took me a moment to realize that I had been transferred to another room. I found it hard to believe that I'd slept through the move, and that I had slept so long.

Unlike the emergency room, this one was quiet. The curtains were a pale green. They were pulled open, but the bed was positioned so that I couldn't see outside of the room. I imagined an empty hallway with a shiny floor. I heard the hum of machines outside my room. My arm with the IV was strapped to the bed railing next to a handset with a nurse call button. I reached across with my other arm and pressed my thumb on the button.

"Can I help you?" said a tinny sounding voice in the handset speaker.

I said, "I'm awake."

I felt immediately embarrassed because I sounded as if I expected them to think that my waking should be world news.

The voice said, "I'll send someone."

The needle in my vein confounded me because I wanted to get out of bed. I needed to get home. Wolfears would be expecting our morning run and breakfast. I wanted my world to be normal, but that was too much to wish for. I glanced at the clock. The minute hand hadn't moved, and I realized it was stuck.

A nurse came into the room. She was cheerful for it being the middle of the night.

"There's our little sound sleeper," she said.

"I didn't even know they moved me."

"The midazolam really knocked you out. I was told in a matter of minutes you were sound asleep. It is very unusual to react so strongly. You've been switched to only saline."

"Can you take it off? I don't need it."

"I'll need to check with the doctor," she said. "They usually keep you on saline until you're ready for discharge."

"I'm ready," I said.

"How are you feeling?"

"Fine, but I need to leave."

"Patience, patience."

"I need to pee."

I sat up and felt a cold draft on my backside from the opening in the hospital gown. The nurse unnecessarily helped me to my feet and instructed me to roll the IV stand with me. She walked beside me to make sure I was steady on my feet, again unnecessary. She hovered outside the bathroom door.

When I returned to bed, I said, "I need clothes for when I leave."

She gave a bright smile and lifted a finger in the air. When she opened the closet door and saw the bag with my clothes, her smile dropped.

"Oh my, they're wet. That won't do."

She rinsed them, hung them in the bathroom and realized they wouldn't be satisfactory even when dry.

"Lucky for you," she said. "the hospital volunteers take clothing donations exactly for your situation. It's quiet now. That's why I work the night shift. I'll run down and see if I can find you something."

"Thanks," I said. "My boyfriend is supposed to bring me some."

"That reminds me. You're a popular young lady, you've had two night-time visitors. One of them even dozed off in the chair waiting for you to wake up. Tall, handsome fellow. He must have been your boyfriend."

Knowing Garrett had been there lifted my spirits.

"Two visitors?" I asked. "Who was the other one?"

"A detective. I told him you were not to be disturbed."

I was left alone wondering why a detective would want to see me when Garrett came into my room with a can of coke in his hand. When I saw him, my breath stopped and my face couldn't decide whether to smile or cry. It did both.

"You're awake!" he said.

Still holding the coke, he bent and reached his other arm around me and gave me a delicate hug as if I might break. I wrapped my free arm around his neck, not wanting to let him go of him. When he finally managed to pull away, the collar of his shirt was wet with my tears. After assuring him I was fine, he wanted to know what happened.

"It was an accident," I said, speaking barely above a whisper. "Something went wrong with the car. It wouldn't stop. My father drove it straight down the center of the pier to avoid hitting people. It was the only thing he could do. It was a miracle that he didn't hit anyone. Some of them almost didn't get out of the way. It was awful. The looks on their faces. But he didn't hurt anybody. He's a hero. He sacrificed us for everyone else."

"The gas pedal must have stuck. The car was defective," Garrett said. He looked away, then took a sip of his drink. "With a good lawyer, you should be able to settle for millions."

Desperately wanting to change the subject, I said, "Did you bring my clothes?"

"I didn't know what your message meant. I just wanted to get here as soon as possible. My boss let me leave my shift early."

As if she'd been waiting outside the door for her cue, the nurse entered the room bringing a paper sack with clothing for me.

"I hope these will do," she said. "They're probably too large, but better that than too small."

"Anything will be fine," I said.

She pulled out a set of matching track sweats, navy blue, accented with double white stripes on the side seams of the pants and the arms of the top. They were obviously several sizes too big for me.

"If you don't need anything further, I'll leave you with your company."

"Thank you," Garrett and I said simultaneously as she left us.

"That solves that," Garrett said.

"Yes, now I need to get out of here."

"Have you been discharged?"

"Yes," I lied. I didn't want to argue with him. "Wolfears missed his dinner. Not to mention Sneakers."

I felt a catch in my throat when I said Sneakers, my father's Savannah.

Garrett said, "I think a dog and a cat will be fine if they miss a meal."

I bristled. "They are the only family I have left. And taking care of family is everything." At least that is the saying, I thought.

"We'll be family soon," he replied.

"I'm sorry. I shouldn't have snapped."

I sat up and again felt the cold draft on my back. I started untying my wrist from the bed rail. Garrett looked skeptical.

I said, "I only needed it tied up when I was sleeping."

When it was free, I looked at the needle in the back of my hand. It was held firmly beneath the tape. I started pulling slowly on the edge of one of the tapes.

"I'm sure you're not supposed to be doing that," he said. "Let me get the nurse."

He started to reach for the call button. I grabbed it first and jerked it away from him.

"I need my arm free. It makes me feel panicky not being able to move freely. The sooner I'm out of here, the better. Here, you take it out," I said and held out my hand.

Garrett shook his head, and said, "I don't think I'm supposed to."

I ripped off the tape. Before I could think about it, I pulled out the needle. A trickle of blood flowed from the wound. I tied a knot in the tubing to keep it from leaking. Garrett had a shocked expression.

"I'm going to change. Guard the door and let me know if someone is coming," I told him. "And don't turn around until I tell you."

I was surprised when he went to the door without protesting. I changed into the sweat clothes and a pair of flip-flops I found in the bag.

"Okay," I said, rolling up the pant legs to my ankles. "Is the coast clear? Let's get out of here."

He put a hand on my shoulder. "Wait, easy baby, I don't think the doctors want you leaving like this. I'm pretty sure you are leaving against medical advice."

"Doctors don't know everything," I told him. I said it with a certainty I knew to be true. I peered around him and saw the hallway was clear. It looked just as I had imagined it. "Just walk naturally like we're late-night visitors."

I slipped away from his hand into the hallway and started walking. I had to keep one hand on my waist to keep the pants from slipping down. Garrett caught up to me.

When we reached the elevator, he said, "I didn't want to mention it before, but the receptionist said there are couple of reporters nosing around trying to find you. I think I saw one of them sitting in the lobby. A guy with a hat like they wore in old movies."

We took the stairs and found a side door leading outside of the hospital.

Chapter 8

Garrett's faded red Ford Escort, which we called The Chugger, lived up to its name as we drove up the coast. On the incline from Malibu into the city of Yitha, it sputtered and rattled. I wondered if it would make it to my home. Garrett was probably exhausted, because he hadn't talked much on the drive. That was fine with me—maybe he sensed I didn't want conversation. I had enough questions rattling in my head without dealing with any more. When we turned off into Concha Pointe, I found it strange: everything looked the same, yet everything felt different.

The houses in the community where I lived were walled, gated, and landscaped for maximum privacy. If there weren't walls or fences, hedges hid the homes. It wasn't always that way. Once there were ranch-style homes with open yards and even horses. I'd heard stories and seen pictures. Even in my lifetime there was an evolution toward greater isolation if I stopped and thought about it. As the more affluent and famous moved into the neighborhood, it transformed into an exclusive, private community. Every few years a proposal was put forth to gate Concha Pointe, but thus far they were unsuccessful at even further closing us off from the outside.

Often, especially on my morning runs, I zigzagged through the streets, but driving through them now as a passenger, I saw them as an outsider might see them. The people who lived here were like decorator crabs. Their houses were shells camouflaged to conceal their inhabitants. Concha Pointe wasn't so much a neighborhood as a cluster of shields to provide an illusion against mortality. Maybe this was a remnant effect of mind alteration from the hospital sedative.

Garrett pulled up to our front of my gate and I got out of the car. The rich, fruity scent of flowers hung in the night air. I went over beside the bushes on the left. Having lost my keys, I was dimly thankful that the gate intercom also had a keypad. Luckily, my father hadn't changed the code recently.

The wrought iron gate rattled along its track as it rolled open. There was a soft grating noise from the motor that I'd never noticed before. With a lurch, the gate stopped. I motioned to Garrett to drive in. I pushed the close button and the gate started rolling back. I paused and looked at our house as if for the first time, seeing it as my shell, my fortress, my shield against the fragileness of life.

Unlike most of the houses, you can actually see it through the gate on the street. It is set on the edge of the cliff above the ocean, but you can't see the ocean from the front when standing in the cobblestone driveway. It is a two-story and looks like an overgrown English cottage with rough, off-white walls and broad wood beam accents. That's how I describe it. It's English Tudor or Country German, depending on if you'd asked my mother or father. It is peculiar in that on both front corners of the house there are round towers. Perhaps the architect had flip-flopped between building a castle or a home. There was a guest house for a maid's quarters above the garage, but we'd never had a live-in housekeeper.

Garrett parked his car next to mine, Mister Aphid. When he got out, he tilted his head back and stared up. He seemed fascinated with the whale weathervane on one of the steeples. The matching steeple on the right has a weathervane for the compass points. I always imagined that migrating birds used it to verify they were on course when flying over.

I walked down and stood beside him. When he noticed me, he turned and said, "I wonder if you're going to be able to keep the house?"

It struck me as an odd thing to say; something I'd not had a chance to worry about myself.

I reached my arms around his waist and pulled him toward me. He is so much bigger than I am that what I did was pull myself into him.

Pressing the side of my head against his chest, I said "Am I going to get to keep *you*?"

He put his arm around my shoulders and gave me a squeeze.

"How can you even ask that?"

With his other arm, he jangled his car keys in his hand.

Sharp, joyous barking erupted from the side of the house. Wolfears must have been asleep in the back because he'd finally noticed our arrival. Before I could unwrap my arms from Garrett, a streak of black fur was racing toward us. He's a big dog and trained not to jump on people, but when he can't contain his excitement, he jumps up and down as if on a trampoline. Garrett stepped back.

"He thinks he's a little dog sometimes," I said.

When I'd petted Wolfears enough, he sniffed at Garrett and pressed his head against his thigh. Wolfears has good instincts about people. At least he seems to know how I feel about them. Garrett awkwardly petted the top of Wolfears' head.

"Wolfie won't break," I said.

"You know I've never had a dog," he said, defensively.

"You won't hurt the furry beast," I said, and gave Wolfears a solid slap of affection on his side.

In response, he snuck in a lick on my hand with his pink tongue and twirled in a three-sixty. When he stopped his spin, he sniffed and licked my hand where the IV had been attached.

"Is the house locked? How are you going to get inside without your keys?" Garrett asked.

"The doggy door," I said. "Not that you could fit through it. Wait here. After I turn off the alarm, I'll let you in the front door."

Keeping one hand on my waist to hold up the sweatpants, I went around the side next to our neighbor's three-story contemporary.

The walkway ran between our house and a tall row of junipers between our yards that shielded the neighbor's view of our backyard. Wolfears ran ahead of me as if encouraging me to move faster. The doggy door in the kitchen door has an electronic sensor that unlocks when the transmitter on Wolfears collar is nearby. Wolfears scrambled through and I followed.

The first thing I noticed when I crawled inside was the smell of French bread. I turned on the light. There was a fresh loaf on the counter waiting for me. Seeing my favorite food for breakfast and lunch made me realize I was hungry. I was tempted to snatch up the loaf and gnaw off a piece on my way through the house.

I heard Wolfears nails clicking on the floor as he headed toward the front door. I was often home alone, yet now the house felt hollow and breathless, as if it knew my parents wouldn't be coming home again.

I paused, stood still, and listened. There was a soft hum from the refrigerator, and I could hear the ticking from the grandfather clock down the hall. I hadn't looked in the direction of the ocean when I crossed the backyard and realized that was quiet now too. No waves crashed on the rocks below.

I felt paralyzed standing in the kitchen, afraid to walk through my own house.

Wolfears returned to see what was taking me so long. Sensing something was wrong, he sat and fixed his eyes on me. I started shaking and hyperventilating. He came over and pressed his head against my leg.

If he weren't there, I think I would have slithered back out the doggy door to escape.

I rubbed his furry ears between my fingers, feeling their softness between the insides of my hands. I pressed them against his head. When I released them, they sprung up. I refolded them. They sprung up again. It calmed me down, and I began to feel better.

I stood there so long playing with his ears that Garrett came around to the back and knocked at the kitchen door.

"Hey, when are you going to let me in?"

"I'll be right there," I said in the best upbeat voice I could manage. "Sorry, I got distracted. I still need to turn off the alarm."

Chapter 9

When I let him in, I said, "Thanks for rescuing me and seeing me home, my knight in shining armor. You better go home and get some rest."

"What? I'm not leaving you. Not now."

"You can't stay, you must be exhausted from work. I know you've got exams coming up too. You can't risk your scholarship."

"I don't feel right about leaving you."

"What would you mother say if you spent the night?" I asked, attempting humor and failing.

"It doesn't matter what she thinks," he said.

I knew that wasn't true. He'd told me repeatedly that his mother had a big thing about our saving ourselves until marriage. Spending the night together would be taboo. I remembered when, after one of his basketball games, it was late and everyone else had gone home. Things were getting hot between us. We were lying on the grass at the edge of the school parking lot, kissing, breathing hard, our hands exploring each other. I'd unbuckled his pants and put my hand inside—he'd jerked away from me as if I'd slipped a red-hot poker into his jeans. No doubt he'd heard his mother's voice inside his head. The truth is that I wanted him now, not out of lust but to make me forget. Still, I knew how much school mattered to him.

"I've got Wolfears with me. I'll set the alarm when you go."

It took me a little longer, but I convinced him to leave. The Chugger sounded like an asthmatic bowling ball as he drove away.

I headed upstairs to my bedroom to change into clothes that wouldn't trip me if I didn't hold them up. At the landing is a full-length mirror. Normally, I stopped on my way up or down to check myself out, admire myself when I felt pretty and find imperfections on insecure days.

I didn't want to look in the mirror this time. I didn't know whom I'd see. Would it be me? Would the face looking back at me be a stranger's? My feet stopped on the landing. I stared at them before slowly raising my eyes. In the mirror, I saw an empty-eyed girl in baggy clothes staring back at me. Though her flattened hair clung to her cheeks in tangled strands, it perfectly followed its natural part down the middle. I knew the face belonged to me because I recognized my hair. It had a will of it's own. No matter how I might attempt to style it, it never felt comfortable any other way than parting down the middle. Changing it was like fighting nature.

After dressing in my own clothes, I went downstairs to feed Wolfears. He must have been starving, but he didn't gobble his food with his normal enthusiasm. Next I prepared Sneakers' food—she was always fed separately because she became territorial around food, no doubt due to the wild, Serval, half of her genes. She didn't show herself, and I realized I'd not seen her since I'd been home. Usually, she comes when she hears the can opener. Maybe the disruption in her feeding schedule had thrown her off.

I started to worry that she'd escaped. I wasn't afraid of her running away, but being a hybrid with her spotted coat and exotic beauty, I worried she might wander the neighborhood and someone might snatch her. Also, she needed to be watched around wildlife. One time she'd pounced on a young gull that was resting on the wall. My mother was horrified and screamed at the sight of the mangled body, blood, and feathers. My father had disposed of the bird. Later I'd found a few scattered feathers. I'd picked them up and dropped them over our cliff wall and watched them float down to the sea and rocks below.

"Where's Sneakers?" I asked Wolfears.

He ran to the basement stairs and stopped. He never took stairs unprompted, unless there was a reward waiting at the other end.

Our home has two basement rooms—one is devoted to Sneakers. To keep her active mind stimulated, it was set up with cat towers, furry cat toys, balls and even remote-controlled toys on timers for her to stalk. It wasn't surprising considering my father's fondness for the cat. She was one of many gifts he'd received from friends and colleagues. No matter how busy, he always made time every day to leash her up and walk her. And Sneakers had bonded with him much more than with my mother or me. With us, she acted with the aloofness more typical of her domesticated cat ancestry. How I would take care of her from now on, I didn't want to think about. One meal at a time, I told myself as I stood at the top of the stairs.

The other basement room was my father's office. Rather than having his office above, he preferred the quiet location because he found the noise of the ocean waves a distraction.

I suddenly felt afraid to go down the stairs, as if my father's ghost was waiting for me in his office. It was a stupid thought. I don't believe in ghosts. For a moment, I wished I'd not sent Garrett home. Taking a breath, I took hold of Wolfears' collar and forced myself to go down the stairs, past the plaques, awards and pictures of babies my father had helped bring into the world for his patients.

The door to Sneakers' room was shut. Sometimes she accidentally closes it and traps herself, which is exactly what she'd done this time. When I let her out, she paused only long enough to take a playful swipe at Wolfears before leaping up the stairs.

My father's door was shut too. I couldn't help but wonder if, inside, there might be clues as to why my father had done what he'd done. Standing in front of it, I felt my anxiety rising. I needed to kill my irrational fear.

I pushed the door open and turned on the light. I forced myself to step inside. The air felt colder. Maybe it was my imagination.

Unlike me, my parents kept things neat and orderly. His office was no exception. A row of black file cabinets lined the far wall with their drawers closed and typed labels on each. There were no decorations on the walls or personal effects in the room, other than a framed picture on his desk of my mother and me taken on a vacation in Hawaii. There was something about the room that gave it a feeling of business being completed.

When I opened his top desk drawer, I saw that even his office supplies were neatly organized in trays. Picking up a paperclip gave me the feeling I was violating his personal space. I didn't know what to do with the paperclip or even why I'd picked it up. I waved it around before dropping it back in place. The drawer clicked when I closed it, sounding like a piece of puzzle box being slipped back in place. The backs of my legs bumped his office chair. I sat down and spun in a circle. I remembered being a little girl and my father spinning me in the chair. I stopped rotating, and my eyes rested on the Hawaii picture. My mother had her arm around me and we both had big smiles. I stared at the picture and wanted to be inside of it.

When I slid the picture toward me for a closer look, an envelope resting behind it slipped out. Curious, I picked up the envelope. It was stamped and addressed to Maria Nogales, a name I didn't recognize. It was unsealed, and the only thing inside was a check, dated two weeks ago, made out to her for ten thousand dollars.

My mouth hung open as I wondered what it was for. Then, I remembered my father complaining about the cost of the interior decorator for the recent renovation they'd done at his practice.

Maybe Ms. Nogales was the decorator, and it was part of her payment.

I put the check back in the envelope and positioned it and the picture to where they'd been on his desk, as if it mattered that they looked undisturbed.

As I sat there, I felt my mother's arm around me, just like in the picture. It took me a minute or two before I realized I was imagining it. My body ached, and I was exhausted. I forced myself to stand, turn off the light and head up to bed.

Chapter 10

It was late morning when Wolfears pressed his snout against my face to say, "Hey, what's going on? Get up, lazy bones."

I must have fallen asleep about five-thirty, which is usually when I wake up. Typically, we start the day with a run. Like it or not, he seemed determined to hold me to our normal routine.

I sat up, feeling sore and stiff—nothing too bad, considering. I ignored my aches, got up, dressed, and put on my sneakers.

As we crossed the driveway, I noticed a big, boring car parked across the street. It caught my eye because the entire street is posted for no parking. A man and woman were inside. I wondered if they were the reporters from the hospital Garrett had told me about. When I opened the wicket gate, which is down from the driveway, they stepped out. The man called out hello and walked toward us. Wolfears spread his front legs, lowered his head, and sighted the man's every move as he approached us. The woman remained standing by the car.

"It's okay, Wolfie," I said, and rested my hand on his shoulder.

The man wore dark sunglasses. His skin appeared almost translucent, as if he were freshly scrubbed or made of wax. He didn't look like he spent any time in the sun or, if he did, he covered himself in sunscreen. I could relate.

As he came closer, I saw that his thinning blond hair was combed back from his forehead in straight rows with furrows between the rows, as if combed with a large-toothed comb. He removed his glasses as he stepped into the shadows of the tree towering across the street. Stopping several feet away, he smiled. His smile was nice, almost shy, or nervous. I caught a whiff of his aftershave. It smelled like mandarin orange and lavender.

"Sit," I told Wolfears, who did, though I could still feel the tension in his body as I slid my hand up his neck to his head. He was ready to uncoil in a flash.

"I'm Detective Yates," the man said. "With the sheriff's department."

I thought a shy smile was strange for a cop, not that I really knew what cops were like, other than from books and movies. With a flip of his hand, he opened his wallet and showed me a shiny badge. He could have been a magician the way his fingers fluidly removed a business card. He handed it to me. It had bolded black printing with a blue and gold image of a badge in the center. I was nervous and hardly glanced at it because I was concentrating on Wolfears. The last person I wanted him biting was a policeman. Detective Yates curled his hand into a fist, lowered it and extended his knuckles. Wolfears went over and cautiously sniffed it, then stepped back beside me.

I nodded when he said, "You must be the young lady who's supposed to be in the hospital. I'm terribly sorry to bother you, but I'm investigating the accident and need information that only you can provide."

Do we have to go to the police station?" I asked.

"Not unless you want to," he said and gave a small smile.

For a cop, he seemed easy to talk to. He motioned for the woman to join us, and introduced her, but I didn't catch her name. She had the serious demeanor I expected from a detective. Rather than stand in the street, I held open the gate and invited them inside.

As we walked across the cobblestones, he said, "I'm sorry for your loss."

"I still have my dog," I said in a lame response.

He paused and looked up at the house.

"Look at those wonderful wood accents throughout the stucco. I love the English cottage architecture," he remarked. "Although your home is more the size of a castle than a cottage."

After locking up Sneakers, I led them inside to the living room. They sat on the couch, while I sat in the chair that my father often used.

I felt very small.

"We've talked to a number of witnesses," he said. "I was hoping you could tell me what happened."

"I don't really know," I said, trying to pretend it happened to someone else, and I was simply repeating it. "It all happened so fast. We'd just started home. The next moment the car lurched over the divider from the parking lot onto the walkway. We kept going faster and faster until we reached the end of the pier."

The detective didn't say anything, just looked at me with a concerned expression, waiting for me to tell him more. I wanted to blurt out that my father had gone insane. However, I felt if I told the truth, I would be betraying him.

"That's all," I said.

His partner's eyes had stopped wandering and bored into me. Detective Yates leaned back. I managed to not say anything by looking at the carpet.

"One couple told me they thought your father was trying to run them over," he said.

"What? That's crazy. He wouldn't do that. My dad was trying *not* to hit anybody. That's why he sounded the horn. People scattered to the railing on either side to get out of the way. Something was wrong with the car. The gas pedal got stuck, or something. My father was a hero for not hitting anybody. We came really close several times. It's a miracle nobody else was killed."

Wolfears yelped. I realized I was squeezing his neck and my fingernails were digging into him. I let go and he went to lie down in a safer spot by the fireplace. He rested his head on the brick and closed his eyes, but his ears were up, turned forward.

"Did you notice if your father pumped the brakes or attempted to turn off the ignition?"

"He probably did. I don't know, maybe they didn't work. We were bouncing so badly, I couldn't tell what was going on. Probably just steering the car took all his attention."

"We're having a team inspect the car to assess it for mechanical issues."

"That's good. I don't know how people could think my father would want to hurt anybody." The thought shook me.

"He was a doctor, wasn't he?"

"Yes, he was a reproductive endocrinologist. His patients loved him, and he loved his work. I can show you pictures of babies that his patients have sent him. Some of them even send letters and pictures, updating him as their children grew up."

He nodded and said, "I do need to ask some routine questions, if you don't mind? Did he exhibit any unusual behavior lately? Anything out of the ordinary? I'm sure his profession is stressful . . . might he have mentioned any financial difficulties?"

"No," I said curtly to each of his questions. My head seemed to snap involuntarily.

"How about your time on the pier?"

"It was very normal. We had dinner to celebrate my birthday." I felt my mouth becoming dry. I thought I needed to mention something out of the ordinary. "He was in a good mood. The only unusual thing was that, on the way out of The Pelican, he didn't hand money to the homeless guy that hangs out on the pier. Usually, he gives him some cash."

"Ah, Ronald," the detective said.

I was surprised he knew the guy's name.

"Did you interview him, too?" I asked.

He gave his reserved smile again. "That's a good idea. Maybe you should be a detective."

I almost laughed, but didn't. The female detective didn't laugh either.

I began feeling sick to my stomach. I hate not telling the truth. It bothered me how easily I had lied.

I sat there wondering if I knew my father at all, or even myself. I had told them what I wanted to believe.

Maybe if I repeated the lies enough, they would become true.

Chapter 11

Detective Yates rested his hands on his knees and leaned forward. I thought he was about to get up to leave, but then his hands came back to his lap.

"May I ask about your relatives?"

"I guess," I said.

"Do you have any family living nearby that I could contact?"

I was puzzled as to his question. "Nobody close by. My father has a brother and his parents—my grandparents—but they are all in Japan. That's it."

For some reason, I kept looking at his hands. One hand was over the other, fingertips resting on the knuckles.

"Why do you want to know about my family?" I finally managed to ask.

I looked up at his face. He pursed his lips. I dropped my gaze back to his hands. His index finger tapped on the knuckles of his other hand in an uneven rhythm as if tapping out Morse code.

"I'm sorry to have to bring this up, but there's the formality of identification of your parents. I was hoping someone else could come to the medical examiner's office, considering all you've been through."

"So, I have to do it?" I asked, horrified at the thought of seeing my parents' lifeless bodies. "My mother's only relative is her sister, but they don't stay in touch. I don't really know her—I haven't seen her since I was little."

"I'd be happy to contact her," he said.

"She doesn't have a phone. She sends me birthday cards. Her return address is a P.O. Box in Yarnell, Arizona."

Not that it mattered or made any sense, but I knew my mom wouldn't want her estranged sister identifying her. They hadn't spoken in years. Talking about her always upset my mom.

The clock above the mantel clicked loudly.

"I'll do it," I heard myself say. "When does it have to be done?"

His partner spoke. "It would be advisable for you to come before the M.E. begins the autopsy."

I jerked. My expression must have been alarming because Yates raised all the fingers on his top hand stretching them like Sneakers' flexing her claws. I thought he might take a swipe at his partner. Instead, he merely lifted his hand. She became silent. He narrowed his eyes when he looked back at me.

"I'm so sorry," he said. "There's no rush. It can wait until you're ready." I nodded, and he continued. "At a time like this, it can be helpful to be with friends or see a professional."

"My boyfriend will take care of me," I said. When he didn't say anything, I added, "My mother sees, I mean she *saw*, a psychologist. I can call her if I need to."

"You have my card, please give me a call when you're ready. I'll be happy to accompany you to the examiner," he said. "Thank you for your time, and again, our sympathy on your loss."

He placed his hands on his knees again. This time he rose from the couch. His partner gave me a strained smile and followed him. His shoes creaked in the entryway, hers clicked. Funny, they looked like they were wearing identical shoes.

When he reached the front door, I blurted out, "I want to go now. I'd rather get it over with, so I don't have to think about it."

Detective Yates offered to drive me there in his big, boring government car. His offer seemed both unusual and kind. I wondered if sheriffs normally do that. I was thankful because I felt dread at the thought of driving. Strangely, I didn't mind riding as a passenger.

Before leaving, I let Sneakers out and locked the doggy door to keep her from escaping. I let Wolfears outside to roam the yard while I was gone.

When I met them at his car, I was mildly surprised that his unmarked police car hadn't been ticketed or towed. The Concha Pointe private security regularly patrolled and called parking control on violators. I supposed cops didn't worry about such things. Then I noticed the license plate only had a short string of numbers and thought that maybe that alerted parking enforcement and tow truck drivers not to mess with it.

Out in the sunshine, his partner seemed to relax and commented on the quietness of the neighborhood. She offered to let me ride in the front seat. I declined, saying her legs were longer, and I'd be comfortable in the back. In contrast to his quiet demeanor, Yates drove aggressively, changing lanes often and braking at the last moment. I wondered if all cops drove like that. Like my first ride in the ambulance, I'd never ridden in a cop car before. Going to the morgue would be another first. I'd had enough of them. I wanted to say I'd changed my mind, but there was no moisture in my mouth and my lips were glued together.

* * *

The weathered red bricks and gray concrete of the medical examiner's building presented itself with a stately dignity that modern government buildings lack. It appeared as a monument to the solidity of death in contrast to the ephemeral wisps of living.

We parked in a reserved space in front and climbed the stairs. The wooden doors opened into an expansive lobby with detailed craftsmanship. Across the room in the center, a regal-looking staircase with royal blue carpeting led upstairs. The floor had honeycomb-shaped tiles, mostly white with staggered embellishments that looked like heraldic crests. I wondered if they were the coat of arms of a family lost to history. In the center of the room, a pair of burgundy couches faced each other, divided by a wooden table. The table held an empty glass bowl and several magazines. Along the sides of the room were aged wooden doors with arched windows above them. None of the doors had any nameplates that I could see. Detective Yates motioned for me and his partner to take a seat on the couch and disappeared through one of them. Not one for small talk, his partner crossed her legs and picked up a magazine.

She'd only turned a few pages when Yates returned with the medical examiner, a man of South Asian ancestry who had graying temples and wore wire-framed glasses. He had a long name that Detective Yates pronounced with precision. I was glad I didn't have to repeat it.

As we followed him, the ME spoke in a soft, melodic voice that contrasted with the echo of our footsteps on the marble walls. We didn't take the stairs. He led us toward the back of the building to the morgue.

Unlike the lobby, the storage room of the morgue was cold. The room was a bloodless white and a row of mortuary cabinets stretched along one wall like file cabinets for a stainless steel purgatory. I managed to keep my feet moving forward and followed the ME. He opened two cabinet doors in the second row above the floor and slid out the two shelves. The bodies were covered with sheets. I recalled my ride in the ambulance.

"Are the sheets soft?" I asked. I didn't want to touch them, but I needed to know.

"Yes, they are," the ME said, and brushed his fingertips along the sheet where it hung over the edge.

He motioned me beside the first shelf. Detective Yates stepped next to me as if ready to catch me if I fainted. My heart shot up, stuck in my throat and rocketed to my skull where it pounded inside of my head like a sledgehammer. The ME's hands moved in slow motion as he grasped the top of the sheet.

He lifted it back as if revealing a great treasure, but it wasn't a treasure, only lifeless clay, an imitation of my mother's beautiful face, a shell of whom I loved.

I didn't faint. I wasn't there. Someone else was standing next to the metal shelf and identified her body.

The ME moved to the other sheeted body.

"Ready?" he asked.

My head nodded and he began his ceremonious lifting of the sheet. This time, I thought I might faint because I expected him to reveal the head of a monster, someone I would hate. But there was no monster beneath the sheet, only the bruised, lifeless face of my father. Another shell of someone I cherished.

In a tiny voice, I said, "I love you, Daddy," and reached out to touch his swollen, purple cheek.

Chapter 12

Yates dropped me off on the street in front of our home. I punched the code on the keypad and the driveway gate rattled as it opened. A streak of black fur shot across the driveway towards me. When Yates saw Wolfears coming to greet me, he smiled and started away. His partner gave a wave.

With Wolfears beside me as we crossed the driveway, everything felt the same, until we stepped through the front door and Wolfears scrambled ahead of me. His nails clicked on the tiles. Their sound echoed as they always must have done, but I'd never noticed how hollow the entry sounded, like a mausoleum. As I followed him, my own footfalls echoed too.

Wolfears skidded to a stop where Sneakers was sleeping on top of the China cabinet, her tail and one paw hung over the edge. With an indifference common to cats, she took no interest in my arriving home, if she'd even noticed. Not even her tail twitched.

A red flashing light on the telephone answering machine pulsed insistently. I would have ignored it, but I hoped I hadn't missed a call from Garrett. I listened to the messages, counting them by marking hash marks on the notepad beside the phone. Many of them were from neighbors and friends of my parents. News travels fast in the community of Concha Pointe. Several people mentioned attorneys they knew that handled lawsuits regarding wrongful deaths. Three calls were from real estate agents inquiring about listing our home for sale. Two calls from sickos wanting to know the details of my parents' last moments.

I was listening to call number fourteen when the phone rang again.

It was Garrett. He was between classes and said he could drive over to see me before going to work if I wanted. I told him I was fine, and he didn't need to, but I didn't mean it. He promised to come over tomorrow, on Saturday, before work.

Message number eighteen was spoken in a whisper. Still, I recognized Mysti's voice instantly. Hearing her filled me with emotion. I hadn't known if we would ever speak again.

"I heard what happened. Call me." That was the entirety of her message.

She was my best friend, but we'd not spoken in months. I'd said some pretty bad things to her the last time we saw each other and I'd never apologized. I picked up the phone and then put it back down. What would I say to her?

I wanted to return to the beach to see if my pants had washed up—and my ring. I was trying to get up the courage to drive there when the phone rang again. It was Mysti.

"Hi," I said.

"Are you home?" she asked.

"Yes."

"I'm coming over."

She hung up without saying goodbye.

I felt anxious about seeing her and went out to the backyard.

Unlike inside the house, being in the backyard seemed as if nothing had changed. In contrast to the house's English Tudor style, the backyard has a Mediterranean ambiance. The pool is the centerpiece. Against the south-east side of the yard is a lemon tree and four of my mother's sculptures. In front of the sculptures is a circular, brick fire pit that matches the waist-high brick wall that borders the cliffside back of the property. Beyond it, the ocean stretches to the horizon. Perhaps I should have felt anger at the sight of the ocean.

I did not.

Being in the backyard was an oasis for my turbulent mind. I inhaled the crisp ocean air and almost felt as if I could slip back in time. As I wandered around, an acrid scent pricked the fresh air. Ashes and a few curled pieces of paper rested in the fire pit. Seeing them reminded me of roasting marshmallows with Mysti. She and I often hung out in the backyard.

Mysti was the most uninhibited person I knew. Whenever we were alone—which was often with my workaholic father and my mom's active social life—Mysti would drop her clothes on the deck and jump in the pool. After swimming, she'd lie beside the pool, and not dress again until we heard one of my parents coming home. She claimed being naked was the natural human state.

"You vain creature, I think you just don't want any tan lines," I'd tell her.

"Besides, it's just the two of us here," she'd say in defense. "and hippie blood runs through my veins, don't you know."

It took a while, but she finally convinced me to give a naked swim a try. I had to admit it felt good, but as soon as I'd get out, I'd wrap myself in a towel. While she bronzed, I'd climb up and lie on top of a section of the wall that hung over the cliff, which I'd dubbed the half-moon. Mysti called it the suicide spur. The double row of bricks on top was just wide enough for me. At the right times of day, it was shaded by the broad leaves of the white bird of paradise beside it. Lying there I could look out at the ocean or peek over the edge of the cliff and look down at the rocks below. Depending on the tide, only the tips would being showing or they could be exposed like jagged rows of crooked teeth.

One day, while half-asleep lying on my back with my towel wrapped around me, a gust of wind had blown my towel open. I'd wrapped myself again, but the wind was persistent and kept blowing it open. I'd given up trying to keep it around me and had laid there with the warmth of the bricks through the towel on my back and the coolness of the wind off the ocean caressing my skin. Mysti had converted me to what she called "being a naturist."

"You're a free spirit now," she had said.

We spent many fun days by the pool being naturists until one warm, cloudless day. I was at my usual spot on the wall lying on my green towel with the Bigfoot footprints. Mysti was on her stomach lying on her towel beside the pool. I'd been on my back with my head turned outward, watching the ocean swell and listening to the waves crashing onto the rocks below. As it was warm even in the shade, I was getting thirsty and had decided to get a drink from the fridge. I swung my feet onto the bench seat that wraps below the half-moon and stepped down from it into the yard. I'd called out to Mysti to ask if she wanted something, too, but she hadn't answered. I thought she'd fallen asleep.

As I started to cross to the kitchen, I happened to glance up and saw my younger, next-door neighbor, Donny, in an upstairs window leering down at us over the tops of the junipers.

I'd let out a cry and had run back and snatched my towel to shield my naked body from his gaze. Mysti had raised her head and looked at me. Clutching my towel against me, I'd pointed at the window. Unlike my instinct to immediately cover myself, she'd left her towel on the deck and had stood, naked and unembarrassed, with her breasts jutting out as if they were the prows of ships. She'd strutted a couple of steps in Donny's direction, a big smile on her face. She'd raised her hand as if to wave to him, and he'd looked like he was pressing his forehead so hard against the glass that it might shatter. She'd rotated the back of her hand toward him, her smile turned into a sneer. Then she'd thrust her hand up and flipped out her middle finger. His head jerked back from the window. She'd laughed, while my mouth had hung open.

Having Donny leering at me seemed such an insignificant thing now.

I must have been in a trance staring into the pool water because I was startled when I heard Mysti's voice. She was standing on the other side of the pool.

Since I'd last seen her, she'd had her hair cut to shoulder length, like my mother's. She looked more like my mother's daughter than I did.

She ran around the pool to me, while saying, "You didn't answer the buzzer. Luckily, the gate code hasn't been changed."

I bit my lower lip and stood there watching her with my arms hanging at my sides. When she reached me, she wrapped me in a bear hug. I buried my face into her neck and tears came. My body shook. I couldn't hug her back because she had my arms pinned against my sides.

Chapter 13

When I told Mysti about losing my engagement ring and wanting to look for it on the beach, she looked skeptical.

"I wouldn't count on it," she said. "The odds of finding your pants are pretty low."

"It could happen. Life is full of impossibilities. Some of them must be positive. Like you—you came back into my life just when I needed you most."

"Are you sure you're okay going back there?" she asked. "I could go look for you."

"I'll be fine. I have to try."

"Okay then, but I'll drive."

When Mysti parked on the gray asphalt beside the pier, I saw a ribbon of yellow crime scene tape that had broken loose and was fluttering in the wind. Mysti opened her door to get out. I remained sitting, suddenly feeling as if I could not inhale enough air to breathe. I knitted my fingers together. I couldn't tear them apart to open the door.

"What's wrong?" she asked.

I banged my clutched hands against my chest to indicate that I thought I was having a heart attack. Mysti slid back into her seat and put her hand on the back of my neck.

"Try and slow your breathing," she said. "I think you're having a panic attack. You're going to be okay."

"I can't do it." I said between gasps. "I can't get out of the car."

Mysti stroked my neck and hair. After several minutes, I managed to slow my breathing.

A jogger wearing headphones ran by.

"Can you turn on the radio?" I asked.

Music helped.

I looked over at Mysti and said, "It didn't happen the way I told the police."

"What do you mean?"

"I don't think anything was wrong with the car. My father wanted to drive us off the pier."

Her eyes widened and she jerked back in the seat. "You can't even think that. No, not your father. He would never do that."

"Something inside him snapped."

"You mean like a brain tumor?"

"I don't know. I *don't* know, but I need to figure out why."

Mysti looked at me sympathetically. I could tell she didn't believe me.

"I found a check in his office made out to a woman. Do you think he was having an affair?"

Mysti laughed. "Your father? He's not the type. I'm sure he writes lots of checks. Why do you think it had something to do with an affair?"

"It was for ten thousand dollars. Maybe she was blackmailing him."

"I don't think that would make someone drive off a pier. Couldn't the check be for something else?"

"I guess it could be something for work . . ."

"Exactly. Look, you just had something horribly stressful happen—it's playing with your imagination. Do you want to go home?"

I shook my head, took three deep breaths and got out of the car.

Since the current runs down the coast, we figured the most likely place my pants could have washed up would be on the south side of the pier. Walking under the pier, I shivered. I took off my shoes and walked barefoot down by the water's edge. As the waves spread up the sand, they tickled my feet and soaked the bottom of my pants with the chilly water. I hardly noticed, lost in thought about what could have driven my father to do the unthinkable.

I wanted to believe Mysti; believe that I was wrong, but I knew I wasn't. I don't know why it mattered, but the need to find out the reason felt like a hot stone caught in my throat.

Mysti walked farther up the beach to scan there. We found nothing more interesting than seaweed and a plastic, blue toy shovel.

When we'd gone a mile, Mysti said, "Too bad jeans don't float."

We turned around and walked back together. Clouds moved in front of the sun. The dispassionate ocean pushed the remnants of a wave a bit farther up the beach and soaked my pants to my knees. I realized that my feet were cold and I shivered.

Just before we reached the parking lot, I gathered my courage and said, "I didn't mean what I said about you."

Mysti stopped. "That I'm a slut or that I hit on Garrett?"

Her voice sounded tight, like her vocal cords were piano strings. I didn't want to look at her.

"Neither. I freaked out when he told me that *you* hit on him at the party."

"That's not what happened. Like I told you, *he* hit on me."

"You've got to understand, I thought you were trying to steal him. Garrett is the only guy I'd ever gone steady with. You can have any guy you want."

"What? Hardly."

"You're built like a Viking goddess. If you smile, guys start drooling."

"What? You're prettier than I am. Guys don't like me more. I'm just more friendly and approachable. I'm the girl next door. You're a bit aloof, more reserved, intimidating. That's all."

"You mean introverted? It does take me a while to warm up to people. I'm not like you. I've always been a little bit jealous of your social skills."

"I'd never hit on a friend's guy. It hurt me that you'd even think that I would. I didn't want to tell you, but I thought that you needed to know what happened. You'd just started going steady with him. I didn't tell you to hurt you. He probably told you that to cover his tracks in case someone told you what actually happened—that *he* hit on *me*."

I knew she believed it, even if it wasn't true. She was probably high at the party and didn't remember it clearly. Garrett wouldn't have lied to me, but the last thing I wanted was to lose her again.

"I believe you," I said. "I'm sorry,"

"Thank you."

"Obviously, we're engaged now, so I don't need to worry about his straying anymore."

Just then, I heard a familiar voice. It was Del on his way to work.

"Hello, gorgeous. I bet you're here to pick up your father's phone. When the busboy found it, I ran after you, but you had already left. A good thing too because right after, a madman drove onto the pier and—"

I don't know what my expression looked like. Del's eyes grew wide when he saw it. He stopped mid-sentence and took a step back.

"The gas pedal stuck. My father was not a madman. He was a hero."

Chapter 14

When Mysti dropped me off back home, I fixed myself lunch, but didn't have much interest in eating. I wished I could see or at least talk with Garrett, but I didn't want to interrupt his studies. I thought about how we used to talk for hours on the phone—I don't even remember what we talked about now. It's funny how in many ways we didn't have a lot in common, but we'd always felt so comfortable just hanging out with each other. Just being with him made me tingle. Of course there was also the physical. He was as attractive as hell with his long legs and eyelashes that I hoped our kids would inherit.

As I sat there with my half-eaten lunch, the phone rang and startled me. Maybe he was calling me between deliveries. Then, I realized it was my father's phone. I was scared to answer it. What would I say? I let the call go to messages.

I started to worry that it was my father's turn to be on-call and one of their patients had an emergency. Then, I thought about it. He'd said he was taking the weekend off, so he wouldn't be on-call. I decided to listen to the messages anyway. Maybe they'd hold a clue about my father's secret life that would help me make some sense of what had happened.

The first message puzzled me. It was time-stamped during my birthday dinner, when he'd ignored the call. The number was from Cummings University, where he'd done post-doctorate research.

The caller said: *"Robert, where are you? I've already left you two messages. I know you're a busy man, but call me right away. You know how important this is."*

The man's voice sounded older, and he was obviously impatient. For some reason, I envisioned him as a small man with a ferret face and jittery eyes. He didn't bother leaving his name, so my father must have known him well. What also struck me was that he called my father "Robert" not "Dr. Otomo." The only person I knew who called my father by his first name was my mother. I might have thought the message was a wrong number if he hadn't used my father's name. I jotted down the number. With the push of a button, I deleted the message and moved on.

The next few messages were from patients, non-urgent calls that could be referred to the office. Then came a message by a woman who enunciated precisely.

"Hello, Dr. Otomo, this is Brenda Delgado. I'm sorry for the delay in getting back to you. We just got back from Puerta Vallarta. Orlando and I would be delighted to take Sneakers, and I'm sure that Boots won't have a problem. They're from the same litter, after all. Perhaps a bit jealous at first. Just let us know when you're ready, and we'll be happy to come and pick her up. Or, of course, we'd be thrilled to have you drop her off and see her new home. Just let us know. I'm sure she'll be incredibly happy here."

The message stunned me. I couldn't believe my father had ever thought of parting with Sneakers. He considered her part of the family. The possibility he would give her up for adoption chilled me because it indicated that what happened on the pier wasn't a momentary break with sanity, but something he planned.

The messages raised more questions about who my father was and what was going on in his life. Whatever it was, I wanted to know, and I didn't want to know. Was it something illegal? That sounded way out of character for my father. He was a man whose life was ordered by routine and rightness. Or was it, I wondered? My father had always been a good man. I needed to understand. I knew it was best to keep busy, to keep my mind from spiraling, so I called the university number. I expected to get no answer or a machine.

"Professor Pinsky's office," said a male voice.

"Hello," I said. "Is Mr. Pinsky available?"

"*Professor* Pinsky," the voice said, correcting me. "He's not here right now. Can I take a message?"

I didn't think I should leave a message that my father was dead. It seemed like a cold way to inform him.

"No, I'll call back later. Do you know when he'll be in?"

"His office hours are Mondays and Wednesdays from 3:30-5:00, or by appointment. Other than that, who knows? Are you sure you don't want to leave a message?"

On a whim, I asked, "How old is the professor?"

"I dunno. He's old. That's a weird question."

"What does he teach?"

"Cellular biology, mostly."

"Oh, he's not a medical doctor?"

"How do you not know anything about him and you're calling for him?"

"Someone recommended him," I said.

I had no idea where I was going with this, but the guy on the other end of the line seemed more amused than aggravated by my questions.

"Recommended him for what?" he asked.

"I'm deciding on classes."

"Oh, you're a student. Now I know why you're calling. If you want to apply for one of the internships, you need to submit your application and get on the waiting list like everybody else." He paused and laughed. "You don't want to talk to him on the phone. He can be cranky if you waste his time. Although, I can tell you he really knows his stuff. He's way into research, so if you want hands on experience, he's the best."

"Are you an intern?"

"Duh, why else would I be answering the phone on a Friday night?"

I took a wild stab, and said, "Do you know Dr. Otomo?"

"Sure, the guest lecturer that gave the talk on mitochondrial replacement therapy and cytoplasmic transfer."

I had no idea what he was talking about, but said, "Yes."

"Cool. Why?"

My instinct was to hang up. Instead, I said, "I'm his daughter."

"Wow, you're so lucky. You must have absorbed so much just by osmosis. You'll go to the front of the line."

I didn't have any more idea of what osmosis was than I did about cytoplasmic whatever. I needed to head to the library.

"Yes," I said, fumbling. "I think so. No, not really, I guess."

"You're funny. Hold on. I've got another call."

The phone clicked and music came on the line. I realized that Professor Pinsky must have been calling my father to ask him to do another lecture. There was no nefarious connection to him. My imagination was running away with me.

I didn't wait for the intern to come back on the line and hung up.

Chapter 15

The only clue I had was the unmailed check to Maria Nogales. I went to my father's office and retrieved the envelope. Her address was in Sun Valley, a neighborhood in the San Fernando Valley of Los Angeles. If I delivered the letter in person, maybe I could learn something. I'd have to drive, but I'd have to get over that fear eventually anyway.

With all that had been happening, I felt like things were closing in on me. Even my clothes felt restricting. I just wanted to wear something loose that made me feel a bit free. Besides, it was likely to be hotter once I went over the hill. I chose what I called my relief dress, a casual olive-green number, which hung off my shoulders to just above my knees, a bit shapelier than an oversized T-shirt, but not much. To complement it, I slipped on a pair of flats and was ready. Hardly practical attire, but all I was planning to do was drop off the letter and hope to meet this woman, to learn her connection to my father.

Once I began driving, I found my anxiety about it disappeared. I liked the feeling of being in control of something.

Even in the late afternoon, it was hot in the Valley. I drove the freeways until taking the Sunland Boulevard exit toward the hills. In about a mile, I came to Maria's street, La Tuna Canyon, and turned right. Unlike the freeways and the boulevard, there was very little traffic. It was more rural than I expected. It was in the shadows of the hills and a bit cooler, but still warm. Nice homes—some with horses in corrals—were mixed with others that looked like hovels. Like where I lived, there were no curbs with street numbers. Only some of the homes had visible numbers on them. I was curious what Maria's address would look like. I didn't see the number for her house. The numbers above and below hers were on either side of a dirt driveway next to a telephone pole. I made a U-turn and parked beside the pole.

I sat listening to the engine click as it cooled. It was still daylight, but everything was in shadow except the top half of the northside hills. I rolled down the window and smelled the fragrance of chaparral with a hint of jasmine. Quiet hung in the air, except for the occasional sound of a passing car or the neigh of a horse.

I missed the rhythm of the waves.

Maybe coming here wasn't such a good idea, I thought. I could come back another time with Garrett, but then I'd have to tell him about the letter.

I didn't want to do that.

I rolled up my window and opened the car door. I picked up the letter and licked the flap to seal it and stepped out of my car.

Walking up the driveway to what I hoped was Maria's house, dogs began barking. I was glad it wasn't dark yet. I was accustomed to well-paved driveways and trimmed hedges, not rutted dirt and thirsty, untamed bushes. The neighbor's fence ran up the side of the driveway. There were gaps in the pickets and only a little white paint remained on the weathered wood.

I maneuvered around the large ruts in the hard-packed ground of the driveway, now wishing that I'd worn something more practical than a dress and sandals. The dress was pocketless, so I held my car keys in one hand and the envelope in the other.

A curve in the driveway blocked the house from the street. When I went around it, I saw the house.

From its dilapidated appearance, I would have thought it was vacant except for the noise of a television coming from inside, and an old blue truck with oversized tires parked by the garage. I stopped, thinking how I couldn't run as fast in sandals as in my sneakers. At least I hadn't worn high heels—not that I would need to run. It was just an old house. I tamped down my instinct to turn around and go back to my car.

The shutter on one side of the front window was hanging crooked as if held up by a solitary nail. I could only imagine that it was rusty and would one day give way, and the shutter would fall onto the brown, dead shrubbery below the window. The window itself had a crack crossing the lower corner next to the opposite shutter. Behind the window, a pink curtain was pulled to one side, likely it had once been red, but the morning sun had baked it pale.

A small face pressed against the glass beside the curtain.—what I'd thought was a child's face was only a faded doll.

What had once been a lawn looked as if it had not been watered in years. A few clumps of stale yellow grass with tinges of green remained, but most of the yard had been reduced to no more than dirt. The exception was where a foot-high patch of weeds grew along one edge where runoff from the neighbor's yard led to the ruts in the driveway. The wooden garage door was warped, bowed enough to make gaps on each side. Perhaps whoever lived there was sick and unable to care for the place.

By the stairs to the porch, I noticed a pizza box resting in the dirt. The lid was closed, but several flies were investigating, puzzling a way inside. The pizza chain Garrett worked for sometimes transferred him to Valley stores when there were staffing shortages. He often said he felt people looked down on him when he made deliveries. I thought he wouldn't feel that way if he made a delivery here.

My courage was emboldened by my curiosity about what my father's connection would be to a person living in this place. I went up the wooden stairs to the door. A television laugh track crackled from inside. On the porch were recent newspapers still wrapped in plastic—I recognized the cover on the *L.A. Times*. It was the issue with the story of our car plunging off the pier and the death of my parents.

My mouth felt like it was full of stale peanut butter. I felt dizzy.

I kicked the *Times* off the porch and it landed by the pizza box. The flies flew off, but quickly returned.

I couldn't find a doorbell and rapped on the screen door instead. No one answered.

Thinking my knocks couldn't be heard over the television, I pulled open the screen door. In the center of the door was a knocker below a peep window. I lifted and tapped the knocker twice. It didn't echo, but clacked, sounding as worn out as the house and the yard.

"Go away," a man's voice shouted from inside.

Ordinarily, I would have turned around. If I hadn't driven so far, I would have. Twice again, I lifted the knocker and struck the strike plate. Its dead thuds sounded bleak. The television volume lowered.

"What the hell?" the voice called. "I said go away. Scram. You'll get your rent when you get it."

Plucking my courage, I spoke to the peep window. "I'm not here for the rent. Does a Maria Nogales live here?"

The voice didn't respond. The television went silent. I heard footsteps from inside.

I closed the screen door and stepped back. The little window in the door opened and revealed a blinking eye.

"Who wants to know?"

"I have a letter for her."

"Are you a process server?" he asked.

"What's that?"

The eye pulled back and the peep window slapped shut. I heard a bolt being undone and the door swung back.

A man of maybe thirty in a T-shirt and boxer underwear stood in the opening. He nudged the screen door out a few inches and stuck out a thick hand through the opening.

"I'll take that," he said. "Give it here."

His stale, alcohol-soaked breath assaulted the air and felt as if it scraped my cheeks. I stepped back to the edge of the porch and pressed the letter to my chest.

"It's for Maria," I said, in a voice sounding bolder than I felt.

The man snorted and gave me the once-over, his eyes crawling down and up my body like a spider with hairy legs.

"She's cleaning up out back," he said. "Come on in."

He pushed open the screen door and stepped to the side to make room for me. I shook my head and took another step back.

"Be that way. Maybe she's too busy if you don't come in."

"I'll come back another time," I said.

"Who the hell is it?" a woman's voice called out from the back of the house.

"It's an angel with a message from God," the man called back. He laughed, which made his belly jiggle beneath his once-white T-shirt.

"What are you talking about?" the woman asked. "God, not another process server?"

"She don't look like a process server. She's wearing a dress. Says she's got a letter for you."

"For real?"

"I think so. She don't look smart enough to be cagey," he said.

I heard hurried footsteps almost running across the floor. She pushed aside the man and stood in the doorway.

I don't know what I expected her to look like, but she didn't match the house and certainly could have done a lot better than the slob she was living with. She wore a pair of old blue jeans and a yellow blouse that was too tight, probably to show off her figure. She was petite and somewhere around forty. I could see how some men would find her attractive, but my father? She couldn't compare to my mother.

"Are you Maria?" I asked, attempting to conceal my shock.

"Who are you?" she asked. "You don't look like a courier."

"I work in Dr. Otomo's office," I said.

The man clapped his hands.

"What did I tell you, baby?" he exclaimed. "What'd I tell you?"

She flung a hand behind her and gave him a thump on the chest.

"Why don't you mind your own business?" she told him.

"I knew you could squeeze more money out of him. I'm a friggin' genius."

She ignored him and locked her eyes onto the envelope in my hand.

"Com'on, baby, it was my idea. Give me some credit," he said. "I told you life would be good with me."

He put his hands on her shoulders. She shook them off. He made a horse-like snort and retreated inside. She stepped out onto the porch and closed the door behind her. When the television blasted again, her eyes widened and her lips parted, revealing two rows of teeth so white that I wondered if they were fake.

She thrust out her hand, palm up, and said, "I'm Maria."

Unlike the man's wandering eyes, her cat eyes remained focused on the letter. I pressed it against my chest, realizing that once she had what she wanted, she'd not be motivated to tell me anything. I suddenly felt thirsty and wished that I'd brought a bottle of water with me.

"He told me to ask, how you are doing?" I said, and forced myself not to look down at the newspaper.

"I'll be good if that envelope has what I think it has," she said.

Taking a wild stab, I said, "I don't remember you. Are you a patient of his?"

"You're pretty curious for an employee. What are you up to?"

"Just doing my job," I said, stumbling for what to say next.

Her hand darted out, quick as a gecko's tongue and snatched the letter from me. She eagerly tore it open. Her eyes brightened when she saw the check.

"Tell the doctor I'm fine," she said.

She stepped back and shut the door in my face.

Chapter 16

For a moment I stood on the porch, stunned at the rudeness of the woman. By the time I drove away, my astonishment had turned to a mix of emotions: anger, contempt, and a touch of pity. It felt as if I'd stepped into another world.

As the flush of anger lessened, I told myself how lucky I was not to be her. I knew I lived a privileged life, but it also dawned on me that it had been a sheltered one too, at least until it was shattered. Sure, I wasn't an idiot. I knew many people lived their lives in various circumstances unlike mine. I'd read about different kinds of people, seen them portrayed on television and in movies, but I'd never actually stepped into their world like I had just done.

The worst part was that I wasn't any closer to understanding how she was connected to my father. The only thing I'd learned about her was that she didn't appear to know that he was dead. If she'd been a patient, why would he be sending her money? If it were medical malpractice, such things would be managed through legal channels.

Obviously, it was something under the table, which was so unlike my honest father.

What was he hiding?

Could it be an affair? I couldn't believe my father would have been attracted to someone other than my mother—it seemed impossible. If not that—if she were simply blackmailing him—I couldn't imagine what for.

Nothing made sense. Certainly, from where she lived, these surroundings, she didn't look like a typical patient of my father's. They were mostly wealthy people, often professionals who had delayed having children until their childbearing years were nearing their end and nature needed a bit of assistance.

I didn't like the woman. She was so unpleasant that I felt it hard to find much sympathy for her. I wondered if I lacked empathy. It made me worry that I wasn't the good person I believed I was. She probably didn't have a lot of choices, but she did have the choice to not be rude and live with a dirty pizza box in the front yard that she was too lazy to put in the trash.

What disturbed me most about her was the look in her eyes when she saw the check. It had the look of a ravenous predator.

She was ten thousand dollars richer. I wondered what she would spend it on.

The car behind me honked. I'd been so lost in thought that I hadn't noticed when the light changed green. I took my foot off the brake and pressed the gas pedal to head toward the freeway and the comfort of home. Instead of heading straight at the next light, I made a right turn onto Glenoaks Boulevard, a main street before the freeway.

The experience of seeing a different lifestyle up close seemed to heighten my awareness beyond myself. I drove through an industrial area and saw people living on the street and in their cars. Litter blew like tumbleweeds from the gusts stirred up by passing cars. I drove through areas with liquor stores and houses tucked between businesses. There were churches with sharp-edged crosses guarding green, well-trimmed lawns, and cars that looked like they belonged in junk yards and not on the road. I passed a gigantic hole in the ground, a landfill with garbage trucks descending into it. Yellow earth moving machines stood motionless in the pit, like gigantic praying mantis insects patiently waiting for their next victims.

A semi-truck and trailer rumbled by me. Black exhaust rose from it. I wondered about the lives of truckers who spent so much time on the road. What were their lives like, rolling from place to place, being away from home day after day?

Around me was civilization. I tasted the dust of people's lives.

I suddenly felt very alone and drove faster.

Eventually, I came to a freeway and headed back toward my home, to where I belonged. At least I hoped I still did.

I suddenly tightened my grip on the steering wheel as I recalled the detective asking if my father was in financial trouble. I hadn't thought that could be possible. Now that I didn't seem to know him at all, I feared there was a chance I couldn't keep our house. It was just another thing I didn't know.

By the time I pulled up to my driveway, it was dark. I couldn't shake my perplexity about what connection my father had to Maria. The question gnawed at me. I supposed that contemplating the puzzle of Maria was unimportant in the scheme of things. Whatever it was, it was in the past. The past is the past, but it occupied my mind, which, in one sense was good because it kept my thoughts from sinking into those that would drag me deep below the waves of life, where the light was dim and little fish nibble at flesh until the skin is raw and the only balm is depression.

My mood lightened when Wolfears greeted me with a wagging tail. He snuck a kiss on my cheek when I bent down to pet him. The first thing I did was feed him and Sneakers. I hadn't eaten either, but nothing sounded appealing. When I went upstairs to change into my jeans, the house was quiet.

It felt spooky in my home, as if it were too big with too many places for mysteries to hide. Luckily, Wolfears was with me. I don't think I could have stood being there without him.

I called Mysti. By the way she slurred her speech and paused to gather her thoughts, I could tell she was intoxicated.

"You're high," I told her.

"Are you mad at me?"

"No."

"You're not?"

"I said I'm not."

"I'm going to a party. Do you want to come? We could pick you up."

I thought I should be around people, but realized that now I had an invitation, I didn't want to be.

I said, "No, not tonight."

"Is everything okay with you?"

"Yes," I told her.

"Why did you call?"

"I just wanted to hear your voice because I'm happy we're friends again."

I heard a horn honk in the background, and she said, "My ride's here. Are you sure you don't want to come?"

"No, thanks. Don't get too crazy."

"I love you," she said. "I love everybody."

When I hung up, I wandered into the backyard. Except for the stars directly overhead, most of them were obscured by an early fog that covered the ocean with a charcoal gray blanket.

I sat up on the half-moon wall and looked out into the murk. With my legs dangling over the precipice, I listened to waves below gently slapping the rocks. Normally, sitting there listening to them calmed me, but not tonight. I swung my legs up and sat sideways with my feet flat and my knees pointing at the sky. Hugging my legs, I rocked back and forth.

My mind wandered. Now that I had my general education classes done at the community college, I needed to decide on a major for when I transferred to a four-year college. Perhaps it would be best to just be Garrett's wife and focus my energy on supporting him. He'd suggested that once.

The wall was becoming slippery from the dampness so I went inside.

Wolfears followed me to my bedroom. I opened the sliding glass door to the balcony and shut my bedroom door to let Sneakers roam the rest of the house. I didn't bother changing out of my clothes and threw myself on the bed. My body felt stiff.

Before I fell asleep, I told Wolfears, "Tomorrow morning, we'll go for our run. I promise."

Chapter 17

When I woke, Wolfears looked at me expectantly.

"I don't think I'm up for a run," I told him.

He lowered his head back on his paws and looked away.

"Do you hate me?"

For some reason, asking him that caused me to collapse back into bed. I lay there feeling as if all the bones in my body had melted, and I'd become a blob of aches and heartbreak.

In the late morning, a phone call from Garrett telling me he was coming over motivated me to get out of bed. I began feeling better.

When he rang the gate buzzer, he asked me, "Do you want me to bring in the flowers?"

"What flowers?"

"The ones left at the gate."

"They're not from you?" I asked, teasing. "I wish they were."

"They are not."

He wasn't in a playful mood. I released the gate and rushed out to greet him. To my surprise, his mother was seated next to him. Garrett handed me an arrangement of white orchids and baby's breath.

"Hello, Mrs. Deacon, welcome to my home," I called out.

She said, "Please, call me Betty." Her head wobbled from side to side and she waved. "Pretty soon you'll be calling me mother."

I hugged Garrett and felt self-conscious because she remained sitting in the car watching us. After our hug, I saw why. She handed a cane to him and he helped her out of her seat. The only two times I'd met her before were when I'd attended church with Garrett. She'd been seated then and I didn't recall she had a cane.

She pointed at the flowers and said, "You don't have another suitor, do you?"

I couldn't tell if she was joking or not.

"No," I said. "I'm sure they're sympathy flowers. I have no idea who sent them. It doesn't matter. I'm so happy to have you here. Please come in."

Her stare withered me a bit, so I snatched the envelope from the flowers. I couldn't decipher the signature on the card. It could have been from any of my parents' friends, though I knew so little about my father's life and the people he spent time with.

"They're from my father's office," I told her. Then, I went to take her arm and said, "Be careful on the cobblestones. They're a bit uneven."

"No, dear," she said. "I'm fine now. Getting up, that's the tricky part. You bring the flowers inside. Flowers are precious."

Garrett opened his car's trunk. He lifted out a stack of newspapers. Why he'd brought them, I had no idea. And then he took out a plate covered with tin foil. I inhaled the delightful smell of something freshly baked. I realized that I'd forgotten breakfast and stopped wondering about the magazines. Mrs. Deacon was standing, staring up at the house, much as Garrett had done yesterday. Her eyes seemed to be focused on the whale weathervane too.

When she noticed I was looking at her, she said, "My, my, my, what a lovely house."

Garrett's hands were full, and he asked me to close the trunk. We all went inside. Garrett put the magazines on the coffee table in the living room and placed the plate on top of them. He and his mother sat next to each other on the couch where the detectives had sat. He peeled back the tin foil to reveal a stack of chocolate chip cookies.

"I made these for you," his mother said. "There is nothing like home-baked cookies to cheer up a person's spirits, that's what I say. Do you have any milk, dear?"

"I don't have cow's milk," I said, "but we have soy and rice milk."

His mother made a face as if I'd suggested we drink vinegar with the cookies.

"I'm mildly lactose intolerant," I explained.

"You can't drink milk? How awful."

"I can drink a little, just not too much."

Her expression brightened and she said, "Garebear, why don't you be a dear and scoot down to that market I saw by the highway and get us some milk."

He looked like he didn't want to, but said, "I'll be right back," and left.

"Just leave the gate open," I called after him.

When he started The Chugger, his mother said, "This is nice. While Garebear is out, it'll give us girls a chance to get to know each other."

I smiled and tried not to look uncomfortable.

Though the plate was much closer to her than me, she said, "Can you pass the plate?"

When I did, she told me, "I'm going to sneak one cookie before he's back—don't tell Garebear. You can go ahead too, with your plant milk."

"I'll wait for Garrett," I said.

She gave a nod of approval. I couldn't bring myself to call him "Garebear" like she did. I wondered if she expected me to. Never had I heard anyone else call him anything but Garrett. She took a bite of her cookie and pointed at the magazines.

"I brought these for you. Maybe you already have them?"

I looked closely and saw they were tabloid magazines. "No, I haven't. I've seen them in grocery market check-out lines."

I had never been one to pay attention to the news. I wasn't politically active or much concerned about the world. To be candid, I was self-absorbed, living in my own little bubble. I suppose to some extent, I can blame it on youth when little things in one's life seem much larger, and the world seems much smaller.

Chapter 18

"Well, I'm so glad that I brought them. Whenever you start feeling blue, these will take your mind off things. Not only that, but they are also quite educational. They report on the stories that the mainstream press is afraid to print."

"Oh, thank you for bringing them."

"Garebear says they're a bunch of foolishness, and I shouldn't believe everything I read. I don't, but you'll be surprised how much you can learn. I'll admit the ones written about aliens are fake. Everyone knows that aliens are make believe."

I nodded, hoping Garrett would be back soon. She picked up several, leafed through them, and held them up as she commented on them. The cover of the first one held a picture of an actress who happened to live three houses down.

"You might think movie stars live glamorous lives, but they have their troubles too. The lives they lead. You won't believe what some of them get into: drugs, extramarital affairs, all kinds of temptations." She stabbed her finger on the picture. "She was once so high that when she drove by a traffic cop, she thought he was a hitchhiker and pulled over. She lost her driver's license. Now she has a chauffeur named Rex.

"Here's one about a man who ate a jar of peanut butter every day and was a hundred and thirty years old. This same issue has the story about a wrestler who murdered twelve people and sold paintings he'd done of his victims to museums all over the world.

"There's other amazing stories too. Here's a disturbing one you *must* read."

She showed me another newspaper. I had kept a straight face so far, but when she showed me this one, a small laugh escaped my lips. I thought she would be offended, but she took my snicker to be a gasp.

"I know, shocking, disturbingly perverse," she said.

On the cover was a photograph of a woman with a horrified expression, looking as if it were snapped mid-scream. She was sitting in a hospital bed with a baby chimpanzee in her hands. The headline read: "*Woman forced to give birth to monkey child.*" Printed below the photograph, it read: "*Secret government experiment creates half-human baby.*" I covered my mouth with my hand to hide my smile.

Mrs. Deacon let out a breath and said, "Lord knows, some scientist is going straight to hell without passing go. Just imagine that poor woman bringing such a ghastly creature into the world; a baby without a soul. What an abomination. The kind thing to do would have been to put it down. If they keep doing experiments like this, we'll soon have beasts with brains running around, and we'll be living on *Planet of the Apes.*"

I didn't know what to say other than, "Oh."

"Listen to me prattling on about the magazines. Well, Garebear won't be gone long. The truth is that I had an ulterior motive for sending him off for milk. I wanted to have some alone time with you so we can talk girl to girl, or should I say mother to daughter?"

I didn't know where this was going, but I felt my anxiety level rising. I reached for a cookie, just to have something to do with my hands and nibbled on it.

"As I'm sure Garebear has told you, his father was no good. You've obviously recognized that Garebear is golden, not like his father, or his older brother who was also nothing but trouble. With Garebear going away to school in the fall, and all that has happened to you, I started thinking. Long-distance relationships can be difficult, and you wouldn't want to let him slip away. I think you two should talk about marrying before the summer is over."

The moist cookie in my mouth turned into sawdust.

"Not to get ahead of myself, but that wouldn't mean you'd need to live with him while he's at school, because once you're married you're bound for life. I came up with an inspired idea: why, with Garebear away, I will be lonely all by myself—I suppose you will too, rattling around in this big house—so, I'm sure we girls can figure out a solution."

I attempted to smile. My lips were stuck together. She didn't seem to notice my strained expression as I moved my mouth into something that wasn't a grimace and forced my eyes to blink.

"Bringing up two boys, I always wanted a daughter. The hand of God is at work here. Garebear will be away at school before we know it. Now that we've gotten to know each other, I insist that you call me mother. Wouldn't you like that?"

When I didn't answer, her head swiveled as she looked around the room. I thought it might do a three-sixty. I don't think she even noticed that I was choking on my cookie until I made a funny noise in my throat.

"You'd best get some of your plant milk to wash that down," she said.

I made my way to the kitchen and got a glass of water. I managed to swallow the crumbs in my mouth. Wolfears had trotted after me. He was watching my every move.

"I'm okay," I told him.

When I went back to the living room, I asked, "What does Garrett think about all this?"

"You and I both know what he thinks is not really important."

"What do you mean?" I asked. My tongue still felt sticky.

She laughed, then said, "Oh, child, there is so much I must teach you. We women have so much power, if only we choose to use it."

She stopped talking for a moment when her gaze fell on my hand.

"How come you're not wearing your engagement ring? Your fingers are so delicate, does the ring need to be resized?"

Just then I heard the tattooing of Garrett's tires on the cobblestones as he drove back down the driveway.

I jumped up and said, "I better make sure the front door is unlocked."

Chapter 19

When Garrett brought in a carton of milk, Mrs. Deacon smiled benignly. It sent a shiver down my spine.

I got glasses for us and we munched on cookies, talking about trivial things until his mother said to Garrett, "I told you the ring would need to be resized. Why didn't you have that done before giving it to her?"

Garrett looked at my hand, not having noticed before that I wasn't wearing it. His eyes lifted to mine. A million excuses ran through my head, but none of them seemed to offer a good outcome. A reached down to steady myself on Wolfears, but he'd not followed me back from the kitchen.

I heard myself say, "I lost it during the accident."

"What?" Garrett said with shock or anger in his voice. I couldn't tell which.

"It's only a ring, dear," his mother said, and put a hand on Garrett's knee. "Your love is stronger than any piece of jewelry."

I was surprised by the calmness of her reaction.

"But it belonged to your mother," I said. "I'm so sorry."

"Yes, God rest her soul. Don't give it another thought," she said. "It couldn't be helped. It was too large for your finger. Did it slip off in the water during the accident?"

"I think so. It all happened so fast, I'm not sure when I lost it. I dreaded telling you."

I looked back at Garrett. He had that set-jawed expression that he did when he was bothered about something. His mother squeezed his knee.

He looked down, and said, "No big deal."

They didn't stay much longer because Garrett needed to get to work, Saturday being a busy night in the pizza biz. As they were leaving, Sneakers crept up and brushed herself against Mrs. Deacon's leg, startling her. She typically didn't show herself around strangers. Perhaps her unusual behavior was caused because I was late feeding her.

"Oh, my," his mother said. "Animals don't belong in the house."

She nudged Sneakers away with her cane.

When they were gone, I felt drained and dropped myself back in the chair. Wolfears came back into the room and laid down next to me. My fear that Garrett and his mother would react poorly to my losing my engagement ring was, like most worries in life, overblown. Her reaction was unnervingly calm and understanding. He showed only mild irritation, the way he often did when something didn't go the way he planned, but no worse than the time I lost a sweater he'd given me.

My thinking about the ring was now replaced with the possibility of a summer wedding. I liked the idea. At least I think I did, but everything was changing too quickly. I still needed to have a memorial for my parents. If you'd asked me about moving up our wedding a week ago, I would have jumped at the opportunity. Now—and maybe because it came from his mother and not him—I felt intimidated by the prospect. We'd never even talked much about a date or time of year. It was understood we'd wait until after he got his bachelor's degree, which was at least two years away, and probably until after he got a master's, which would add another one or two years. The more I thought about it, the more I found the possibility of getting married in the next few months overwhelming. I had no idea what Garrett thought of it.

It made me question my commitment to matrimony. Was being engaged something I was serious about? Although, I realized that the thought of losing him was more frightening. I told myself that if it was what he wanted, then I would too. Wolfears thumped his tail as if in agreement.

There was too much to think about. I needed to stay busy, but I couldn't decide what to do after feeding Sneakers. I took the glasses to the kitchen and set them on the counter and stared out the window. The housekeeper would be here Tuesday, and my mother usually let the dishes pile up for her. Not wanting to deal with the disruption, I wished she wasn't coming. There was only me now. I picked up the glasses again and put them in the dishwasher.

Sneakers made a hissing sound. Having eaten, she wanted attention.

It should have been a harder decision—she had been so important to my father. I knew if I thought about it, it would be. Before I could change my mind, I picked up the phone and returned Mrs. Delgado's call.

She answered the phone saying, "Golden Paws, how may I help you?"

"I'm Dr. Otomo's daughter," I said.

It turned out that in addition to having their own exotic cats, they ran a shelter and boarding facility for them in Riverside. I made plans to rehome Sneakers with her. She would have more attention and stimulation there.

"Don't worry," I told Wolfears. "You're not going anywhere. I might even let you to continue staying in the house. Just don't tell Mrs. Deacon."

I took Sneakers into the backyard for fresh air. Even though I knew I'd made the right decision, I felt guilty about sending her to a new home. She played with a wind-blown leaf until it disintegrated from her repeated pouncings. Watching her, my mind drifted to my father's relationship with Maria. An affair seemed the most obvious connection. Still, if I knew my father at all, the most implausible one too.

When I went back inside, I returned to the living room and plopped into the chair again. The woman with the horrified expression, holding the baby chimpanzee, on the magazine cover stared at me. I took another magazine from the stack. The blurb on the cover read: "*Multiple Movie Stars Report Having Sex with Elvis Presley's Ghost.*"

Oh, brother, I'm being as silly as these ridiculous tabloids. How could I imagine my father having an affair with that woman?

Mysti's suggestion of a brain tumor made more sense.

Chapter 20

Sunday was a day lost in memories.

There was a chill in the air, and my bed was warm. I didn't want to get up, but I couldn't break another promise to Wolfears about taking our run. Not that he actually runs with me, which I've heard isn't all that good for dogs. He runs ahead, around or behind me and explores. Often, he'll take a shortcut to catch me.

I'd practiced laziness when I was younger, before ambition set in and discipline structured my life. I even scheduled my relaxation. Running has the double duty of relaxing and keeping me fit. I always wake up at 5:30 AM, ever since I was on my high school's dive team, no matter the time of year, whether it was dark or light, clear or rainy.

I heard the gentle hum of my bedroom's coffee maker when its timer clicked it on. I'd strategically placed it across the room so that I was forced to get out of bed to get my morning coffee.

This morning, I felt tired as I woke from a pleasant dream—something rare nowadays. When I stirred, I began feeling the bruises on my body that I'd been ignoring. How could they feel worse on the third day? I'm normally a fast healer. Where the shoulder belt had restrained me, a purple bruise stretched diagonally across me. My flesh, ribs and the inside of my right breast were tender. I hadn't noticed much before. I'm tough. At least I like to think that I am. I lay back in bed and attempted to close my eyes, but they kept popping open. There are little springs of discipline in my eyelids. Surprisingly, Wolfears wasn't snouting me to get me out of bed. He was having pleasant dreams too.

When I heard the drips of the coffee slowing as it was nearing the end, I put my feet on the floor. I always wait until the drops are near the end so as not to have to hold my cup underneath to catch them. One must not waste precious resources. As I padded across the floor in my bare feet, Wolfears opened his eyes, raised his head, thumped his tail once and watched me. I looked out at the morning's fog. Though it was still twilight, I saw there were sheets of mist. A misty-fog morning I call such times.

The ocean was silent.

After my coffee and a cracker, I put on my own sweats, ones that actually fit, and started out the sliding glass door to take the stairs down from the balcony. I'd never thought of locking the glass door, but this morning I did.

When we go on runs, I leave our house by the wicket gate whose path cuts through the boxwoods and opens onto the street up from the driveway gate at the edge of the property. Once outside, I headed toward the Edler Nature Preserve. My footfalls sounded dull in the heavy air. Even Wolfears seemed more stealthy than usual, with the weight of the morning. He disappeared ahead in a thicker patch of fog and startled me when he reappeared from the side and joyfully batted his head against my thigh.

The nature preserve is at the headland of Concha Pointe. Most locals seldom visit it, and with only a small strip of roadside parking with a one-hour limit, there are rarely many people there. The dirt paths are bordered by low chain-link fences and boardwalks leading to lookout platforms to keep visitors from trampling the native vegetation. They form a maze, and on particularly ambitious mornings I run the gamut of them. This morning, a couple of cars were already parked roadside, but I didn't see any people as I zigzagged my way to the path at the edge of the bluff that leads to the metal staircase. It spirals down to the isolated strip of beach that disappears when the tide is high. The stairs are the one place where I can move more quickly than Wolfears.

The beach is mostly rocks and pebbles that rattle when the waves push them back and forth. A thin band of sand hugs the bottom of the cliff. From the top of the staircase, I couldn't see the beach or the ocean through the fog. Once I was at the bottom, the soupy air was less dense, and I could see most of the length of the beach. Wolfears found a piece of driftwood and we played stick-fetch until he became distracted with the scent of something intriguing by the section of the cliff where an overhang creates a waterfall from the runoff when the rains have been heavy. I went to inspect his find, but whatever the scent, it was undetectable to my human nose. I remembered one of the few times when Mysti had run with me. We'd showered in the cold waterfall. With our teeth chattering, we'd run back home trying to get warm.

Today, in the dry summer, there was no waterfall. I left Wolfears behind to explore whatever intrigued him and headed back up. At the top of the stairs, I had that eerie feeling of being watched, though now the visibility through the fog was only a few yards.

I thought about calling Wolfears, or whistling for him, but the stillness of the morning enfolded me into inertness. I paused with my mouth open to better hear. There was no rustling coming from the bushes or any unusual sounds, only the gentle lapping of the water on the beach pebbles below. My feeling was my imagination, but I sighed as I let out my relief when I heard Wolfears scrambling up from the bottom of the stairs. I waited until he caught up to me before resuming my run.

The eerie feeling triggered the memory of a day when there was no fog. That day, the air was dry and seemed to crackle, even with the moisture from the ocean. The sharp tang of smoke from the recent wildfire hung in the air and seared my nostrils and lungs. It was a ridiculous day to run, but I'd missed several days because of the fire. There was another more pressing warning for my not being out alone. I'd ignored it.

Chapter 21

When I was sixteen, there was a small brush fire on the other side of the mountains. Only thin ribbons of smoke were visible from our house. Nothing had touched Concha Pointe for sixty or seventy years, when there were only scattered ranch houses, horses, and livestock in the area. Wildfires are a natural occurrence in the chapparal biome of Southern California. They bring rebirth to the land. Human mitigation has caused them to be less frequent, so that when they do erupt, there is far more fuel, and they can come with greater destruction.

Since there had been no fires that had threatened the Pointe since we had lived there, we had gone to bed that night with no concerns. We were woken in the middle of the night by the sound of sirens. During the wee hours, the Santa Ana winds had kicked up, bringing with them the dry desert air. The winds had whipped the fire towards the ocean with surprising speed.

Soon after, police cars had driven through our neighborhood announcing an evacuation order through megaphones. We'd hurriedly left home, having little time to grab a few possessions. On the other side of Pacific Coast Highway, we'd seen a wall of fire that had crested the mountain. The orange flames had lit the sky, shooting high in the air as it clawed its way down. White smoke had risen above the flames like the steamy breath of a hungry monster devouring everything in its path; the chaparral, hillside homes, any animals that could not escape. As we'd fled south, we'd wondered if we would even have a home to return to.

Due to the valiant effort by the firefighters, the fire was stopped at the highway. Only one house in Conche Pointe had been ignited by flying embers, and a few trees damaged on the ocean side. I was thrilled when we'd returned to our untouched home. I'd found a new appreciation for it and promised myself not to take it for granted.

The destruction across the highway left behind a lunar landscape of black and gray char. Many homes were lost. One of the homes deep in Concha Canyon, that the fire consumed, was owned by an eccentric. He'd kept a hidden and unlicensed zoo on his property. With no time to safely evacuate his animals, he'd opened their cages. The authorities found the burnt body of a leopard who'd run in the wrong direction and had become trapped by the flames.

Soon after, sightings of a wolf were reported. The zookeeper had claimed the leopard was the only dangerous animal he'd kept. He'd said if somebody saw a wolf, it was a wild one. That was considered implausible considering there hadn't been any roaming in the southern half of California for at least seventy years, and maybe more than one hundred. Humanity is not known for its compassion for sharing real estate with other intelligent life. Wolves had been vilified and exterminated. Of course, there were also sightings of displaced coyotes, mountain lions, bobcats, and rattlesnakes.

The wolf sightings had all been reported across the highway, where the human population was less dense. The expectation was that the wolf would not cross the highway and retreat into the unburned ranges beyond. Hunters were scouring in the inland mountains in pursuit of it. Then, a motorist on Clover Street had reported seeing it by the realty office at the edge of the highway in Concha Pointe. My father had suggested what somebody saw was a scrounging coyote blackened with soot, and they'd imagined it to be larger. Nonetheless, he'd forbidden me to run alone.

Though mildly concerned about meeting a pack of desperate and hungry coyotes or a mountain lion, I was far more immortal at sixteen than I became at twenty. I'd snuck out while my parents were still asleep—what they didn't know wouldn't hurt them.

My feet had kicked up ash as I'd run. The air had burned my eyes, nose, and throat. As I'd neared the nature preserve, I'd come to Murphy's place. He was an old hippie with a beat-up VW van with flowers painted on it. He often parked it on his grass in front of his house. Having lived in the neighborhood longer than anyone could remember, he was the last of the old guard from mellower days. He no longer fit in the neighborhood that had transitioned to the expensive homes of celebrities and wealthy business people. His double-sized yard didn't have a gate, a wall or a hedge shielding it. He'd decorated it with a fence made of old, mostly broken surfboards to the displeasure of his neighbors. There'd often been rumors he was moving to Hawaii, which I'd suspected he'd mischievously started. The scent of pot often wafted in the air before I reached his home. That morning, I hadn't smelled any, but with the smoke hanging in the air, its aroma could have been masked.

I'd glanced at his porch as I went by. He hadn't been there to call out, "Hello, wahine," in his froggy voice. I'd felt disappointed because seeing him would have given a sense of normalcy to the morning, otherwise oppressed by the heavy smoke-fogged air. His van hadn't been there either. I'd wondered whether the fire might have prompted him to make the Hawaii move.

I'd hoped not. I'd have missed him. When I was learning to surf, he was patient and gave me lots of pointers.

I'd run on to the nature preserve and looped to the far end where the vegetation grows higher, and had started through the path. The morning had been quiet, particularly in the thick vegetation. I'd thought I heard rustling in the bushes. As I'd come to the clearing in the center, I'd caught a glimpse of tawny fur, the color of a mountain lion, on the other side. Electricity had shot up my spine and my shoulders had tensed. I'd felt a cold sweat compressing me in the warm morning.

Mountain lions seldom attacked adults. The only cases I'd heard about were ones when people were running or on a bike, and their prey instinct was triggered. I'd stopped and raised my arms above my head to appear larger, and had called out, "*Hey!*"

With the fire, I'd had no idea how desperate one might be. I'd taken a step backwards, my eyes locked onto the spot across the clearing where I'd spotted the fur. Yards away from where I was staring, the lion had stepped out of the bushes. Her massive head was low, her magnetic, amber eyes held me. My instinct had prodded me to turn and flee, but an equally powerful force immobilized my feet. I'd managed to wave my arms. I'd called out again, but from my dry throat, only a raspy sound had come out.

The lion had taken a slow step forward. Her tail had twitched, brushing up puffs of soot from the ground. She'd stopped, her eyes locked on me.

My mind had raced as the world had stalled in time. I'd thought there was a possibility I might live if only I could find my voice. Then, I'd heard rustling in the bushes behind me. Mountain lions are solitary hunters, a small voice told me, but it was quieter than the rushing blood in my ears. There was more than one.

The lion crouched. Her eyes looked on fire. Her muscles pulsed beneath the skin of her shoulders like steel cords. A snarl had rumbled from deep within her. The terrifying sound reverberated to my core. I'd wanted to start waving my arms and shouting, but to remain standing took everything within me.

I'd heard a growl behind me, a different sounding one, throatier, like an engine stuttering, no less spine-chilling. Out of the corner of my eye, I caught movement, something black had been approaching my side.

The wolf.

I was caught between two predators, deciding which one would eat me for breakfast. My knees began shaking. Not collapsing at that moment was the bravest thing I had ever done.

Chapter 22

The lion had opened her mouth, baring her fangs. To my surprise, she'd made a hissing sound and retreated, disappearing into the plants across the clearing. A bark sounded at my side. The hair on the back of his neck had remained standing as I'd turned. If it were possible, my mouth opened wider. No wolf stood beside me—it was a black dog. His filthy fur was matted and covered with soot and burrs. The dog's ears were upright like a wolf's. I'd realized he must have been who the passing motorist had mistaken for a wolf.

Large as he was, he was no match for a mountain lion, but in a fight the lion would have risked injury, and an injured wild animal is soon dead.

When I'd got home, my parents had been furious. It was the only time my father had ever yelled at me. I was grounded for weeks. It was worth it because when no one claimed Wolfears at the animal shelter, I'd got to keep him.

Now, though it had been years since the wildfire, Mr. Murphy was still in his house with the surfboard fence. When Wolfears and I ran past on the way back, his van was on the lawn, and he was sitting on the porch with a cigar. I didn't smell any weed.

Seeing me, he called out, "Hey, wahine, I'm still waiting for you to move to Hawaii with me."

It had become our running joke. I laughed and kept running.

"Your dog can come too," he called after me.

My body felt better, and my mind was more at ease by the time I got back home. Wolfears had lagged. While I waited for him by the wicket gate, I caught a whiff of smoke. I thought I'd imagined it because I'd been thinking about the fire, but there were cigarette butts on the ground by the gate. I was sure they hadn't been there when I'd left.

Someone cleared their throat, which startled me. Hardly anyone was ever out this early on a Sunday morning. I was about to call Wolfears when Donny, the scrubby little weasel next door, stepped out from behind the overgrowth of bushes.

"You scared me. What do you want?" I asked.

I tried to sound harsh, but relief sounded in my voice that it was only him. We hadn't spoken since the window incident. I'd not even seen more than a glimpse of him for a long time. He still had creamy smooth skin and deep-set eyes. He didn't look so little now.

"I was waiting for you," he said, as if that were explanation enough.

"Were you following me? Were you at the nature preserve just now?"

He looked confused. "No, why? I never go there."

"Never mind," I said. "Are those cigarette butts yours?"

He looked down at the butts. His eyes darted back and forth as if he were watching ants scurrying on the ground.

"Why don't you quit that disgusting habit? You'll wreck your skin and dry it out. It'll make your pores large," I said, sounding like my mother.

He shrugged with indifference.

"My dad had the house soundproofed after my mom left," he said. "He doesn't have to listen to the ocean anymore. He always hated the waves, not that he's home much."

"What does that have to do with anything? Why are you telling me this? You came over to tell me that?"

His eyes darted more rapidly, as if the ants that only he could see were moving faster. He nudged a cigarette butt with his toe.

He said, "I wanted to say sorry about your parents. Did you get the flowers?"

"Those were from you? I couldn't read the signature."

"Yeah, my father called from Thailand. He's shooting a film there. When I told him what happened, he told me to order them."

"Thanks, Donny. Thank your father too, please."

Wolfears joined us and sniffed at the cigarette butts. Donny glanced up at me, said "Bye," and left. He was so awkward that I felt sorry for him.

The phone rang just as I walked into the house. I rushed to answer it.

"Hello," I said and heard the voice I wanted to hear.

"Hey, baby, how are you?"

"Oh, I'm doing good. I did my run. I'm feeling better."

"I'm glad to hear that."

"Are you coming over after church?"

"About that. Behavioral finance isn't logical. I don't quite have it down yet. I was thinking, since you're doing okay, I should spend the day hitting the books."

"I don't want to spend the day alone. Could you come over just for a little bit? You could study here."

"Nah, I've got to ace the final. It's for our future. You understand."

I tried not to sound disappointed. "Sure, I'll give Mysti a call."

"Mysti? What?"

"I didn't get a chance to tell you yesterday. She came over. Everything's good between us now. She even invited me to a violin recital she's got coming up."

"I'm glad you patched things up, but you shouldn't be hanging out with her."

"Why not?"

"Did you forget she hit on me?"

"No, of course not. It won't happen again," I said to avoid getting into that.

"Besides, she's not the best influence. I mean, she's got no shame, walking around naked in front of your neighbor like that. That's acting like an animal. I don't want her corrupting you again."

"You think I'm corruptible?"

"I didn't mean it like that."

I wanted to yell at him, but I kept my voice calm. "Speaking of Donny, he's the one who sent the flowers."

"I better not catch him nosing around or I'll give him a thumping he won't forget. Nobody messes with my girl."

The last thing I wanted to do was fight with Garrett, so I changed the subject.

"Your mom suggested we move up the wedding. Do you think that's a good idea?"

"I don't know. It doesn't matter what she wants. It's what *we* want. I've got to focus on exams. We can talk about it after. I need to get back to my studies."

When we hung up, I called Mysti, but she wasn't home.

I went to the backyard. Rather than mope around and feel sorry for myself, I decided to clean out the fire pit. The ashes and remnants of paper were still there. They bugged me, as did the check to Maria Nogales. Maybe there was a connection. With the papers burned to indecipherable scraps and Maria not communicative, it didn't make much difference. They both led to a dead end, at least for the moment.

I thought I'd take another look around my father's office. Besides, it was a lot less messy than shoveling ashes and soot. As I went down the basement stairs, the gate buzzer sounded.

It's Garrett, I thought. My heart leaped. He'd changed his mind about seeing me and had come to apologize in person.

Chapter 23

I didn't bother saying hello on the intercom and activated the gate to open. Then, I rushed out to greet him. Wolfears trotted out after me. The car pulling down the driveway wasn't Garrett's, but a white, older model Audi. Mrs. Deacon was behind the wheel. I fought to keep the disappointment off my face.

She parked, popped the trunk, and opened her door. I extended my hand to help her out, but she waved me off and got out by herself without any trouble, now that Garrett wasn't there to help her. I hadn't noticed how bright her copper-colored hair was before and wondered if she dyed it.

I looked up at her and asked, "Where's Garrett?"

"Garebear said you didn't feel like being alone. Since he couldn't make it, I came to visit you."

"What? Really? Aren't you going to church?"

"I think the Lord will forgive me if I miss one Sunday. God comforts me, and I shall comfort you."

"Oh," was all I managed.

"I hope your neighbors won't complain," she said. "My old car hardly looks like it belongs here. How did you know it was me at the gate?"

"I thought it was Garrett."

"You should be more careful. It could have been a thief or a murderer. They target neighborhoods like this. You really shouldn't be living alone. It's not safe."

"I have Wolfie," I said.

"And you have that wonderful cat," she said, either completely missing my point or ignoring it. "What's her silly name? A cat such as she should have a regal name."

"It's Sneakers. Guess what? I've found a new home for her."

"Why on earth would you get rid of a cat?"

That confused me because she'd said before that it didn't belong in the house.

"It's what my father wanted," I said.

"Your father isn't here anymore. You'll have to get used to that, my dear." She shut the car door with a shove of her hip, leaving her cane inside. "It's breezy out here. Let's go inside. Do you have any more of those cookies and milk left?" she asked when she sat on the couch.

After two cookies, she waved her hands in front of her like an orchestra conductor, and said, "Your mother must have photo albums with baby pictures. If you wouldn't mind getting them, I'd love to see them."

I wanted to ask why, but there was something in the way her voice commanded that made me set off without questioning.

"They're in the other room. I'll go get them."

Wolfears didn't follow me and stayed by the fireplace, as if guarding or keeping an eye on her. I couldn't tell which.

The photo albums were in a barrister bookcase in the reading room. As with all things in my mother's life, they were neatly organized, dated sequentially. I gathered up the two earliest with my pictures. When I returned to the living room, Mrs. Deacon patted the couch beside her, indicating for me to sit there. I sat and sunk into the cushions, but not as deeply as she did. With her being such a large woman, I felt tiny next to her. Garrett must have gotten some of his height from her. I'd never met his father and knew nothing about him because Garrett never mentioned him. I'd assumed that his father had left the family when Garrett was young.

We opened the books and thumbed through them. She oohed and ahhed at the photos, especially ones in which I grinned through chocolate cake smeared on my face.

"That reminds me of Garebear playing in the mud," she said. "You two have so much in common. I don't believe you're any younger than one year old in any of these. Where are your newborn pictures?" Mrs. Deacon asked. "You must have missed an album."

"No, there aren't any baby pictures of me," I said and stuck out my lower lip.

"Oh, my, were you adopted?"

"No, I wasn't adopted. When we moved here to Seabird Lane, the moving company lost the box with my baby pictures."

"How absolutely awful."

"Yeah, my mom was really upset about it. She didn't even like talking about it. She said I was irresistibly adorable. My parents didn't plan to have any kids, then I came along. She said I was the best surprise that ever happened in her life."

"That certainly turned out for the best. Thank God she didn't believe in abortion," she said and slapped my thigh. "I bet you were a cutie. You still are."

To change the subject, I gathered my courage and asked, "What made you want to look at baby pictures anyway?"

A smile spread over her face.

"I have an adorable picture of Garebear swaddled in a blanket when he was only a month old. I was hoping to find one like that of you. No matter, there's lots of cute toddler pictures I can match with some of yours."

"Oh, what for?" I asked, perplexed as to what made her think of such a thing.

"I thought it might be nice having them on the wedding invitations. Don't you think?"

I tried not to look startled. I suddenly felt I was sitting too close to her, as if I were about to be smothered.

"Mrs. Deacon, we haven't had a chance to talk about moving up the wedding yet."

"How many times do I have to tell you? It's Betty. Once you're married, calling me mother will be best."

"There's just so much happening."

"Please don't feel like I'm pressuring you about your wedding. I'm just so excited for you. One can never start planning too early." She tucked back her chin, looked away and added, "I want you to have the wedding I never had, that's all."

"Thank you."

As she was leaving, she asked me, "Would you be a doll and give Garrett a jingle to let him know I'm headed home? He always likes to know my whereabouts. He should be back from church by now, if he didn't see Pastor Andrew afterwards to seek counsel. You know, the pastor has been like a father to Garrett; very generous with his time."

"He went to church? I thought he was studying."

"Yes, it's more important for a man not to miss church than a woman. I've raised him to be a good husband."

Chapter 24

When Garrett's mother left and couldn't hear me, I said, "Goodbye, Mrs. Deacon."

As I waved to her, I realized that it would be my name too. I'd never considered that before. Mrs. Deacon.

I'd never written out "Mrs. Garrett Deacon" to see how it looked. I wasn't one of those girls. I liked Prima Otomo. Prima Deacon was nice, but didn't have the same ring to it. I decided I wanted to use my maiden name.

Would Garrett be okay with that? I wondered. I couldn't think about that now.

When I called him, he startled me when he answered on the first ring in a low, sexy voice.

"Hey, Babycakes."

I ignored his unusual endearment. "You mom's on her way home. She's making me panic. She wants us to get married this summer."

"Yeah, well, we've been talking about it."

"*We* haven't talked about it. It's too much right now, with all that's happened."

"Nothing changed. You know, she's a worrier and doesn't want you to slip away."

"I'm not going to find someone else why you're away. You know that."

"She keeps pushing."

"Calm down. I'll talk to her. We'll work this out. She doesn't mean anything, it's just her way."

"Do you want us to get married now? I mean, we haven't discussed it. We said a couple of years."

"Slow down. You're not making any sense."

"*I'm* not making any sense? She's *your* mother. She acts like we're getting married in a few weeks. Is she crazy?"

"There's nothing wrong with her. You're the one who's acting wacky. She really likes you, and she's excited about our getting married. That's all."

"Why did you answer the phone like that?"

"Like what?"

"You said 'Hey.' You never say 'Hey, Babycakes.' How did you know it was me?"

"Who else would it be? I'm in the middle of studying and trying not to think about you. So, you were on my mind when the phone rang. It's a new nickname I thought of for you."

That slowed me down.

"Really?"

"Um-hum."

"Come over and show me what you were thinking," I said.

"You know I can't. I've got exams."

"I'm stressed out. I think I need one of my mother's pills."

"Slow down. Just chill. Once exams are over, we'll spend more time together."

"But I need you *now*."

"What is wrong with you? You're acting like one of the groupies that hangs around the team."

"Do you call them Babycakes?"

"You know I don't pay any attention to them. You're the only one I think about."

"Studying and practices are all that you think about."

"For our future."

"You sound like your mother."

"What's that supposed to mean?"

"She said the same thing about your not coming over with her. How you'll be a good provider."

"Isn't that what you want?"

"I don't know what I want anymore."

"Don't worry. Everything is going to work out fine. You'll see."

Even though we'd argued, just talking to him made me feel better. We talked a little more and then I let him get back to his studying to prepare for "our future".

I returned to my father's office. The starkness of it struck me again, the row of black file cabinets, the unadorned walls, the desk top in perfect order as if it held no unfinished business within, now that I'd delivered the check to Maria. His room was like a puzzle box camouflaged so well that it didn't appear to be holding secrets within it.

I decided to check the file cabinets first.

Everything was labeled and meticulously organized, going back for years: the deed to our house, mortgage payments, a grant deed for when our home was paid off, birth certificates, passports, an envelope with thousands of dollars in cash labeled "Emergency Cash." Leave it to him to be prepared for the unexpected. It seemed amazing to me that, as busy as he was, he could find the time to be so organized. But maybe that was his secret, his efficiency, never having to waste time hunting for something or wonder where it had been placed.

In the cabinet closest to the desk, I discovered some files for current patients. I would need to get those to his colleagues, along with the patient messages on his phone. The last cabinet against the far wall was filled with papers from his college and med school days. Even copies of his report cards and research papers. By the time I opened its bottom drawer, the room was filled with the vanilla musk of old papers. Inside was a row of army green hanging folders labeled "Case Studies B1 to B12 and C1 to C12." They were research papers from his post-Ph.D. project with Professor Pinsky. The case subjects were identified by numbers and not names, which seemed dehumanizing. I could see some people viewing them as nothing more than test subjects, but not my father.

Most of the scientific jargon in the files went over my head, no less than if written in another language. Thumbing through them, what I easily understood was that none of them resulted in success. They were all rubbered stamped "Miscarriage." I noticed the B9 file was missing. Thinking it was misplaced, I searched for it in the vain hope against my father's methodical nature. It was nowhere to be found. Maybe B9 was a participant who dropped out before the study began.

I thought it odd there were no "A" files. I felt a cold shiver and the hairs on the back of my neck rose as I remembered the ashes in the fire pit. My father was an enigma. Something told me I should let sleeping dogs lie. Whatever he wanted buried or burned was probably best left unknown.

Maybe it was a curiosity gene that I'd inherited from him, but with each added mystery of his actions that I uncovered, I felt a stronger pull to know more.

I took a deep breath and went to his desk. I tackled the bottom right file drawer first. In it were investment statements. Not that I'd taken much interest in such things, but from all I could tell we were quite affluent. I thought about Detective Yates' question about the possibility of their being distress from debts. From what I could tell, we didn't have any. The only items of interest I found were three checkbook registers. The joint checkbook register with my mother was filled with various household expenses. The business one looked to have been seldom used. The third one was a personal checking account.

Monthly checks for one thousand dollars to Maria Nogales were listed going back to the beginning of the register, except for the ten thousand dollar one I had delivered to her.

Was it a final payment for something? I wondered if she'd read the newspaper I'd kicked off her front porch.

I was stumped for the moment, until I thought my father's business partner, Dr. Snead, might be able to tell me something about her.

Chapter 25

On Monday morning, I took the patient files to my father's medical office. Strange as it may seem, or maybe not, I'd never been there before. The six-story medical tower was all straight lines with alternating white walls and bands of gray windows. It looked like a giant box resting on its side and dwarfed the purple-flowered, well-tended jacaranda trees spaced uniformly around its base. I couldn't help but contrast its utilitarian architecture with the personality of the brick-and-mortar morgue. Of course, the morgue was now called the more clinical Medical Examiner's Office. Likely, it would be torn down one day and replaced with an efficiently constructed modern building.

I found the contrast of the two buildings ironic, considering the one for discarding the vessels of the dead embodied more life than the one that served the living. The hospital across the street was a blend of the two styles, with its white concrete walls and small windows grouped in pairs like eyes watching the world.

I managed to find a spot on the street under the shade of a parkway camphor tree and parked there, glad that I didn't need to use the multi-level parking structure adjacent to the building.

Walking to the building, I noticed that being inland, the morning was already warm. Two sparrows hopped cautiously towards me as if I might feed them.

The automatic doors opened and I went inside. At the elevator, a woman with a tool belt hanging on her hips slapped a door bumper to reopen the doors for me.

A bell chimed. The doors opened on the fourth floor. The woman stepped out. She blocked the doors from closing with her work-booted foot.

"Oh," I said, "I'm going to the sixth floor."

"You better push the button, or you'll be going back down," she said, and removed her foot.

I must have been nervous. I pushed the button for the sixth floor with my knuckle. When the door opened, I took a deep breath and stepped out.

A cushioned bench placed in the foyer seemed to call to me: *come, rest for a moment. I'm soft, not hard, like the concrete benches outside.*

I pushed on the cushion with my hand and felt it give with the pressure.

"Another time, maybe, okay?" I asked.

I paused, waiting for an answer, wondering if I were having a mental breakdown.

Across from the elevators was a pair of oak doors with a placard that read, "*Drs. Otomo, Snead, and Associates. Reproductive Endocrinology.*" Their office took up the entire top floor.

As I entered, a woman brushed past me. I avoided eye contact.

The waiting room was large, with gray-toned chairs around the walls and a group of seats in the center. Most of them were occupied. There were two women at reception windows. Neither looked up when I entered. I went over to the one with the placard that read "*New Patients.*" While I waited, I fingered a dark green, waxy leaf in a potted plant. Her perfume reminded me of my mother's. She glanced up and gave a cursory smile.

"I'm sorry to keep you waiting. We're swamped this morning. One of our doctors is out. You'll need to fill out these forms," she said, while nudging a clipboard toward me. "Which doctor are you here for?"

"I'm here to see Dr. Snead. I don't have an appointment."

My voice sounded squeaky. She gave me an exasperated look.

I said, "I'm Prima Otomo."

The crease between her eyebrows vanished. She motioned me toward the inside door. When she escorted me inside, I felt dirty looks from some of the waiting patients. She took me to Dr. Snead's office. I looked at the sky through the floor-to-ceiling windows. He joined me moments later.

He had a full head of hair that my mother must have approved of, and the perpetual tan of someone who played tennis regularly. I held up well when he offered his condolences. He was considerate to not ask about details of the accident. I handed him the files and phone messages. The fingers of my now empty hands knitted together, squeezing so hard that I thought they might break.

"Do you know a Maria Nogales?" I asked.

His eyebrows raised. Maybe it was my imagination, but I thought the question made him uncomfortable.

"Her name doesn't ring a bell. Was she a patient of your father's?"

"I don't know. She left a message, but no telephone number," I lied.

He checked his computer and told me, "She's not a patient."

"Oh, she might have been calling for my mother," I said. "I know you're really busy, but the detective that was investigating the accident asked if my father had any financial problems."

Dr. Snead laughed. "Your father? That would be a shock."

He pressed a button on his intercom. "See if Arthur is available. Dr. Otomo's daughter is here. I'd like him to meet with her."

While he waited for an answer, he explained that Arthur Doi was the accountant who handled their professional corporation and also prepared my parents' taxes. His office was just down the street. As it turned out, Mr. Doi was available to see me. I thanked Dr. Snead for taking time out of his busy day and left to see the accountant.

Mr. Doi had owl-like eyes, thick, black-framed glasses and looked as if he were born to be an accountant.

"Yes, yes, I prepare your parents' personal tax returns. I can assure you that, from what I can see, their finances look to be in exceptionally good shape. I can't imagine you'd have anything to worry about. However, the best person to talk to you about their numbers would be their financial planner."

"Financial planner? I didn't know they had one."

He gave me a business card for Frank Volden and told me I should contact him for details.

Walking to my car, a man was lurching toward me. He swung his arms wildly as he held an animated conversation with himself. He paused to yell at a couple passing by, screaming that they were possessed. I scooted to the side of the building as he was nearing. He stopped just before we were to cross paths, stared and pointed his finger at me.

"You're okay," he said, before continuing his spasmodic walk, swinging his arms chaotically.

Maybe he wasn't completely crazy and knew something about me that I didn't, because I didn't feel okay.

When I got home, I called Mr. Volden's office and made the first appointment I could. I made myself lunch and sat on the half-moon wall. It was the place where I often felt a calm exhilaration, something about the height gave a tingle in my stomach that made me know I was alive. It inspired clear thinking. Wolfears sniffed the yard in patrol fashion to update himself on any goings on that were beyond my senses.

I tried to think about future things and not everything that was happening at once. There was a lot to discuss and decide with Garrett, especially now that his mother was inserting herself in our affairs. I felt more apprehensive than excited about moving up the wedding.

The clarity that the half-moon often brought me was illusive. I watched the smooth, rolling waves, perfect sheets of glass in motion.

When they hit the jagged rocks below, they shredded into white rags of foam. Staring at the slate gray water, I saw myself reflected in it. For the first time in my life, I understood why people considered suicide to escape the onslaught of stress in their lives. Having recently seen Donny, I got a creepy feeling and thought about him at the window.

I glanced back toward his house. The slightly swaying tips of the junipers were now grown above his windows and blocked any view from them.

Wolfears had curled up by the wall near me. He looked up at me with a worried expression.

"Don't worry," I said. "I'm not leaving you. I was just thinking how I could understand how some people felt."

What pulled me out of my lethargy was curiosity. The connection between Maria and my father nagged at me like a small rock rolling around in a shoe. There was so much about my father's life that I didn't know. Now that he and my mother were no longer here, not only did I miss them as if part of my flesh had been ripped out of me, but I also wanted to know more about them. Who were they as people, not only as parents? So much I had taken for granted.

I pondered my suspicion that Dr. Snead knew Maria. I thought of a way to check if I was simply becoming paranoid. I went inside and called the office, hoping the woman at the front desk wouldn't answer and recognize my voice.

"Hello," I said. "This is Maria Nogales. I've misplaced my calendar. Can you tell me when my next appointment with Dr. Otomo is?"

"Let me check," the woman who answered said, and put me on hold.

Luckily, she didn't sound like the same receptionist and I couldn't smell her perfume through the phone line. I held my breath hoping she'd not ask me for a date of birth. I didn't know how to get around that.

When she came back on the line, she said, "I'm not seeing an appointment under your name."

"Maybe it was with one of the other doctors," I said.

The woman sighed. "It'll take a moment. Hold on, please." When she returned, she said, "I'm not finding any appointments under your name."

"Okay, thank you. I must have the wrong office," I said and hung up.

The call hadn't gotten me any closer to discovering how Maria was connected to my father, other than eliminating the possible connection of her being his patient.

Chapter 26

I went into the backyard and stared into the depths of the pool, not that it was deep compared to the ocean beyond. It was a puddle. Its turquoise water was the color of the Caribbean Sea in a vacation brochure. Its surface, as smooth as a mirror, reflected a V formation of brown pelicans flying over the ocean near the shoreline, as those ancient birds had done for millions of years.

There was a cloud bank coming in from the south. In the reflection, it looked as if it were chasing the pelicans. The pulse of the ocean against the shore was a soundtrack for my thoughts. It felt like the heartbeat of the Earth. For sparkling moments, being alone in the backyard, it seemed as if nothing in my world had changed.

I lifted my eyes from the water and watched the pelicans. The symmetry of their formation was broken when one of them suddenly dropped like an arrow into the water. Its scoop missed its target. The prehistoric bird pulled out of the ocean with labored flaps of its large wings. When it caught up with its squadron, it fell in at the end of one of the V's arms.

In the southeast corner of the yard was my favorite sculpture of my mom's: a bronze of a woman rising out of a tangle of seaweed, her arms clawing the sky as if she were pulling herself up through the air. I'd always wondered if she was a human or a mermaid because below her torso, the clinging seaweed made it impossible to see if her body rose from legs or a tail, be she human or half-fish. I had decided she was a mermaid.

Now that the sculpture had acquired a green patina, the smile on the mermaid's lips reminded me of my mother's. I wondered if the sculpture was intended to be a self-portrait, though, unlike myself, my mother wasn't a water lover.

Behind the mermaid, a stack of custom bricks was neatly piled. They were replacements for the bricks in the wall when they became damaged. Mismatched bricks would have bothered my father. For some reason, the top bricks on the wall suffered short lives, as if creatures were crawling up the cliff from the sea and digging claws in them to hoist themselves over the wall, to find refuge on land.

I walked to the deep end of the pool. Beneath my feet were the sawed-off bolts in the concrete that once held a diving board. Strange they'd not been removed, because they tarnished the otherwise perfection of the yard. My mother had wanted to place a sculpture there. It was one of the few times my father had put his foot down. When I thought about it, it also was out of character for him not to have the rusting bolts removed.

I wandered over to the wall and stood at the cliff's edge. The ever-changing Pacific Ocean stretched beyond. In one moment it might be hiding monsters, the next it could be playful, and sea nymphs would surface. I couldn't decide if I loved or hated it. Maybe both.

I went back to the pool and stood over the bolts. With my bare feet, I liked to dig my toes into the little divots and press them against the metal. Now wearing shoes, I couldn't feel them beneath my feet. I stood staring at the light blue water. A shaft of sunlight broke through the clouds, illuminating the pool in a beckoning glow. I looked up in the sky. The opening in the clouds was ringed with a luminous golden light. I closed my eyes. Not diving or jumping, I tilted forward and fell into the water.

I crumpled as I hit the water, but the impact still stung. I contracted into a fetal position as I sunk to the bottom. Pinching my fingers on my nose, I blew air and cleared my ears before floating back to the surface, feeling heavy with the weight of my clothes. My head bobbed above the water. Gasping, I drew several breaths and kicked my shoe-burdened feet to propel myself to the side. I grasped the coping with one hand, my fingers tight as if it might crack. Hand over hand along the edge, as if I could no longer swim, I traveled to the steps at the shallow end. I pushed my hair back from my face and climbed the steps feeling like something unnatural that had a home in neither sea nor land. I'd become a being in transition.

My shoes made sucking sounds and my wet clothes clung to me as I went over to the half-moon in the wall and stared at the ocean. It beckoned me as though I belonged beneath the surface of its waters.

I stood there dripping, as wet as the ocean.

I sat on the wall, took off my shoes and pulled up my top. It stuck to my skin like an octopus not wanting to let go. After I managed to free it over my head, I peeled off my pants. My clothes lay on the pool deck like a molted skin. I lay on my back on the top of the wall, feeling the sun warming my naked body. The height gave me a feeling of exhilaration. With the cliff dropping down beside me, I felt the tenacles of life stroking my skin, knowing that if I rolled over, I would plunge onto the rocks far below. It felt as if by, falling into the pool, I had been transformed. I felt at one with the world.

My paranoia and crusade to understand had dissipated. I was part of something larger. Whatever had caused my father's actions, be it madness or contorted logic, it made sense to him. If he had wanted me to know what his reasons were, he would have told me. I had to trust that somewhere within his mind was a benign lucidity.

The shifting wind was now pushing the clouds back. The pelicans had disappeared. A lone kitesurfer was skimming the ocean's surface. Above him, a bright red sail pulled him whatever direction the gusts of wind took him.

I inhaled the fresh salt air. My body tingled as if it had become lighter. In that moment, I knew the wind would push me toward happiness if only I would let it.

Chapter 27

The following days went by in a blur. Attorneys circled above our house like vultures, I shed more tears when I gave Sneakers to the Delgados, the maid quit over superstitions about my parents' death, and I made the big decision to skip school in the fall because I couldn't see how to keep Wolfears if I went away. Yet, the weight of sadness seemed not as heavy.

A big chunk of my time was taken by planning my parents' memorial. Mrs. Deacon helped set it up at their church.—Pastor Andrew and a Shinto priest officiated. Mrs. Deacon wasn't happy about the priest. Even though my father had no religious beliefs, I'd invited him out of respect for my grandparents, who'd flown in from Japan.

Other than my aunt, there was no one to notify on my mother's side. I'd mailed a letter to my her, but hadn't heard back. I hoped she was okay because I'd also not received a birthday card from her this year.

Due to the concern of some of the church members about having other ideology spoken in their church, the service was held outdoors on the church grounds. That was fortuitous because, though I'd expected a small gathering, hundreds of people had attended. The church would have overflowed. Garrett said most of them showed up because my parents' deaths were a tragedy, and people were drawn to the drama.

I didn't want to believe that. I like to think people came because they respected and liked my parents.

I told Pastor Andrew that our family wasn't religious. He was respectful and kept the ceremony mostly secular, occasionally mentioning a benevolent deity who directed our affairs beyond our comprehension. The Shinto priest seemed more connected to ritual, and I related more to him. It made me think that I should get in touch with my Japanese heritage. Still, listening to both, I wondered if superstitions are woven in the fabric of our DNA.

To receive guests, I stood beneath an arched pergola. Two white marble benches were within each side, vines with trumpet-shaped purple and white flowers woven through the lattice. Sunlight sparkled on the ocean far below. Being outdoors, I was able to bring Wolfears. Dog is God spelled backwards, after all. He sat patiently beside me. Garrett stayed nearby.

Most people offered condolences and shared fond memories. Garrett was right about some, who asked questions about how my parents died. One asked me what it felt like when the car drove off the pier. Garrett put a hand on his shoulder and ushered him away. But most others confirmed my belief that they cared about my parents. My mother had more friends than I imagined, and many patients of my father attended. Some brought their children, who had been conceived with my father's help. One boy of nine, with spiky hair and anxious eyes, was named Robert after my father. He awkwardly petted the top of Wolfears' head and told his parents he wanted a dog just like him.

The couple next in line were also patients of my father. The woman clasped her hands tightly in front of her and spoke in a whisper. Her husband showed me a picture of their daughter, a girl of four with a bright smile.

"Your father was a great man," the woman said through sniffles.

"If only there were more people in the world like him," the man said with great solemnity, before they departed.

When Mysti neared her turn, Garrett drifted away. She'd dressed in black, even wearing a veil, which reminded me of her Goth phase. When it came to her turn, she hugged me without saying a word. She didn't need to say anything.

I was surprised to see Detective Yates, who'd since finished his investigation. A hat covered his slicked blond hair, and the lavender of his cologne dominated the smell of the freshly cut grass.

Old friends from my high school came, even Kathy, Garrett's ex-girlfriend, showed up. I didn't like her, for no other reason than she had been his girlfriend before me. My opinion of her softened now that she had come, even if she'd worn a short skirt. If I was at all objective, I couldn't blame her for being attracted to Garrett. That is, as long as she stayed away from him.

My opinion of her dropped again when, a little later, I saw her chatting with him. Luckily, he was as devoted to me as I was to him. Garrett and Wolfears—my rocks.

As I greeted those who knew my father, I realized that, though he had impacted many lives, he had no social life unrelated to his work.

With the seemingly endless line of people, I was socially strung out well before the event was over. Part of me wished we'd had separate services for my mother and father, but I wouldn't have wanted to go through it twice. By the time the end of the line neared, I was quite weary from shaking hands and chatting with people.

The next to last person in line was a hump-shouldered woman, an artist acquaintance of my mother's. She admired one of the sculptures in our backyard, which looked like a gigantic strand of DNA draped over an elephant. Butterflies on wires above the elephant waved in the wind.

"If you ever want to sell it be sure to let me know," she said, and handed me her business card as if she were presenting me with a great treasure.

Finally, it came the turn for the last person. He was a large man who wore a black suit jacket over khaki pants. The jacket might have fitted him at one time, but now the shoulders were loose, and his belly was too wide for it to button.

The flaps of his coat flared. He had been stepping back to the end of the line each time someone got in behind him. He never chatted with other guests. I had no idea who he was, but was quite curious by the time his turn came.

Chapter 28

With his white shirt and unbuttoned coat, he reminded me of an overgrown penguin.

I don't know who I might of guessed who he would be, but I was surprised when he extended his hand and said, "I'm Professor Pinsky from Cummings University, a close friend of your father's."

For some reason, perhaps because of his name, I would have expected him to be a small man. I shook his hand, and he held mine in both of his longer than felt appropriate for someone who I had just met.

His voice, unlike his appearance, was polished, confident, precise. He peered at my face as if I should know who he was or, at the very least, be honored to be in his presence. I was too tired to bother.

"Thank you for coming," I said.

He sucked in a breath and stared at Wolfears as if he'd never seen a dog before. Wolfears, who had been exceedingly indifferent to the other guests, responded by standing and making a low growl that almost sounded like a purr. I didn't know if he didn't like the professor or was venting his frustration that the affair hadn't yet ended.

Pinsky let go of my hand, put a hand on his chin and nodded as he looked over at me. His eyes drifted above my head when he spoke.

"As it has been through the ages, a woman, your mother in this case, changed the course of history; a crescendo as if in an opera, that she and your father should leave this world together. And you, young lady, are the proud result of her coming into your father's life."

He was making me uncomfortable. I looked around—Garrett was nowhere to be seen. No one other than the purple and white flowers and Wolfears was within earshot. Wolfears sat back down and watched attentively.

"I'm sorry, I don't know what you're talking about."

"When your father met your mother, he left academia. The world lost a great researcher. Brilliant, no less than brilliant. A man ahead of his time. Not that I'm saying he didn't use his insights henceforth, but oh, where we might be now. We were so close to greatness." He brought his eyes down to my face. "And you? Do you possess your father's intellect? Have his genes gifted you?"

"I'm not following. It's been a long day," I said.

True that the halls of ivy are known to hold within them those who are a bit eccentric and lost in worlds uncommon, but I was beginning to think that this one had gone off the deep end. To put a bit more space between us, I sat on one of the benches.

"Again, thank you for coming," I said, expecting that he would take it as his cue to leave.

Instead, he took a seat on the bench across from me, mistaking my sitting as an invitation for him to do likewise.

He leaned forward so that we were at eye level. The flaps of his jacket spread like the wings of a bat. He smiled.

I glanced around again, wondering where Garrett had gone off to. I wondered if he was still chatting with Kathy.

"Do you mind if I take off my jacket?" he asked. Without waiting for my response, he removed it. "The only other times I wear this are when I'm presiding over a graduation or giving a presentation to government types. I don't normally attend funerals, but this is a memorial, not a true funeral. I've seen lots of people far more casual than I'd expected, but it is a beach community, so there you go. Personally, I think they have the right idea. By they, I mean beach people. Too many important things going on to worry about how one dresses."

Now that he was sitting, chattering, and not looming over me, he had lowered the volume and pitch of his voice as if it dawned on him that he was not in a lecture hall. In the intimacy enveloping us within the pergola, he seemed to have shed his formality with his jacket. He gave a self-deprecating laugh, which made me feel more at ease. I decided that he was simply a nerdy man out of his element.

"How is it that you knew my father well?"

His expression looked puzzled, or surprised, as if he found it odd that I did not know. I think he thought I was joking because he seemed to go in an entirely different direction.

"I must tell you my shock, my absolute shock, to hear the news," he said. "I had only recently spoken to your father about a new development concerning our past research. I left him a couple of updated messages and did not hear back. He must have thought I was barking up an empty tree, as I've been known to do. Yes, I must admit, there have been many times I've caught a whiff of a promising development, only to be disappointed. Ah, the search for immortality in the pages of history."

"What are you talking about?" I asked, beginning to feel uncomfortable again.

Luckily, at that moment, Garrett finally reappeared.

"Do you mind, sir?" Pinsky said to Garrett. "This is my turn. I won't be long."

Garrett just stared at him, so I said, "This is Garrett, my fiancé."

"Lucky man, you are," Pinsky said and rose.

He shook Garrett's hand and said to me, "This is hardly the time and place to discuss such things. I came today to pay my respects."

"What's going on here?" Garrett asked.

The professor didn't answer him, stared at Wolfears, and asked, "What breed of dog is that?"

"I don't know."

"There is genetic testing available. You can find out what he is made of."

"Oh," I said.

He grunted and turned away. Pressing his bat wings against his sides, as if to keep himself from taking flight, he walked with long steps across the lawn away from us.

"Who was that?" Garrett asked.

"An old friend of my father's. One of his professors."

"What was he talking about?"

"I have no idea," I said.

"He was weird."

"Tell me about it. You abandoned me. Where have you been? Talking to Kathy?"

"Gosh, don't get all jealous on me. I was just saying hello. She's been saying prayers for your parents."

"I was surprised she came. How did she even know about it? Did you invite her?"

"She goes to church here too, you know."

"The two times I came with you, I didn't see her."

"She goes to the later worship. Pastor Andrew announced your parents' service to the whole congregation last week. That's probably where she heard about it. She just wanted to show her support."

Garrett flung his arms out and then clapped his hands.

"I know," I said, and stroked Garrett's arm. I felt his muscles ripple. "I'm being silly."

He embraced me in a hug and kissed the top of my head. He seemed more relaxed than usual.

In his arms, the anxiety about moving up our wedding vanished. Though I'd dreaded it, the memorial helped to bring a sense of closure.

Chapter 29

The next day, on Sunday morning, I felt better. I was glad the service was over and felt that I had done right by holding the memorial for my parents. I woke up late and felt more rested than I had in ages. My bruises were hardly noticeable now—I've always healed quickly.

I went for my morning run under a sky with a few scattered clouds that looked like seahorses drifting across. Unlike the other day, it was a peaceful run. When Wolfears and I had just finished our late breakfast, the phone rang. He raised his head and looked at me as if inquiring if I would answer it.

I let the phone ring and told him, "Don't worry, it's just you and me today."

He put his head back on the floor, seemingly contented that I wasn't answering the phone. When the answering machine picked up, I was surprised to hear Garrett's voice. I rushed to the phone, nearly tripping over Wolfears.

"Why aren't you on your way to church?" I asked. "It's almost ten."

"We're going to the eleven-thirty service." Garrett said.

I couldn't help but remember that he'd said Kathy went to the later one.

"That's a surprise. You always go to the early service."

"I know, but Mom's tired after yesterday."

"I bet. She was very helpful. I couldn't have done it without her."

"Since I had a few minutes, I just wanted to call and see how you're doing."

"I'm fine," I said. "I could be even better if I could see you today."

"You know, after skipping studying yesterday, I've got to buckle down this afternoon."

"I miss you."

"I miss you too, but we saw each other yesterday."

"Hey, I've got an idea. I could go to church with you."

"Are telling me you felt some of the holy spirit move you yesterday?"

"No, I can't tell you that," I said.

"That's okay, I'm sure you need to rest too. You don't need to come to church. I love you the way you are."

Garrett was seldom overtly affectionate, and that he so quickly dismissed the idea of my going with him made me suspicious. Where was my paranoia coming from?

"I want to come with you today," I said.

Garrett paused before responding. "No, it's best if you don't. You'd get my mom too excited if she thinks there's a chance you'll join the church. We both know that's not going to happen."

Still, I couldn't help feeling jealous that Kathy would be there. I needed to cajole my way into going.

"I never got a chance to thank Pastor Andrew for the fine job he did."

"I'll be sure to tell him for you."

"Maybe I should go so I can tell him in person."

"You'd hardly get a chance after the service. His Sundays are super busy."

"I just feel like I should go. I want to see you."

"We wouldn't get to spend time together. I'm just going and coming straight home. My statistics course is really a bear."

"Don't you want me to go?" I asked, knowing I sounded pathetic. "Kathy will be there, won't she?"

"What's this thing about Kathy? I don't care about her. She's just a friend now. You know that."

I made a small noise.

"You're getting so needy," he said.

I didn't respond.

"Sorry, I didn't mean to say that. You know you're the only one for me. I've got to get going. Mom needs help with something."

"Bye," I said, sounding hurt and not caring.

I hung up and sat back down in the kitchen.

I told Wolfears, "Like I said, it'll just be the two of us today."

Less than a minute later, the phone rang again, I jumped up, thinking Garrett had changed his mind.

It was Mysti.

"Oh, hi," I said.

"Don't sound so disappointed."

"I'm not. I'm glad you called. What's up?"

"Wanna get some yogurt and hang out? Maybe go bike riding on the boardwalk?"

"Nah, I just ate, and I'm kinda drained today. I think I'm just going to stay home and recharge."

"Don't tell me you're going recluse on me."

"Just for a day. Yesterday was exhausting."

"Yeah, I understand. It's like that for us introverts."

"You're not an introvert."

"I am sometimes," she said, in mock offense. "We don't have to hang at the boardwalk. I've got big news."

"Good or bad?"

"Mostly good."

"Spill."

"Not on the phone,"

"All right, you hooked me. Let's get together. Do you mind coming here?"

"I'll be right over."

It was a good thing that she was coming over because I was working myself into a dark mood, my thoughts spiraling downward. I tried to comfort myself with the possibility that my jealousy was rooted in the loss of my parents. I'd never been the jealous type before.

I thought about all the people at the memorial service, how they thought they knew my parents, well, maybe my mom. But my father? He was a walnut shell. And as I thought about him, I realized that in some ways he and Garrett were similar. They were both focused, disciplined and didn't share their feelings easily. Considering how little I knew my father, did I really know Garrett?

They say you marry your parent—for the first time, I wondered if I was making a mistake.

Was the solid earth about to vaporize beneath me again? I knew he wasn't having an affair with Kathy, but I never could have believed that my parents wouldn't be here, not now, and not how. So, anxiety had become an undercurrent of my life that had never been there before. Mostly I could ignore it, but sometimes I couldn't ignore the suspicion that anything I thought to be true might not be. I'd come to the awareness or belief that I might not know anything at all.

Much gnawed at me. The future still seemed uncertain, even more so now that I was suspicious of Garrett and his ex. We'd always been honest with each other about things. Trust was a foundation in our relationship. I felt guilty that I was doubting my trust in him.

When Mysti arrived, I hardly greeted her before saying, "Garrett didn't want me to go to church with him. Do you think he cheats on me? He has lots of opportunities. Girls are all over him at the games. Did you see Kathy at the memorial? Remember when she dated Garrett in high school and everyone called them G 'n' K? I think she still has feelings for him."

Chapter 30

Mysti opened her mouth as if to say something, then closed it. I continued spilling my worries to her. She listened without commenting, other than nods and affirming sounds to indicate she was paying attention.

I finally stopped by repeating my question, "Do you think he is cheating on me?"

"No, he's a good guy, and I don't think he was hitting on me either. Just showing off for the guys. Like I told you, I was jealous because you were spending all your time with him and you'd forgotten me, so I built up something harmless into something it wasn't."

"I'll never ignore you again," I said. "We'll get together lots from now on."

Mysti gave a funny expression that I couldn't decipher.

"What?" I asked.

She lifted her head and had a faraway look in her eyes.

Now that I'd settled down, I had enough presence of mind to ask, "What's your news? I'm being so selfish and self-centered. Tell me."

She pressed her cheeks with the knuckles of her fists. Her eyes danced and her vitality flowed back into her. Her hands flew from her face, fingers spread like a burst of stars.

She said, "I'm going to be a Lion."

It took me a moment to understand what she meant.

"Oh, you got into Columbia! Congratulations!"

"Yes, the history and anthro departments both accepted me, and I got the diving scholarship."

She jumped up and down and then squeezed me. I thought I would have been hugged out from yesterday, but it felt good to be loved.

When she let me go, I said, "That's incredible. Wait, you said there was bad news too. What?"

Her cheeks were still red from her knuckles. She looked away from me again.

"The downside is I'll be leaving soon, not in the fall."

"What? Why? You can't leave now."

"It's terrible timing. But there's a summer program in Germany that I get to be part of. I get to join in a dig in a Wielbark cultural cemetery on the Amber Road. Third century site. It's kinda my thing and will look great on a resume."

"Oh, that *is* kinda your thing," I said. "Clay pots and Goth stuff, right?"

"Exactly."

I tried to sound happy for her, and I was. But I couldn't help feeling abandoned after we'd just reconnected.

"Will you have time to come back here before the fall semester?"

She shook her head, and said, "Straight to Columbia from Germany."

"We'll have to spend as much time as possible together until you leave."

She smiled and gave me another hug.

"You look so sad," she said. "I know something what will make you feel better—let's go to the pebble beach at the preserve."

Wolfears looked at me expectantly.

"I was just there with Wolfie. I just want to hang around here. I don't want to be around people."

"I understand, but the tide is coming in. It'll be deserted, except for the surfers out in the water. We can build memory cairns."

"What are you talking about?"

"You know, the ancient Goth tradition."

"By ancient you mean like 1990?

"Well, it has evolved from the Goths in the Middle Ages. They built them for trail markers and arranged them in various ways to leave messages for other travelers. They made them to honor the dead, too."

"How do you know this? Are you making this up?"

"No. Sure, there's holes and gaps in the whats and whys—most things are lost in history. I'm extrapolating, but it is possible. That's what I believe. And why not?"

"That sounds religious. I had enough of that yesterday."

"No, it's more spiritual, an honoring ritual."

I felt myself being sucked into her enthusiasm. Wolfears thumped his tail as if he liked the idea too.

In a last attempt at protest, I said, "I thought you said cairns are bad for the environment?"

"They won't cause any soil erosion on the pebble beach. They'll disappear with the tide."

Mysti's energy is contagious, and with Wolfears on her side, I gave in and we headed to the beach.

As Mysti predicted, the tide was already coming in, but there was still plenty of beach left. A lone, older man wearing a blue baseball cap was huddled next to the cliff watching the few surfers out in the water. Soon after we arrived, he climbed the staircase to the preserve above and left the beach to the three of us. Mysti played with Wolfears while I combed the beach for stones to build the cairns. I was so intent on finding stones and not paying attention that I slipped on the tangles of kelp that had washed up. I let out a cry.

Wolfears bounded over to me to check that I was okay. When he saw that I was, he shook and gave me a shower from his wet fur. I continued my hunt and selected more stones using my top as a basket to carry them.

I built one for my mother first. I made the base with the common gray stones that dominate the beach. For the top one, I used a white stone mottled with brown lines, like a web constructed by an over-caffeinated spider. The cairn arched to one side and looked like the wind might topple it, but it held. The base of my mother's was only three stones wide. For my father, I built a four- by-five base because of the larger, oddly shaped cap stone I'd found. Its shape reminded me of the skull of a carnivorous animal, or a duck's head. I couldn't decide which. I didn't build his cairn as high to have multiple stones to support the larger cap stone. As it rose, it gave the appearance of a twisting pyramid.

When I was done, the three of us sat on the sandy patch where the man had been and watched the tide push the water closer and closer to the cairns. As expected, my mother's cairn was the first to topple. My father's stubbornly resisted the ebb and flow of the waves. Even when it had been completely immersed, it held.

A couple of surfers came in from the water. One of them smiled and waved to us before heading up the stairs. The metal stairs clanged as they ascended.

Mysti said, "Do you think you'll ever go in the water again?"

"I went for a swim."

"Really, you did?"

"In the pool, not the ocean. And that's an exaggeration—I fell into it."

"Did you trip? Like on the beach? What happened?"

"No, I just let myself fall into it. Weird, huh?"

Our conversation ceased and we sat watching the water and inhaling the salt air. The tide rose so that we could no longer get to the stairs without getting our feet and calves wet. Still, my father's cairn resisted the onslaught of the water rolling in as the tide continued its clocklike rhythm.

When the backwash still revealed it to be standing, I became impatient. The next time the water receded, I walked over to it and kicked it down.

Chapter 31

I'd planned to spend time with my grandparents and uncle later in the week. Unfortunately, my uncle needed to return to work earlier than planned, so their flight back home to Tokyo was now scheduled for Monday morning. Because of that, Sunday afternoon was the only chance for us to get together, and they came over to the house.

Kaito, my uncle, didn't smile much, and when he did it looked like it hurt the muscles in his face. It seemed to me that he felt shepherding my grandparents around was a burden. My grandfather didn't smile often either, but when he did, it didn't look painful. In contrast, my grandmother was warm, but not speaking each other's languages, we mostly communicated with expressions and body language. She often tilted her head sideways while looking into my eyes. Occasionally, she touched me in a way that made me feel she viewed me as fragile, though I think she meant the physical contact to be reassuring.

Before the memorial, I had only met my grandparents twice when they had come to visit. My father had flown to Japan many times, but they were always quick trips, and he'd never taken me along. I'd never met my uncle, Kaito, until the memorial. In contrast to my father, Kaito was sloppy and loose-jointed. He seemed self-absorbed and sprawled on the couch with his legs split apart and his arms tossed to either side. I guessed that he had been drinking. I found it difficult to have a conversation with him. My limited communication with my grandparents was only through my uncle's interpreting, which seemed to be an annoyance to him. Still, death had brought us together. We were all bonded by our loss, for which one needs no words.

When they arrived, I had the presence of mind to offer refreshments. My grandmother went into the kitchen with me and showed me how she made tea. She was methodical and took pleasure in the simple act, which seemed infused with ritual. Gestures and smiles sufficed to connect our communication.

I arranged a tray with crackers and cheese slices in alternating circles in an attempt to make them aesthetically pleasing. I had no idea if it was a complement to the tea.

We served the tea and snacks. My grandparents only drank tea. My uncle almost single-handedly consumed all the cheese and crackers. When they were gone, he reached out to the empty plate and brushed his fingers over it as if there might be an invisible piece of cheese hiding there. When he found none, his fingers tapped it, clicking like miniature horses' hooves.

"Let me get another plate," I said.

"No, I've had enough," he said, shaking his head emphatically.

He sat up straight. His eyes averted mine more than usual.

He said, "I suppose you know about the life insurance policy your father recently took out for my parents."

That caught me off guard. I didn't.

"My father didn't share a lot. Especially about financial things," I said.

"That doesn't surprise me."

He grunted and then spoke to my grandparents in Japanese before speaking to me again.

"Unfortunately, as you know, I need to get back. I had intended to start the paperwork before leaving—these things are much easier in person. Perhaps you could help me coordinate the claim?"

"Oh, wait, I might have something that will help."

I sprung up, glad to have something specific to do beyond trying to fill in the gaps in our awkward conversation and serving tea. The death certificates and autopsy reports had arrived the other day. I'd opened them without bothering to read them beyond seeing what they were. I retrieved them from the entry credenza.

"These might help. Too bad you're leaving. I have an appointment with my parents' financial planner tomorrow. I bet he can help."

"Please have him get in touch with me."

I handed the letters to him. While he read them, we returned to polite expressions and uncomfortable silence. My uncle made another grunt. This one was harsher sounding, more than just an expression of mild exasperation. He handed the papers back to me and turned to my grandparents and said something that sounded like, "e-caw shin-git," which I later learned must have been "*ikka shinju.*"

From their wide-eyed expressions, I didn't need to know what the words meant to know it was something bad. My grandfather's jaw tightened. My grandmother put her face in her hands."

"What?" I asked.

My uncle shook his head.

"Nothing unexpected," he said and gave no further explanation.

I knew he was being evasive and mentally repeated the sound of the words so as to not forget them.

"I wish we could stay longer, but my parents are very tired and our flight is early. We'll need to get going so they can rest."

They stood. My grandmother tugged my uncle's arm and spoke to him.

My uncle said, "She asks if you would allow us to see the view from your backyard before we leave."

"Yes, of course." I'd not thought of giving them a tour as they'd spent time at our house on their last visit.

We stood outside on the patio, looking at the ocean. The ocean was a deep blue and sparkling with late afternoon sunlight, indifferent to the weight of the world it carried. My grandmother pressed her hand against my arm, less tentatively this time. My uncle translated her words.

"She says, 'We live on different sides of the same ocean. You are welcome to visit and see the view from our side. Please come any time you wish.'"

Even though being with them was bumbling, when they left, I felt a void.

I went back outside with Wolfears and sat on the wall, staring at the ocean as the sun dipped and flattened like an egg yolk in a frying pan. The blue ocean turned gray and reflected the red-streaked sky before it melted into a colorless expanse. It whispered to me, and I did not speak back to it. I shivered and stepped off the wall, glad to have Wolfears warm and solid beside me.

I called Garrett hoping to convince him to take a break from his studies and spend time with me. As always, he said once his semester ended he'd have more free time. I thought of how my father was always working, how they were similar in their dedication to their goals. I hung up the phone and went to bed early.

Nights are always the worst. All my fears bubble up, undistracted, and with them come things unseen in the light of day when they rise from the depths of the sea and slither into my mind. Some are slimy. Their ooze smothers pleasant dreams. Others have jagged edges that scrape away pleasant or logical thoughts, like the one where my father and Garrett became one person.

I woke before the morning light, from a dream in which I was in a sea of broken glass. As at the pier, I dove again and again, but was unable to reach my parents beneath the waves.

Unable to return to sleep, I lay in bed listening to the ocean slapping the rocks below the cliff. Wolfears moved about as if his thoughts were keeping him from sleeping too.

I asked him, "Do you think I'm marrying my father? Do you think that one day Garrett will try to kill me?"

Chapter 32

I dreaded the drive into the San Fernando Valley, but like it or not it was time to hit the road to see my parents' financial planner. I needed help with that practical facet of life.

PCH was crowded as I expected. I considered taking one of the canyons, but if the one I chose locked up, it could be a long ride over. I headed to the 405 freeway, which would take me near his office. At least I wasn't coming from the valley where the southbound traffic was jammed to a standstill in some places. Even so, there was enough traffic going north that I had to pay attention and couldn't relax. At least, I thought, I didn't have time to miss Garrett.

Frank Volden's office was in Sherman Oaks, in a high-rise attached to a shopping mall. Though I felt trepidation, it was nothing like when I'd gone to my father's office. I found a parking spot on the third level of the parking structure and walked through the lot, dodging the cars of anxious shoppers looking for deals. I took the elevator to the eleventh floor and stepped out into the reception area. The receptionist was a young man with a pompadour like he'd stepped out of an old film. He led me to a corner meeting room with curved glass walls facing the interior.

When he offered a refreshment, I opted for tea. Not the simple choice I expected, he rattled off multiple varieties. I chose green tea, thinking of my grandmother. He brought it in a coffee mug.

While I waited, people walked by looking without looking. I felt like a goldfish in a fishbowl. I thumbed through the autopsy report of my mother. I noticed the checkbox for current pregnancy was left blank. No surprise. If it had been checked, I would have been shocked. It made me realize she'd never talked about being pregnant with me.

As I was about to start reading the note section of her report, Mr. Volden appeared. He was a tall, thin man with large, pale eyes set in a moon face. He shook my hand timidly and motioned for me to sit back in the chair across the table from him. When he sat, he steepled his fingers and rested his small chin on them. He reminded me of a cartoon turtle because his chin disappeared into his neck. Though he spoke softly, his voice was deep and resonant.

After condolences and pleasantries, he said, "Your parents have done an excellent job in providing for your future. In fact, if you manage your money wisely and don't squander it, as people your age often do, you'll never need to work a day in your life. Not that I'm suggesting that you don't work. You do have the luxury of that option."

I gave a weak smile. It was something. I immediately thought how Garrett wouldn't need to push himself so hard for us to have the life he wanted. At the moment, I was more concerned with how to access money to pay the bills and keep things going, the mechanics of daily living. That and the hope he could give me some insight into my father's mystery.

"I understand my father had a life insurance policy," I said, and handed him the death certificates and the coroner's reports.

When he finished reviewing the papers, he re-steepled his fingers, but didn't rest his chin on them this time. His voice dropped in pitch when he spoke.

"There may be an issue with the life insurance policy. Policies have a suicide clause, which means that, if a death occurs in the first two years, and the death is determined to be suicide, the benefit will not be paid. Because of the unusual circumstances of your father's death, they are likely to challenge the claim and do an investigation."

"I understand," I said, more calmly than I felt.

He said he'd be happy to deal directly with my uncle during the process. I decided that I would help my grandparents with money if they needed it. We then discussed other aspects of my family's finances. Before I left, I showed him the checkbook register with the entries of checks to Maria Nogales.

"Do you happen to know what these checks are for?"

He looked genuinely puzzled and couldn't offer me any insights as to why they had been given to her.

When I left his office, I crossed over to the mall. I decided to splurge on something for myself since Mr. Volden had assured me that I had more than enough money.

The mall reminded me of a teen movie that I guessed had been filmed there. I liked riding the elevator with the glass ceiling above that let in natural light. I wandered past the store windows and drifted inside a few of them but couldn't find anything I wanted to buy for myself.

I've always had everything I wanted, so things for their own sake are not important to me. I did find a scarf for Mysti that would warm her in the colder weather.

I passed a jewelry shop and spotted a gold chain with a diamond encrusted basketball pendant. When the shop keeper removed it from the case, he gave me a patronizing expression without moving his caterpillar eyebrows. I didn't blink at the price and bought it for Garrett.

If I wanted to miss the traffic, I needed to get going.

When I exited the parking lot, I didn't make a right turn toward the freeway and home. Instead, I turned left, in the direction of Maria's place. I felt compelled to find out more about the relationship between my father and her. Since he couldn't give answers, she was the only one who could.

I had no idea what I would say to her when I arrived.

Chapter 33

Driving to Maria's, I thought about Detective Yates asking if my father had financial problems. Now, I knew that whatever had been troubling him, it wasn't a money issue. I couldn't wait to tell Garrett about all the money that I would now have. That *we* would have. It was a ray of sunshine through a black cloud. Now he could quit the pizza delivery job that he hated. He wouldn't need to depend on a scholarship and could go to any university that would accept him. With his grades, he'd have lots of choices. He could take a lighter load in school without the financial pressure. We could spend more time together.

His mother had hinted more than once about moving in with me, and then us. I didn't like the idea of that, but now, I could buy another house just for her. It seemed like somehow at least some things would be working out.

I recalled my mother saying, "Money is the most important unimportant thing there is in the world."

As I thought about it, I could buy him a new car too. He could sell The Chugger. He wouldn't have to be ashamed about driving it any longer.

The day was heating up in the valley. I turned on my air conditioner. I couldn't remember the last time I'd used it because I seldom needed it by the ocean. It blew warm air, musty at first. Another thing to get fixed. I rolled down the windows down to let the air circulate. Someone honked as they drove by. I'd slowed down while daydreaming.

In the late morning light, La Tuna Canyon felt less ominous and more welcoming than the last time I was there. I appreciated it's being more rural and less dense than most of the San Fernando Valley.

When I came to the telephone pole that marked Maria's, I made a U-turn and parked behind the entrance to the dirt driveway. I stepped out of the car and found it was cooler in the canyon, but still warm. I caught a whiff of the hay and sweat scent of horses. I walked up the rutted driveway. It didn't seem so treacherous as before. The leaves in the trees rustled as if they were having a conversation. At the driveway's bend, I saw a two-toned, red and black, Chevy truck parked by the house in the spot where the faded blue truck sat rusting last time. I was glad that the blue truck was gone because it probably belonged to Maria's male companion. He gave me the creeps with his burning blue eyes.

The pizza box was still in the yard, now by the garage next to an overflowing garbage bin. The lid was open, but the flies had lost interest. The front door and the screen door were both open. The screen door hung at an angle, pulled away from the top hinge as if to match the crooked window shutter. I went up the creaking wooden stairs and heard someone moving about inside.

"Hello," I called out.

An older man, probably of Mexican descent, came to the door. On his head was a bucket hat, with a patch of a marlin on the front. A red and black band that matched the truck's colors circled the brim. He held a screwdriver in one hand and there were black smudges on the knees of his khaki pants. He stood in the doorway and didn't say anything.

"Is Maria home?" I asked.

He made a sweeping motion with his free hand. "Your mom's not here."

I jerked back and said, "She's not my mother."

My reaction amused him. He smiled, then said, "Lucky you."

"Do you know where I can find her?"

"I'm sure I'd be the last person to know where she went. I imagine she took off with her new boyfriend. I figured he was trouble when he moved in with her. They skipped out owing three months' rent, on top of trashing the place."

He shook his head, waved the screwdriver in the air as if imitating a tornado and stepped back into the house. Then, he turned back to me.

"Are you looking for a place to rent?" Before I could answer, he continued. "It's nice here when it's fixed up. We used to live here before we turned it into a rental. Quiet, if you don't mind the roosters crowing and the nicker of horses. It won't be ready for a month. Of course, if you're a friend of hers, you'd not be a good tenant."

"I'm not like her," I said defensively. "I don't know her. I only met her once."

He smiled. "You seem all right to me. I'm usually a good judge of character. Just the same, you'll have to fill out an application. My wife has the final say."

"I'm not looking for a place."

"Figures. You look clean and neat compared to most of them that are looking to rent."

"Wait, she could have paid the rent. I just gave her a check. My father gave her money. I don't know why. Do you know anything about her that might help me find her?"

I didn't know why I'd blurted that. I expected him to ask me to explain. I didn't know what I'd say. The truth would sound too confusing. He didn't ask.

"Just because she *could* have paid the rent, doesn't mean she *would*. People like her don't. It's anybody's guess where she went."

I noticed another pizza box inside and said, "She liked pizza."

"Yeah, there's plenty more empty boxes in the kitchen and a couple out back. She liked flies too, evidently. You're welcome to look around for clues to her whereabouts if you want."

He stepped back and I went inside. Just walking inside made me feel like I needed a shower.

I poked around through the mess she'd left. A foul and dusty smell hung in the air. I couldn't imagine someone living in such filth. Not only was the place dirty, but there were holes in the walls, as if someone had punched their fists through it. A stack of old car tires rested in the corner of the living room. The furniture that was left behind was half broken and ripped. All kinds of personal items were left strewn on the floor, counters and in the sinks. The lid of the toilet tank was missing, and the toilet looked like it had never been cleaned. A music CD was floating in the bowl. I found an envelope with her name on it and an old address, but nothing that gave me any clues as to where she might have gone. Still, the landlord didn't mind if I took the envelope just in case.

"Thank you for letting me look around. I'm sorry you have to deal with all of this."

"No *problema*," he said, shaking his head. "Rentals aren't a free ride."

As I started to leave, he said, "I just remembered something that might be helpful in tracking her down. Though, if you ask me, best to stay away from people like her if you can. The neighbor said when they moved out, a Tally Ho moving van backed up the driveway. Ran over her marigolds. Maybe the moving company can tell you something. Funny, she had money for the movers, unless she stiffed them too."

He gave a chuckle and shook his head again.

"I hope you get a good tenant next time," I told him.

He tipped his hat to me, and I left him to his repairs and cleanup.

As I walked down the rutted driveway, a sudden blast of wind swept through the narrow valley, bending down a row of willow trees across the street. Their leaves rustled noisily as if in protest of their quiet conversation being interrupted. They sprung back from the momentary gust. I guessed that with the hills being so close on either side that the wind was funneled like rushing water through the narrows in a river.

As I got in my car, a Lincoln town car pulled up and parked behind me, stopping only inches from my bumper. In my rearview mirror, I saw a man wearing a tweed cap and blue sweater get out of the Lincoln. He held a newspaper rolled up in his hand.

I did a double take. Even without his tight-shouldered, bat-winged coat, I recognized him. He looked much more comfortable wearing a sweater.

Chapter 34

I couldn't help but wonder if Professor Pinsky had followed me because, at the memorial, he'd said something about another time. I thought about locking the door before he approached. To my surprise, he ignored me and walked back to a row of metal mailboxes on posts and checked their address numbers. Then, he came back and walked beyond my car. When I thought he was about to turn into the driveway to Maria's place, I got out and called to him.

He turned around and this time he was the one who did a double take, looking genuinely surprised when he recognized me. I discarded the disturbing thought that he had been following me. We stared at each other wide-eyed, until he said, "You're Dr. Otomo's daughter. What are you doing here?"

"I was going to ask you the same question."

"This can't be a coincidence. You obviously came to see her," he said, and held up the rolled newspaper.

"What?"

"The woman in the story."

"I don't know what you're talking about."

With a shake of his head, he stepped closer and stared down at me. He unfurled the newspaper and showed me its cover as if that were an answer. The newspaper was the tabloid with the picture of the woman holding the furry baby. I must have looked as bewildered as I felt because he stabbed his finger at the cover with such force that I thought he might tear the paper.

"I don't understand," I repeated, wishing I'd driven away.

"You came to see *her*," he said and pointed his fleshy finger at the young woman on the cover.

"I don't know her."

"Then why are you here?"

"I came to see someone about my father."

Oddly, a small smile slowly broke onto his face and at the same time the color drained from it.

In a whisper, he said, "She seems to be playing all the angles. Obviously, your father didn't believe her. I couldn't produce the funds without his help, and she sold out to this trashy tabloid."

"What does this have to do with the woman on the cover?"

"Maria Nogales."

"That's not her," I said.

A pang of fear shot through me. My muscles tightened as I thought I'd given the check to the wrong person. His finger made a circle around the picture of the woman and the baby chimpanzee.

"Of course not," he said as if speaking to a child. "They used a model for the cover picture."

"Thank goodness, for a moment I thought I'd given the check to the wrong person."

"What check?"

"When I saw her, I gave her a check that my father had written and not mailed."

"How much was the check for?"

"Ten thousand dollars."

The professor let out a long breath and pressed his hands together. He walked in circle, stamping his feet on the ground like a child. I couldn't tell if he was angry or ecstatic. He stopped in front of me and grabbed me by the shoulders. His face was now lit with color. The smile he'd given before was a mere shadow of the one now on his face.

"Do you know what this means?"

That you're insane, was my first thought, but I simply said, "No."

"It means your father believed her. We did it! The experiment was a success."

He let go of me and marched in another circle.

When he stopped, he said, "Thank goodness. She must have contacted your father, and he intended to pay her off for her silence. But then, the accident. She didn't know and thought she wasn't getting the money, so she went to the tabloid. Imagine dragging his and the university's accomplishments through the dirt. Did she promise to keep her mouth quiet from now on? I hope you got it in writing."

"She didn't promise anything. What is this all about?"

"I suppose your father didn't bother with the details. He was a trusting soul."

"Details? I don't know anything. I just found the check by accident."

He flapped his arms at his side and again reminded me of an impossibly large penguin.

"Oh, probably for the best," he said. "Just some messy loose ends from our research."

I decided not to mention all the monthly checks to Maria that were listed in my father's check register. Obviously, the professor didn't know that whatever was between them had stretched on for years. As we spoke, cars occasionally zoomed past. Out of the corner of my eye, I noticed a dark blue sedan driving up the street more slowly than the others. Glancing at it, I saw bumper stickers covering the rear bumper and the trunk. It made a U-turn and parked up the street facing us.

Pinsky said, "In any case, this woman has caused trouble. She needs to retract her story because it has sparked a small protest at the university with the religious zealots."

I'd not read any of the tabloids Garrett's mother had left for me. I now wished I'd read the chimpanzee story.

"I'd best get on with the unpleasant task of speaking with her," he said.

"She's not here."

"Do you know when she'll be back?"

"I don't think she's coming back. The place is empty. The landlord said she skipped out."

"Where did she go?"

I raised my hands to show I had no idea. The professor shook his head. I noticed that no one had gotten out of the car that had parked up the road.

"Oh, wait," I said. "The landlord let me take an envelope, but it's probably an old address."

When I handed it to him, he said, "If you already gave her a check, why are you here now?"

"Because I want to know what's going on," I said. "Who is this woman? Why did my father give her such a big check?"

"Like I said, it must have been to keep her silent."

"Silent? Silent about what? Did my father do something wrong?"

"No, not at all. Your father did something *wonderful*. Something brilliant."

I clenched my teeth and waited for him to explain. The people in the car hadn't moved. I suspected they were watching us, thinking we looked out of place and suspicious.

"There were ethical questions raised by small minds around the work we did. Pests from the dark ages. We were working on building hybridized humans to advance the durability and vigorous nature of our species."

The way he spoke made it sound as if what they were doing no more than growing a hardier strain of tomatoes.

"Did you do experiments to create mutants, some kind of monsters?" I asked, straining to keep the edge out of my voice.

"You should be proud. We were advancing science for the benefit of all humanity. Individual sacrifices must sometimes be made."

"Like throwing a woman off of a cliff to appease the gods?"

"I see you have a flare for the dramatic. We're hardly so primitive. Evolution moves forward with trial and error. We make genetic insertions to eliminate errors in the DNA code. We are still learning. Of course they will be—"

"Of what? Putting monkey genes in humans?"

He laughed. "Hardly. No, not a monkey. That's ridiculous. They're not closely related enough to humans. *Apes* are our cousins. We used chimpanzees initially, but found our best success with bonobos."

"What's a bonobo?" I asked, my voice rising. But before he could answer, I shouted, "You created a half-human mutant!"

He remained calm, professorial. "I can only imagine your mother felt the same way. After your father met her, he left the program abruptly. He never gave a reason."

"What happened to them, your half-human creations?"

"Until I read Maria's story, I believed they all ended in miscarriages, but if she is telling the truth—"

"Stay away from me," I said in a near shriek.

I backed away from him, got in my car and locked the doors. He stood looking at me with a perplexed expression, his arms hanging at his sides. In one hand was the newspaper, in the other was the envelope.

I started the engine. I wanted to drive away, but knew that I was too overwhelmed with emotion to not be a road hazard. My chest felt as if a band of metal was tightening around it. Still, if he took a step toward me, I would have pulled onto the street without looking for traffic. Fortunately, he only shook his head before returning to his car.

As I watched him pull onto the street, I finally felt as if I could breathe. I sat there thinking how ignorance is bliss; how only a short time ago, the world seemed stable, the future seemed knowable. Now, it felt as if any step I took or any question I asked could trigger an earthquake and force my world to crumble into the depths of the ocean.

Let sleeping dogs lie, I told myself.

I heard an engine start behind me and glanced in my rearview mirror.

The dark blue sedan pulled onto the street. As it went by, I noticed a woman was driving. The bearded man in the passenger seat looked directly at me with intense eyes, gave a big smile and waved. His head swayed in rhythm with his hand. He was trying to be funny. If I'd been in a better mood, I'd have laughed at his goofiness. When they passed, I read some of the bumper stickers.

On one printed with bold red letters was *Humans are not animals.* On a yellow sticker bordered with diagonal stipes like a caution sign, I read, *Caution: In Case of Rapture, This Car Will Be Unmanned.* The last one I was able to catch before they were too far away read, *Evolution is heresy.* They followed the professor's car and disappeared around the bend too.

I'd never yelled at anyone, let alone someone old enough to be my grandfather. What had come over me? *Get a grip, girl,* I told myself.

Chapter 35

By the time I arrived home, my curiosity had surfaced above my desire for calm waters. I abandoned my vow to let sleeping dogs lie. The first thing I did was grab the supermarket tabloids off the coffee table.

I collapsed into the couch cushions feeling engulfed and small, like when I was a little girl watching the big world and my parents talking about things I didn't understand. I found the issue with the woman and the baby chimp on her lap.

Before, I'd found the shocked expression of the woman to be overly dramatic and laughable. Now, I looked at her face with a creeping feeling of horror. Certainly, the picture was a reenactment. The woman was twenty or thirty years younger than Maria—her features didn't look much like Maria's at all.

Yet now that I knew there might be a sliver of truth wedged between the pages of flesh-filled celebrity gossip, the picture no longer looked amusingly absurd. I wondered at the revulsion one would feel to discover that the baby that had grown inside of her was not human. If I had anything in my stomach, I would have retched.

My fingers flipped through the pages to the article. There were more photographs inside. One picture was of a monkey suckling at her breast, while its hand grabbed her hair, pulling a strand of it across her face. Its caption read, *I Gave Birth to a Half-Human Baby!*

Another photograph showed the woman cowering in fear with a pasted image of a large gorilla looming behind her. Beneath it was, *Secret Government Program Breeds Monsters!*

I lifted my eyes from the pages. Why was I reading this foolish entertainment? How could people believe these stories? They weren't even consistent. I watched the second hand on the clock over the mantel. Then, I took a deep breath and returned my attention to the newspaper.

Now revealed: A secret government program that bred gorillas and monkeys with humans.

Prominent scientists have worried for decades about the dangers of toying with human genes. Their fears have already been realized. A monster—a half-human creature—was created years ago in a clandestine program at a major university.

A woman, whose identity is not being revealed for her protection, has come forward and exposed the awful truth.

Trapped in poverty in Central America during the political turmoil of the Nicaraguan Revolution, she was desperate to escape. Along with a group of women, she agreed to become a surrogate mother in exchange for the opportunity to emigrate to the United States and become a citizen. She was implanted with an embryo via in vitro fertilization. Never did she suspect what was growing in her womb wasn't human.

Most of the women in the program had early miscarriages. Only a few of them reached even the sixth month of pregnancy. By the seventh month, she was the only woman in the program to have not lost her baby. She was taken to a private wing in the university's hospital and kept on bed rest while being constantly monitored and checked upon. She assumed the baby she carried must have belonged to important and influential people. How wrong she was!

Labor was induced prior to term, and a healthy baby girl was delivered. Upon holding the child, she didn't want to let her go. At first, the baby appeared normal, except for being a preemie and having a thick head of hair. Her only other remarkable characteristic was the abnormal strength of her hands. Her little fingers were difficult to pry off whatever she held. One time she grabbed a nurse's hair and pulled it with such strength that the nurse had let out a yelp of pain.

When she mentioned this to the doctors, they laughed. She listened when they spoke among themselves. They didn't know she had once worked as a nanny for an English-speaking couple back in Nicaragua. Though she was unable to understand medical jargon, she did *understand some English. One of the doctors referred to the baby as the chimp child. At first, she assumed they were simply making fun of the baby because of her hairiness and strength. Then, another time, a woman who came to observe the baby made the doctors laugh when she reached her hands under his armpits and wiggled his fingers while making hooting noises like a monkey. The woman began to suspect an awful truth.*

She felt a maternal attachment to the child and began to protest that she wanted to keep the baby. They threatened her with deportation if she made a fuss. To calm her down before she left the hospital, a nurse confided in her and revealed that the baby was part of an experiment crossing monkeys with humans. The doctors were playing God and creating a super soldier with a human brain and the strength of a gorilla. Learning that the child was only half-human and would grow into a monster, she agreed to leave quietly and keep this awful secret—until now.

She's lived with the horror of what she helped create all those years ago. The nightmares have never stopped. Many nights she wakes up, sweat-drenched and wondering whatever happened to the child. Even though it was a freak, it was her baby.

When I finished reading, I saw Wolfears by the fireplace with his front legs stretched out before him and his head resting on them. He watched me with eyes beneath knit eyebrows.

"What do you think?" I asked him.

I wanted him to tell me to laugh at the story. Of course, he didn't.

Secret laboratories, the picture of the woman with a gorilla and their monkey child suckling at her breast. It was too much, absurd, ridiculous, written to shock not to inform.

And yet.

I couldn't dismiss it because, buried beneath the sensationalism, was a seed of truth, or Pinsky wouldn't have believed that the woman in the story was Maria. My father had written checks for years, though Pinsky knew only about the last one.

I stared at the magazine, feeling as if I couldn't rise from the couch.

Why had he kept the checks secret from Pinsky? My breath caught. Could it be true? Did my father create an experimental half-human and decide to steal it?

I was letting my imagination get away with me. There had to be another explanation.

I stared at my hands, wishing the engagement ring was on my finger. If only I could turn back time.

Pinsky had mentioned bonobos and the article had not. I had to find out what they were. I guessed they were a type of ape that I'd not heard about. Maybe something not all that different to humans.

A trip to the library was in order.

Chapter 36

The house phone rang. It never stopped. Thinking it might be an annoying real estate person, attorney or a carpet cleaning service, I stood by the phone and let the machine answer it.

"Hello," a thin, uncertain voice said. It didn't sound like a sales call. She cleared her throat.

"This is your Aunt Ruby."

I twitched and picked up the phone. "Hello, this is Prima."

"Hello, dear. I got your letter. What a shock. I'm so sorry. I've been recovering from surgery and only just read it. How are you doing?"

"I'm okay, I guess. I'm so happy you called."

"Yes, my neighbor, Mr. Johnson, brought my mail to me. I'm borrowing his phone now. I'm deeply sorry, but I wouldn't have been able to travel to the memorial even if I'd got your letter in time. Don't let your knees go bad."

"Are you okay?"

"Rest and physical therapy. I should be up and about before long. I wish things had been better between me and your mother. Life is funny sometimes. I always wanted children and your mother didn't. Then, when you came along, she was the happiest gal in the world. I was so surprised. She and your father had been together for less than a year. I still feel bad that I wasn't with her during her pregnancy. I was in Southeast Asia when you were born. Traveling the world. I didn't even see you until you were almost two. I was jealous. I'll admit that. You were eight the last time I visited. My, you must have grown since I last saw you."

"A little, not all that much."

"Do you remember playing with my mini-poo, Cream Puff?"

"Your poodle. Of course, how could I forget that little ball of energy?"

"She was just a puppy then. She'll be thirteen in a couple of months. She's more pink than white now because her fur is so thin that you can see through it. I suppose I should call her Pink Puff."

I told her about Wolfears. We chatted for a long time, catching up, until I could tell she was getting tired and out of breath.

"I'm sure you need your rest," I told her. "I better let you go."

"Okay, but let's promise to stay in touch."

"Yes, definitely. I'm so glad to hear from you. It would mean a lot if you could come to my wedding."

"I would love that. If you ever want to come out this way, don't hesitate. My little trailer is primitive compared to what you're used to, but you're always welcome."

I was thrilled to have heard from her.

I went back and sat on the couch. I closed my eyes and felt like I was being absorbed into it as I thought about how wonderful it would be to see her.

Suddenly, I let out a cry.

I'd forgotten Mysti's recital was tonight. I looked at the clock—with the after-work traffic on PCH and in the canyons, I'd never make it on time. There would be so few times I could see her before she left for Europe. I hoped she wouldn't be too disappointed.

To distract myself from feeling guilty, I decided to pick up around the house. It was up to me now to keep it clean and organized, at least until I found a new housekeeper. There were so many things that my parents managed that now would be my responsibility. They were things I'd never paid attention to, like paying bills and shopping. As I put stuff away, I came across the envelope with the autopsy reports. The logical place to keep it was in my father's office.

At the top of the staircase, I hesitated. The enclosed stairs looked like an entrance to a cave, the lair of a beast who waited patiently for its prey.

What is wrong with me? I wondered.

I couldn't bring myself to enter. With a shudder, I told myself that I'd feel different in the daylight and went to bed.

I woke to the rhythm of the waves. They sounded steady, like a heartbeat, not an alien tongue. The sun was still behind the mountains, but the morning light gave me a feeling of hope. It's funny how fear and darkness hold hands. The fears of our ancient ancestors are still part of our fabric.

Now, the basement stairs didn't look like a den of wicked demons or the maw of some voracious creature. Still, I called Wolfears after me when I reached the bottom of the stairs.

He sniffed at the door of the room that had belonged to Sneakers. I opened it to show him that she wasn't hiding inside.

Next, I opened the office door and flicked on the light. No monsters were dwelling within. My father's ghost wasn't waiting inside. Only his desk and filing cabinets were there, nothing more than cold metal, stale air, and silence.

Before I put their autopsy reports in the files, I decided to finish looking them over. It just felt like something I should do. I skimmed most of the notes until I read one in my mother's report that startled me. It observed that there were no indications of my mother having given birth. Then, I smiled when I realized it was simply an observation. Being as appearance conscious as she was, I knew that would have pleased her. I wasn't surprised when it noted her blood alcohol content. Whereas in the notes for my father it indicated that tests were negative for drug and alcohol intoxication. That wasn't remarkable. He'd only had my cranberry juice.

After filing them, I went back upstairs.

In the living room, I picked up the tabloid and stared at the cover while shaking my head. Absurd how one laughable article kept me spinning off balance; something that should be worth no more than a few moments of entertainment. It would have been no more than fluff to me if my father wasn't in some way connected to it. I tossed it back on the table.

The professor gave me the creeps, but other than Maria, who had disappeared, he was the only one who could lead me to any answers. And I knew where to find him.

The more I knew before I saw him, the better. No use procrastinating. It was time to get moving.

Just as I reached the front door, the phone rang again. I rushed back inside, hoping it might be Garrett.

It was my father's cell phone in the kitchen cupboard, not the house phone. That was disappointing. I must have forgotten to turn it off. The number of calls on it had diminished to a trickle. Its ringing reminded me I needed to cancel the service.

Garrett had suggested that I carry it so he could reach me when I was away. I didn't want to bother with it. I didn't even like fussing with a purse, and life isn't that dangerous. Besides, sometimes being disconnected is good. I didn't want to be one of those ridiculous looking people talking on their phones in public about when they brushed their teeth. Most of them have nothing more important to say than the guy on the pier who has imaginary conversations. Ronald was the name the detective had said. If he had a phone, people wouldn't think he was crazy.

Canceling the phone service wasn't high on my list of things to do.

Like my father at The Pelican's Roost, I ignored its ringing and left.

Chapter 37

Though the city of Yitha is small, it has its own library, which is a short walk from Concha Pointe. Its librarian, Mrs. Flutcher, had worked there since I'd been a little kid sitting cross legged on the floor, matching words with pictures in books. She was a wonderful person, ever curious and always helpful. She had the knack of making me feel as if my questions were the most important ones in the world. The trouble was that if I asked her about bonobos, she might ask me why I wanted to know about them. I didn't want to tell her, and I couldn't lie to her. It was the way her eyes were magnified behind the thick lenses of her glasses.

As the driveway gate closed behind me, I decided to go down the coast to the Malibu library, where I would be invisible. Being larger, it was also more likely to have something available on the shelf.

I found a parking spot across the street on Civic Center Way. "Malibu Library" was printed on raised, block letters in front of the sun-bleached white building. The turquoise color of the letters reminded me of a tiny triangle bikini with spaghetti straps my mother had when I was ten or eleven—it embarrassed me when she wore it in front of my friends. Remembering it made me start to choke up.

Two guys with skateboards were sitting on the library's front lawn with their legs splayed in front of them. They each had a carton of chocolate milk and were sharing a bag of potato chips. When I walked past them, one of them whistled. The other called out, "Hey, wanna sniff some books?" They laughed.

I wasn't invisible after all. I ignored them and went inside.

Fluorescent lights shone through the rectangles of ceiling panels giving the brown carpet a mustard hue. "Information Desk" was printed in black block letters on a yellow sign hanging over a circular wooden desk. A clear vase with purple and white hydrangeas sat on top. A man and a woman were sitting behind the desk. They had their heads bent with their noses in books. I guessed they might be reference librarians, the smooth, walled conduits that lead to knowledge.

"Excuse me," I said to the woman. "Are you the reference librarians?"

They both looked up and straightened their shoulders.

"Yes, what is it you're looking for?" she asked.

"I want to learn about bonobos," I said.

"Patrick will be able to help you," she told me, and returned her attention to her book.

"You're in luck," Patrick said. "I think we have just the book for you."

He led me to the new arrivals section, slipped a book from the shelf and handed me *Bonobo: The Forgotten Ape*.

"Just remember," he added. "There's only a seven-day check out for new arrivals. Don't forget if you don't want to get a past-due fine."

I sat at one of the round white tables that looked like they belonged in a food court more than a library and opened the richly photographed book.

I'm often surprised how much there is in the world that I do not know. I learned that bonobos are the cousins of chimpanzees. They look a lot alike, but are more gracile. They are so similar in appearance that they'd been called pygmy chimps until they were determined to be a separate species. They were isolated by a river and afraid of the water.

So, they'd evolved in a different direction. Their culture is less violent than chimps—bonobos are the free-love hippies of the ape world. Looking at the pictures, I thought how their sex lives would embarrass Garrett.

I had trouble concentrating on the book because, from what Professor Pinsky had said, there was some truth in the tabloid article. A part of my mind kept screeching the question:

"What mad scientist research was my father involved in?"

I returned to the information desk. Only the intimidating woman was there now.

She unstuck her eyes from her book, looked up and asked, "Did you find what you were looking for?"

"Yes, thank you. I have another question. How can I translate something I heard in Japanese?

I was afraid she might look at me oddly or be impatient with my request, since I was interrupting her reading. She did neither and instead perked up at my question. Her lips formed a smile. Apparently, she found this question more stimulating than leading me to a book about bonobos.

"What were the words?" she asked.

I sounded out my uncle's phrase as best I could. She had me repeat it. She closed her book. Unlike the other librarian, she didn't have me follow her and motioned for me to wait. She disappeared between an aisle of books. While she was gone, the other librarian returned. I told him she was helping me.

The boys from outside came into the library carrying their skateboards. One of them still had his carton of milk.

"You can't bring food inside," the librarian told him.

"It's not food. It's a drink," the boy said.

He tilted his head back, lifted the carton up to his lips and guzzled his milk noisily.

His companion said, "Yeah, I thought libraries were supposed to be full of smart people."

Milk boy laughed, spitting chocolate milk. The librarian looked uncertain as to what to say or do. Then the other librarian emerged from the aisle. Head bent, she marched toward them. They turned and left without saying another word. The library was quiet again. She returned to the information desk and handed me a slip of paper.

"Sorry I took so long. I believe these may be the words you heard," she said.

On it were the words "Ikka Shinju" and beneath them, "Family Pearl."

She said, "The literal translation doesn't make much sense. However, they are an idiomatic expression about family suicide or family murder."

My chest felt hollow, as if a tunnel had been bored through it. I nodded, trying to keep my lips from trembling.

There was no doubt about what had happened on the pier, then.

If she was curious as to the reason for my request, she gave no indication. She sat and returned her attention to her book.

The quiet of the library, which I normally loved, now felt as if it were a physical force pressing on me, trying to crush me.

I heard wind rushing through the hole in my chest. I found myself outside and realized the sound was from the traffic on Pacific Coast Highway.

I looked for the boys because I wanted to yell at someone, but they were gone. Only a milk carton and an empty bag of chips remained on the lawn. I almost threw myself on the lawn, but managed to walk to the street without collapsing or screaming at the sky. I felt the warmth of the sun on my back. It pushed me forward. I hadn't realized how cold I had felt inside the library.

Once inside my car, I sat with my teeth clamped, still as a statue, my scream trapped inside of me. I sat there for a long time, seeing nothing, understanding nothing. I wanted to go home and hide from the world. Instead, I went back to the highway and headed toward Cummings University.

Chapter 38

A few blocks from the university, I found a parking spot on a steep street and walked down to the campus. With its aged brick buildings and majestic trees, it was dramatically different from the utilitarian grounds of the junior college where I'd been racking up credits. Its ambience felt inspirational. As I walked over the sun dabbled walkways as wide as boulevards on the rolling grounds, I wondered why my father had discouraged me from applying to Cummings. Considering the years he'd spent there and the school's vaulted reputation, I would have thought he'd have seen it as a natural choice for me. Instead, he'd actively discouraged me. My father, ever the enigma.

I was disappointed that the biology department was housed in one of the few newer buildings on campus. As if to keep spy satellites from peering inside, its louvered windows made it look like a secret government facility instead of a school building. I climbed a short flight of concrete stairs to the side entrance.

To my surprise, once inside, I saw that in addition to stairs leading to the upper floors, there was a staircase leading to a basement level. The stairs to the upper levels appeared modern, utilitarian. The worn stairs leading down had a wooden banister. Its brass top rail was polished by years of hands sliding over it. I caught a whiff of a strong, sharp scent, like sour pickles, wafting up from below. I surmised that the top of the building was built upon an original basement of an older building. By the elevator, I found a directory—Professor Pinsky's office was located on the second floor. I decided to take the stairs.

On the second floor, the filtered taste of HVAC recycled air replaced the acrid odor hovering by the stairs below. The long corridor stretched before me, looking identical to the one beneath, except this one was empty of milling students. My shoes squeaked on the polished floor, breaking the quiet. I peeked through the door windows into rooms as I went by. Most of them were empty. In the few that were occupied, the students' heads were bent over papers on desks and their hands clenched pens or pencils. Seeing them taking exams made me smile. Soon, Garrett would be done with his. We'd finally get to spend more time together.

I found Professor Pinsky's room number, expecting it to lead directly to his office. Instead, it opened to a reception area with offices in a horseshoe surrounding a reception desk. Behind the desk sat a guy, undoubtedly a student. He had broad shoulders, wavy hair, bright blue eyes, and a chin that couldn't grow a beard if you paid it a hundred dollars a hair. His attention was focused on the legs of a girl in white shorts who was standing in a line of people leading to one of the offices.

When I stood directly in front of him, he ignored me until I rapped my knuckles on his desk. With an effort, he dragged his eyes away from her legs and looked up at me. I felt tall.

"Yeah?"

"Is Professor Pinsky available?"

He gestured with a loose wristed hand. "That's the line, but you won't get to see him today."

"Why not?"

He drew his hand back and looked at his watch. "Because he's got a med science class in twenty-four minutes and twenty-three seconds. He'll leave his office in nineteen minutes and twenty-three seconds, giving him five minutes to walk. So, you understand that even the next person in line will be lucky to meet with him today. Do you want to sign up for one of his scheduled slots another day?"

He lifted a clipboard off his desk.

"I'll wait," I said, and went to the end of the line.

In a few minutes, Pinsky's office door opened. A guy with an angular face stepped out. A girl at the front of the line wearing thrift shop bell bottoms went in to replace him. I didn't have a watch, but undoubtedly when nineteen minutes and twenty-three seconds had passed, the girl exited the office. Professor Pinsky stepped out behind her, clutching a stuffed binder. Staring straight ahead, he walked past the disintegrating line of students, ignoring their pleas. I didn't say anything.

The girl in the white shorts stepped in front of him, and said, "Oh, professor, your last lecture was fascinating. I'm available if you need any more students to help extracting deoxyribonucleic acid."

She emphasized each syllable of "deoxyribonucleic acid." I was surprised she didn't bat her eyelashes with each syllable. I wanted to gag. She could simply have said, "DNA." Even I knew that.

"See Wayne," the professor said to her, and gestured to the guy at the desk.

He walked past me. I wondered if I should chase after him. Then he stopped abruptly, spun on his heels, and looked back at me.

"Come into my office," he said, expressionless, speaking gently as if to a dog that might bolt.

I felt the dirty stares of the students. White Shorts made a huff as I walked past her.

"Professor," Wayne said as he stood. "What about your class?"

"Tell them I'm running behind. You get them started."

He handed the binder to Wayne and motioned me to his office. Wayne shrugged his shoulders and gave an exasperated look to White Shorts.

I had to step over several stacks of books and squeeze myself onto the lone wooden chair across from Pinsky's desk. The seat was still warm from Miss Bell Bottoms' bottom. While I heard him giving instructions to Wayne, the receptionist/teacher's assistant with an attitude, I surveyed his office.

A floor-to-ceiling bookcase stood behind his desk, but long ago it had lost the war to contain his books and papers because every other surface available in the office was covered with them. Even his chair had a pile of papers on the seat. There was barely room for the single chair I sat in.

I kept my elbows tucked in, for fear of bumping a book stack and sending it tumbling. Maybe there was a system or some order to the chaos, but I couldn't see it. I thought how different my father kept his office and couldn't imagine the two of them working together.

When Pinsky came inside to join me, I heard White Shorts say to the TA, "Hi, I'm Candy. I want to learn more about biology."

I wanted to gag again. I was curious to hear their conversation, but Pinsky shut the door behind him.

Inside his office, Pinsky looked bigger than I remembered him from only moments ago. In his haste, he kicked over some of the books I'd stepped over, sending them sprawling. Several slid beneath his desk. He ignored them and slipped behind his desk. I bent to retrieve one, but he waved a hand to indicate for me not to bother. I didn't notice if he moved the stack of papers on his chair before he sat.

Sitting, he seemed to have folded himself like a collapsible umbrella and looked normal sized. He found places for his elbows among the clutter on his desk, stroked the sides of his cheeks with his fingers, and peered at me. When he didn't speak, I felt I needed to say something, but didn't know what. A faint smile flickered on his lips.

When he did speak, he said, "Finally someone I actually want to see."

"I don't want to keep you from your class. I didn't think to call first or make an appointment."

"Not necessary. You obviously got the message I left on your father's phone."

"No," I said, shaking my head, wondering if he was the one who had called just as I was leaving the house. "I've been out."

"No matter. You're here."

"Why did you call?"

"If you listened to my messages, you'd know that I wanted to give you good news. I've found Ms. Nogales, or rather, I should say, *she* found *me*. If you didn't get my message, why did you come to see me?

"I want to know what my father was involved in. When I met you at the memorial, you said there were things about my father that were fascinating. And what does it have to do with this woman?"

"It has more to do with this woman, as you call her, than I imagined. She had a child that lived. She and your father kept it a secret all these years."

Chapter 39

My emotions tumbled chaotically as if I were caught beneath a crashing wave, being whipped and thrust about. In my mind, a dizzying competition of emotions fought for dominance; horror, shock, and a thrill at the possibility that I had a half-sister or brother. I'd discarded the thought that my father had been having an affair with Maria when he died, but I'd never considered that he could have had an affair with her *years* ago.

"Then I have a brother or sister?" I managed to say.

"It was a female. Of course, she's not your sibling. We'd never use our own genetic material in our experiments. That would be unethical. It's not even human, technically. It's a hybrid—an experiment—a combination of human and genetic material with another primate. Ms. Nogales was simply a surrogate."

He had an expression of strained patience mixed with pity at my confusion. It reminded me of a look my father gave my mother when she didn't understand something. It was a look my father had never given for me. Now I knew how it must have made my mother feel.

I glanced down at my lap. I felt deflated, as if I'd gained a sister and lost her in the next moment.

"If she's not my sister, and my father didn't have an affair, why would he give Maria money?"

"Let me back up. Your father and I, our quest was to modify the human genetic code for the benefit of future generations, to create healthier and more powerful humans. Inevitably, there are sacrifices on the path of progress. Some believed that creating babies with the possibility of deformity was immoral. Others objected on religious grounds that God's creations should not be tampered with and polluted by genes from other species. To avoid problems, we decided it would be best to keep our research out of public view.

Surrogate mothers were extensively screened. They signed NDAs and were well compensated."

"What's an NDA?"

"A non-disclosure agreement is a legal contract that creates a confidential arrangement. They're often used by those in power to silence the weaker party, in exchange for something of value. In this case, monetary compensation and the threat of deportation, not to mention severe legal consequences."

While I digested this, he continued.

"Nonetheless, she's taking the risk, propelled by her greed, consequences be damned. If it ever gets to court, she'll claim she was ignorant of the NDA she signed and that she was coerced. But by then, the damage will have been done. She's holding back for now. You may have noticed the article was partly fluff, partly fact. Neither the university nor our names were revealed by her. When the story came out, I immediately contacted your father and learned she'd contacted him demanding money to not reveal more. Hence, the check you delivered to her. When she learned of your father's death, she came to me to extort more money by threatening to reveal the university and our names."

"Are you going to pay her?"

"I don't have the kind of money she's demanding. Besides, as your father told me, blackmailers never stop. My reputation and the university will recover. The public has a short memory. There's something of more importance if she's telling the truth. She claims that your father not only knew about the absconded child, but paid her for years to keep the secret."

"Why would he do that?"

"I have a theory," he said, "but I imagine you're not going to like it."

There were lots of things I didn't like. Lots of things I didn't want to hear, but the truth was a bell in the fog. I didn't know if it was beckoning me or warning me to stay away.

"When your father met your mother, he fell head over heels. I think she infected him with a sentimental morality. She convinced him that our creation deserved a life beyond the laboratory. Animal rights are absurd. They're like a virus some people become infected with. It would explain your father's shift from the purity of scientific discovery to 'compassionate' medicine. I believe that he thought the baby was more than property of the university."

"What happened to it?"

"Most likely it was placed in an animal sanctuary or institutionalized. It could be explained as a natural mutation. Abnormalities like fur-covered humans have been born before. Then, again, it's possible it was adopted if it appeared human."

"Wait," I said. "Maria, her own mother, doesn't know what became of her child?"

"Technically, it wasn't hers, not her egg. She was only the incubator. I doubt she possesses any maternal fondness that wouldn't be traded for cash. The most extraordinary thing she claims is that the child is alive, and your father knew where.

"Maybe my father didn't want her found."

"Obviously. Now, you're the only one living who might have a clue to the hybrid's whereabouts."

"Why does it matter?"

He reacted to my question with an expression of disbelief. I liked that look on his face, brief though it was.

"Because if I can find it, I can do a genetic test and have proof of our great achievement— the creation of the first human hybrid since prehistory. We will be recognized and given our rightful place in history."

"I have no idea where she could be. If she's an adult now, she could be anywhere."

His eyes remained on me, unblinking. They were the eyes of a fanatic, someone obsessed.

"Oh, you must have some idea. Some clue. How old are you?"

"I'm twenty. Are you saying that *I* am the hybrid?"

A surge of fear undulated through me. I pressed my smooth, hairless arms against myself and ran my hands over them. He gave a condescending laugh.

"From what I see, you're far too normal, though she'd only be a year older than you. Think, child. There must have been something your father said or did that would give us a clue."

"There's nothing, just his old files." The moment I said it, I regretted it.

His eyes widened. "I must have them."

"They don't belong to you."

I stood suddenly, feeling an overwhelming need to escape his office. I had to get away from him or his madness would infect me.

I forgot the stack of books beside me and sent them sprawling as I ran out of there.

Chapter 40

I rushed down the stairs to the ground level. After the claustrophobia of his office, the tunnel of the hallway felt like a purgatory. Fluorescent lights buzzed above me as if powering my escape. I took the nearest exit. The rustle of the leaves as I walked beneath the trees and the feel of the air on my skin helped to calm me. Through a gap in the canopy, I stared up at a patch of sky, squeezed my eyes shut and opened them to confirm I was indeed outside. The color of the sky felt like a friend embracing me. I inhaled fresh air.

In my haste to escape the building, I'd gone the wrong way. When I came to a grove of ginkgo trees, I realized my mistake and turned around. When I passed the biology building, I saw a large group of students approaching it. Some held signs. They were attempting to chant, but seemed to have trouble deciding what their rallying cry should be. I stepped off the walkway and onto the grass to let them pass.

When they reached the building, they turned and gathered in front of it. A woman in a grass-green blazer and hair like coiled ribbons separated herself from the group. She marched to the top of the stairs at the main entrance. She motioned and the chanting sputtered. I was too far away to hear her words over the other voices, but saw that she gestured emphatically. The crowd formed a lose ring around the entrance. She organized their cacophony into alternating slogans of "Man is not god" and "People are not animals."

I couldn't help but wonder if their protest had something to do with the tabloid article. My suspicion was confirmed when one of the protesters sprinted up the stairs and handed a newspaper to the woman. She held it above her head.

It was the issue with woman and the chimpanzee infant on the cover.

All heads riveted toward her. Ripples of conversation coursed like electricity through the crowd. She pushed the paper in front of her and swung it around. Several sheets tore loose. The man who'd given it to her pulled a lighter from his pocket. He sparked the flame and held it to the paper. Cheers rose from the group. The fire quickly turned the paper into a torch. She tossed it into the air. The fiery pages scattered and tumbled down the stairs. People began stamping on the pieces. Their chanting descending into whooping yells like troop of baboons in a frenzy. A gust of wind scattered the papers sending them away as if they were attempting to escape. The protestors chased them, laughing, screaming, pounding their feet upon them when they caught them. Fists thrust skyward with each victory. Once all the fires had been extinguished, they regrouped and resumed their chants.

When I got home, I sat on the wall and stared at the ocean. The swells undulated towards the shore as if concealing a giant serpent moving beneath them. The rocks below the cliff, sharp and dangerous, waited for the waves, the serpent beast. The waves crashed upon the rocks, spewing froth like the foaming mouth of a hungry beast. The black teeth waited for prey to come within their grasp.

I clasped my knees and rocked back and forth. The rhythm of the breaking waves became a metronome. I rocked four or five times within each beat.

The colors of the sunset filled the sky. I didn't look at the palette. I only saw the reflection of colors on the darkening water. I knew if I lifted my eyes I would take flight into the sky. If I found I could not fly, I would fall onto the jagged teeth. When darkness ate the sky, I sat shivering. Wolfears poked his snout against my thigh. I hoisted myself off the wall and walked on stiff legs into the house.

* * *

The coast was shrouded in fog at dawn. Wolfears and I did our morning run. Even though, at times, I could see no more than a few yards ahead and moisture clung to me like a chilled coverlet, I felt better moving. In the quiet of mist, anything is possible. The world reveals itself in a slow inhalation. The universe is no larger than one can see and reality beyond has only the substance of dreams.

When we returned, I toweled Wolfears off.

"You smell like a dog. You're going to need a bath soon."

I changed out of my sweats into a pair of faded jeans and a top the color of the sun. It was a new day and I was determined to think of the future, not the past. Garrett's finals would be over this afternoon. When I called him to wish him luck, he promised we could spend the next day together and do whatever I wanted.

"We can just hang out all day," I said. "We'll relax and think about nothing."

"That sounds great," he said, sounding nervous.

Ambition meant everything to him. Goals were the sinew of his world. We both had difficulty getting out of our own heads—we had that in common. I needed to stop thinking and promised myself to spend the day on mundane tasks.

"I'll come over first thing the tomorrow," he told me before hanging up.

As I sat down for my breakfast of a quesadilla and apple juice, my father's phone rang. The caller ID told me it was the Cummings' number. I wanted to throw the phone across the kitchen. Instead, I simply returned it to the cupboard and ignored the call.

So much for my day of not thinking.

I forced myself to finish the quesadilla. The cheese tasted like glue, the tortillas like cardboard, but I washed it down with apple juice, drinking directly from the bottle. That was something I'd never done. But what did it matter? What did *anything* matter?

I was spiraling into a funk.

I went into the backyard. The fog was still thick. By the sound of it, there were slow sets, smooth rollers. They might be big. I couldn't tell. Other than falling into the pool, I hadn't been in the water since the pier.

"Guess what, Wolfie? You get a second outing."

He spun in a circle. I went to the garage and took one of my boards from its rack. It was early enough that there would still be parking at Concha Pointe. I fastened my board on the rack, inhaling the comforting scent of vanilla from the board wax.

Chapter 41

When we got down to the beach, I saw that the waves were three-and four-footers, with an occasional five. A small group of surfers floated in the water on the south side, waiting. I watched one of them catch a wave before hiding my car keys under some pebbles above the high tide line. Wolfears brushed against me. He was always nervous when I went in the water, but he'd learned not to try to follow me.

In my wetsuit, I was warm, but I found myself shaking, feeling chilled at the thought of returning into the ocean. Maybe the water would take me. I knelt and fastened my leash's ankle strap.

"Don't worry," I told Wolfears. "I'll come back."

I paddled out and duck-dived through the waves until I was beyond the breakers. I sat on my board, gently bobbing with the swells and watching Wolfears patrolling the shore. I was up the coast from the other surfers and they paid no attention to me. I liked that. Sometimes being a chick and going out alone, I got more attention than I wanted.

I watched the others catching rides. One of them looked like one of the paramedics. I needed to thank him. I slipped onto my belly and paddled toward them. When I was closer, I saw he wasn't the same guy, whipped my board around and paddled back.

Since I was outside, I was the first one to claim a beautiful outside roller. I slid down it onto the smooth face. None of the guys cut me off. They hooted, cheered, and waved their arms in the air as I shot by them. Like a goofball, I twisted my head to look back and smile. When I did, I lost my balance and fell off.

So much for my glorious ride.

Embarrassed, I kept my head down as I paddled back out. Another few waves passed by. Then, I caught another ride and redeemed myself. I rode it all the way in to the shore. Wolfears rushed into the water to greet me. I felt tired, more than I should have for only catching the two waves, but I'd gotten in the water—a triumph. Wolfears liked the idea of my coming in, so I submitted.

When I lifted the stones to retrieve my keys, they weren't there. I started to panic thinking someone had stolen then, but I'd not seen anyone on the beach and none of the other surfers had come in while I was out. Somehow, I managed to forget under which stones I'd hidden them. Looking around, I realized I'd not paid close attention.

What is wrong with me? I wondered.

As I lifted various stones, Wolfears thought we were playing a new game. With his nose down, he scrambled over the stones. Luckily, his nose was better than my memory. As a reward for finding my keys, we played fetch with a stick of driftwood before leaving.

By the time I got home, the thick fog had dissipated and only a light haze hung in the air. A gray Toyota was parked across from my house, with someone sitting inside. As I waited for the gate to open, a guy got out and walked over to my car. It took me a moment to recognize him—Wayne, Pinsky's TA. His eyes appraised my VW and my board on top, in the same way he'd studied the legs of the girl standing in line.

"Nice car," he said, as if his opinion mattered.

"You're not supposed to park there," I told him.

"I didn't see where else to park."

"What do you want?"

"Is your phone working?"

"What?"

"The professor left you a message telling you he was sending me."

"Sending you, why?"

"You have files that he needs."

"I didn't say he could have them."

"Well, *can* he?"

"I don't know. I'll have to think about it."

PRIMA   185

I didn't really have any need for them. I'd read everything I could understand, but I didn't like his attitude. When the gate opened wide enough, I drove in. He followed on foot. I parked and let Wolfears out first.

When I got out and we were both standing, I looked up at Wayne, not down like when we first met and he was sitting at the reception desk. He wasn't Garrett-tall, but he easily stood above me, looking at me with his cerulean eyes.

"I didn't say you could come into the yard."

"You didn't say I couldn't."

"You and your attitude can go now," I said.

He stuffed his hands in his pockets, shrugged and started back towards his car. I unstrapped my board and went to hose it off. When I finished and went to put it in the garage, I noticed Wolfears was standing erect in the driveway, watching Wayne who had either returned or never left. His hands were still in his pockets.

"Nice dog," he said.

"I told you to leave."

"You locked me in," he said, and motioned to the driveway gate.

I'd closed it automatically out of habit without thinking.

"There's a wicket gate to the right for pedestrians. I'd think a university boy could figure that out," I said, feeling snarky. He was killing my mellow vibe from the ocean.

"Okay," he said. He appeared nonplussed by my comment and didn't move. "The thing is, I was thinking. I don't know how to surf—you could teach me."

"I have a boyfriend. In fact, I'm engaged."

"I'm not hitting on you. I've just never tried surfing."

"You wouldn't like it," I said.

"Probably not, but who knows?"

"You know something? The truth is, I don't want to have anything to do with you or Pinsky. There was a protest yesterday at your school. This is all just too crazy. It's nothing I want to be mixed up in."

"Whoever thought that science would be messed up in politics? I didn't. It isn't fun. I suppose if you give the professor the files, you'd be washing your hands of it."

He had a point.

He continued, "But maybe not. You'll be connected to your father's work. If Pinsky has his way, they'll both be famous. He's like the only student Pinsky ever had who he talks about with respect. Was it hard growing up with a genius for a father?"

"What do you care?"

"I don't. It's interesting. I don't know if they'll be famous or not when all this washes out. If they actually created a human-ape hybrid, that's pretty amazing. It's a whole new leap in evolution. Evolution will no longer be solely in the domain of nature. Man will become God. Of course, the thing they made may just be a blithering lump of flesh, but who knows until we find it. *If* it exists."

"Aren't you the philosopher. You sound like the professor calling her an 'it.'"

"I wonder if the whole thing isn't a hoax. This Maria woman seems pretty sketchy to me. She could be playing everybody."

"How do you know so much?"

"Next to your dad, I'm his star pupil. It took a twenty-year gap for me to come along."

"Good for you."

"If things play out poorly, Pinsky and your dad could look bad. You know, Frankensteins, evil scientists."

"What do some old files have to do with it? It is what it is."

"We can cross reference your files with ours and prove if she is lying, or find a clue to the hybrid. Personally, I think she's just a con artist. Not much chance she was the only one able to deliver a hybrid child. She's just playing on Pinsky's desire for fame. I mean, Pinsky may be brilliant, but his street smarts suck. Ivory tower, don't you know."

"If I give you the files, will everybody leave me alone?"

"Yeah, sure, I don't see why not. You've got nothing else anybody wants."

The way he said it made me want to slap him. When he saw he'd gotten to me, he laughed.

"Get out," I said between clenched teeth.

This time he listened to me and didn't have trouble finding the gate.

He was a genius after all.

Chapter 42

A few minutes after Wayne left, I went to the gate to make sure he had closed it properly and it had locked. As I turned back, I saw Donny standing next to the pink oleander bush by the side of the driveway. He was holding a bag in one hand, and his camera was hanging around his neck. I stopped and gave him a hard stare. He twitched. I marched over and stood across from him behind the gate.

"What are you doing? You better not be spying on me again or taking pictures."

"I'm not spying on you. I lost my driver's license when I crashed my birthday Porsche. I'm waiting for a friend to pick me up."

"I didn't know you had any friends," I said.

"It's a taxi," he said, and looked at the ground.

I felt mean. "I was joking."

"I see you have a new boyfriend," he said.

"He's not my boyfriend."

He looked up and grinned. "Oh? Maybe I'll tell Garrett you're cheating on him."

"Don't you dare, you little weasel. He wouldn't believe you anyway."

"Don't worry. You know I won't go near him. I like my bones unbroken."

When I started to leave, he asked, "What's new with you?"

"Too much," I said. "How about you?"

"Oh, you know, the usual. My dad's still shooting in Thailand. I'm bored. I'm going to go race my slot cars." He lifted the bag. "Want to see my new one?"

"No, I don't. You are such a nerd."

"Thanks," he said and bit his lower lip. His overbite was gone. His orthodontist had done a good job.

For the rest of the day, I did my best to think about nothing. I distracted myself by going grocery shopping and running other errands. I went back to the library and checked out the book about bonobos. I read about them and even found my sense of humor in pretending I had a bonobo stepsister who was a hippie, living in the redwoods. Maybe I was related to Bigfoot.

Still, try as I might, there was too much to think about and sort out.

My distractions hadn't worked because, when I went to bed, I couldn't sleep. I needed to talk to someone. I needed to talk to *Garrett*.

I looked at the clock—it was almost ten when his midweek shift would end. I jumped out of bed and ran downstairs without bothering to change out of my pajamas. When I was about to shut the door and leave Wolfears behind, he whimpered.

"All right, but hurry up."

I rushed back to the kitchen and locked the doggy door. At the car, Wolfears spun a circle before jumping in, having picked up on my excitement and enjoying the change of routine. The driveway gate seemed to roll back more slowly than ever.

When I got to PCH, there was too much traffic to make a left. I was about to head south and turn around at the light, but a break in the traffic occurred and I swung across the highway to head north. We got stuck at the next light, and like the driveway gate, it seemed to take forever. I hoped we'd make it before Garrett returned from his last delivery.

When we reached Atta Patta's Pizza, I made a sharp turn into the strip mall parking lot. Wolfears' front paws slipped off the seat and half of him landed in the footwell.

"Sorry, boy. It's a good thing you don't get car sick."

Scanning the parking lot, I didn't see Garrett's car. It was a few minutes after ten—there was a chance he might still be out on delivery.

I backed into a parking spot in the row at the far end, where I had a good view. I cracked the windows a few inches and we waited. The green Atta Patta's sign cast an unnatural hue on the asphalt and cars. I knew most of their business was take-out, but through the windows, I could see a few people still inside. The manager came over and unlocked the door to let a couple out. Another delivery driver pulled in, got out and rapped on the door to be let inside. Moments later he came out with three pizza boxes. He put them in his trunk and drove off. I guessed they were the night's last deliveries. Garrett might still be out on a run.

The Chugger's muffler announced his arrival before he pulled into the lot. He parked next to Atta Patta's. I got out of the car as he jogged to the door.

He was let in before I'd gone three steps.

I got back in my car and waited, hoping he'd come out without carrying any more pizzas. When I saw him through the windows talking to the manager, I saw that he wasn't holding any.

"Wait here," I told Wolfears as I slipped out of the car.

Moments later, Garrett emerged from the restaurant, stretched his arms, and walked to his car without noticing me.

When I was almost next to him, I called out, "Hey." He spun around as if expecting danger.

When he saw it was me, he said, "What are you doing here? Are you okay?"

"I'm fine. Better now that I'm with you," I said, and wrapped my arms around him.

He gave me a hug and lifted me off the ground.

"You smell like pizza," I told him. "Did you get lots of orders for onions?"

He put me down and stepped back. "Why are you in your pajamas and bare feet?"

"I had to hurry."

"You're going to get cold. Let's sit in my car."

He opened the door for me. I sat in the passenger seat of his Ford Escort. The heater had been on, and it was warm inside.

When he got in, I said, "I don't know what to do."

"About what?"

"Everything."

"Are you still nervous about moving up the wedding?"

"No, it's not just that. There's so much going on. I don't know what to do."

Garrett bit his lower lip.

I wanted to stop thinking. I wanted us to merge and be one somewhere in a different universe, somewhere on another level of being where thinking was impossible.

"Let's not talk," I said.

I twisted and wrapped my arms around his neck and brought my lips against his. His arms slipped around my waist. Under the green light of the Atta Patta's Pizza sign, we engaged in some serious making out. Everything else in life began to disappear. I thought for certain that he wasn't going to stop us this time.

He came up for air and placed his hand against my chest and ran it down the length of my torso until he stopped at my stomach, leaving it pressing gently on my belly button. He pulled back and put his other hand against my shoulder.

"You are so beautiful. I can't wait until we're married," he said.

I took his hand and moved it up until it cupped one of my breasts. His fingers drew across tenderly and he pressed his hand against it. It lingered only a moment before he pulled it away with a jerk.

I felt a surge of anger and hurt. I lowered my eyes to hide my feelings and saw that he was obviously as excited as I was. I leaned against him and pressed my lips against the soft spot on his neck just above his collar bone.

He shook his shoulders, and said, "We have to wait. You're not that kind of girl. It's only another month or two."

I pressed my lips together and wiped the drool from my mouth with the back of my hand. I leaned away from him and rested my back against the door.

Pressing my feet against his thigh, I pushed him away. Then I kicked at him.

"Stop it."

"No," I yelled, but I stopped.

I stared at him until he said, "Tomorrow—like I said—we can do whatever you want."

I knew what I wanted to do, but obviously that wouldn't be included in his version of "whatever you want."

He shook his head. "You're not like other girls."

"Other girls?" I questioned, immediately thinking of Kathy. "What other girls? Do mean all the basketball groupies that come on to you?" Before he could answer, I added, "Or do you mean like Kathy?"

"What is this jealousy thing? I told you we're just friends now. You never used to be jealous."

"I'm not jealous. You treat me like I'm some kind of princess."

"You are. Don't you understand?"

He sighed and his eyes gazed at me with sincerity that softened me.

"So, tomorrow, whatever I want to do?" I asked with a tease in my voice.

"Yes, within reason," he said slowly, cautiously.

"Okay, we're going to the San Diego Zoo."

Chapter 43

All the flushed excitement of seeing Garrett left me as I drove home. Against my better judgment, I began to think. If indeed this ape-child did exist, where was she? Apparently, Maria didn't raise her. She had said the child was taken away from her shortly after birth. Besides, she seemed lacking in maternal instinct. There was no evidence that Maria even knew where the child was, or surely she'd have told the reporter. She just knew enough to stir things up and make herself a nuisance—or dangerous. I didn't know which.

Was the human-ape person tucked away in an animal sanctuary being raised by chimpanzees or bonobos? That was a possibility, being hidden in plain sight. If she were caged in a laboratory, wouldn't the professor know about it? But then everything seemed to lead back to my father, that he had hidden her, but why?

He was the one person I couldn't ask.

Not that I didn't now think that my father was capable of something horrific, but would he ever condemn a child to that?

All the thinking did nothing but make my head spin. I wondered if too much thinking could cause a person to go mad. I wanted to wash my hands of the whole affair, yet I was desperate to know if the hybrid did exist and, if so, what had happened to her. I felt compelled to find her; I felt *for* her.

When I got home, I called Pinsky's number, planning to leave a message saying he could have my father's old school files if he shared what they revealed. To my surprise, Wayne picked up the phone.

"What are you doing there?" I asked. "It's after eleven o'clock."

"I'm going through old papers of the experiments. Digging, digging, digging."

"At this hour?"

"It's quiet. No stupid undergrads bothering me."

Or to ogle at, I thought.

"Please tell the professor he can have my dad's files from their experiments."

"That's great news. We're stuck without them. I'll be right over."

"*Now?*"

"Why not?"

I heard myself say, "Okay."

* * *

The light by the driveway gate was burned out, so I turned on the front porch light. As the driveway sloped up to the street, the light barely reached it, but it should be enough to stop his missing our house in the dark.

As it got closer to when I thought he'd arrive, I opened the driveway gate and went to an upstairs window where I could watch for him. The night was quiet. Headlights lit the street. A car pulled up, but it was a taxi. It stopped just out of my sight. I heard a door shut. When it drove off, I saw the leaves on the bushes across the street in the red glow of the taillights. They swayed from the car's passing. Moments later, a light came on next door. It weakly lit a swath of asphalt in front of our houses. Donny was home.

If he saw Wayne arrive, he'd really believe I was having an affair.

When Wayne pulled up in his gray Toyota, I went outside and motioned for him to pull into the driveway. I couldn't help but wonder if Donny was watching. Wayne drove up beside me and shut off his engine.

When he got out, he said, "I've moved up in the world."

"I didn't want you to get a ticket or have your car towed," I said.

"Ah, you care. You're letting me park in the driveway because you must really like me."

"Don't flatter yourself. We won't need to trek as far to load the files."

"Oh," he said.

He stood there with his hands hanging at his sides. He looked up. A few stars were visible between some high, wispy clouds. The light reflecting off the gray stones and the clouds made shadows on his face. His eyes appeared to be softly lit from within. Now that he wasn't making annoying comments, acting goofy or arrogant, he was attractive, something I didn't realize until his mouth was shut.

When we went inside, I offered him a refreshment.

"Sure, I'll take a coke. I could use the caffeine."

"Sorry, we don't have any sodas. How about tea or coffee? I've got some lemonade in the fridge. Would you like some?"

"Nah, water is fine."

I got him a glass of water and a lemonade for myself.

When we finished our drinks, we went down to the basement office. Wayne was impressed with the accolades my father had on the stairway walls. Wolfears stayed at the top of the stairs.

I opened the door to the office—there were no ghosts inside. I pulled open the drawers and showed Wayne the files. His fingers caressed them as if they were precious treasures.

"I wonder where the A files are?" I asked.

He squeezed his face, and gave me a sideways look, and said, "What would the A be for? Aardvark?"

"I don't know. Don't sequences usually go ABC?"

He laughed. "Well, I suppose. The B stands for bonobo and the C for chimpanzee."

"I'm surprised they didn't try an albatross too," I said, hoping to provoke him.

He was so delighted with the files that he didn't notice, and said, "Yes, these are going to be so helpful. Pinsky has other records we can match up with these. We'll get a good read on the possible hybrid. This is exciting stuff. Your father was meticulous. I wonder why he kept them and didn't give them to Pinsky?"

I shrugged. "Who knows why my father did anything."

"If we find what we hope, one of these files will lead us to the freak."

"Freak?"

"Yeah, the hybrid. If Pinsky can show evidence of success, he'll get new funding to continue the research he and your father started."

I didn't ask any more questions because I wasn't sure I wanted to know the answers. I felt sorry for the being, whatever she was. Garrett often said I was too sensitive.

It took us multiple trips to bring the files to his car. Wolfears thought it was a fun game, racing ahead of us each time. The files filled the Toyota's trunk, and we put the overflow on the back seat.

"I think your dog likes me," Wayne said.

"Wolfie probably thinks more of you than I do."

He stopped petting him, and said, "I really want to thank you. This is an incredible help. I know Pinsky can be a jerk sometimes, but he means well. He told me about your parents and the accident."

"Oh, that, yeah." I looked away.

"I'm really sorry for you."

"You better get going."

He didn't say anything, but remained standing close to me. His breath was warm—I thought he might hug me. I hated admitting it, but I wanted to feel him pressed against me. He reached out and he touched my arm, almost shyly.

"I owe you. Just let me know if I can return the favor," he said, his voice gentle. "I mean it."

Maybe I was imagining he was someone else. He didn't seem like the cocky, self-important guy from before with just the two of us standing alone in the driveway. His hand lingered against my skin, just above my elbow. Goosebumps rose on my arm.

I didn't pull away. I couldn't help but think that if I looked up at him and gave the tiniest of smiles, he would pull me toward him without the restraint of Garrett. I hated myself for thinking it.

His fingertips slowly moved up and down my arm. I swatted his hand away and took a step back, breaking the electrical current between us.

"Let me know what you find out," I said, and turned away.

I went back inside and didn't watch him leave, though I listened to his car backing up the driveway and onto the street. It softly disappeared into the night, unlike the pulsing rattle of Garrett's Chugger. I pressed the button to close the gate.

I tweaked one of Wolfears' ears, and said, "What do you see in him? He's a bit of a jerk."

I think Wolfears smiled, but it's hard to tell with his fur-face.

It was late when I went to bed, but I couldn't fall asleep. I wanted to be fresh for the zoo tomorrow with Garrett, but my mind kept whirring. I believed Garrett's attraction to me was as strong as mine to him, but he could be so restrained. I'd never questioned it before, but perhaps we weren't as compatible as I believed. Sometimes he acted like I was a porcelain doll, not a real person. Was my beauty that he constantly commented on something of adoration, not a connection and entwining of our souls? Did he know I was flesh and blood, not some lofty image he'd created of me? Was I only pretty, something to admire or to touch only gently else I would disintegrate? Something to be worshipped, idolized, held lofty in perfection from which one cannot rise, only topple?

The harder I tried to sleep, the more it evaded me. Never had I questioned whether Garrett was the one. I felt guilty about the connection I'd experienced with Wayne.

Something was wrong with me. I couldn't answer my own questions.

Still unable to sleep, I turned on the lamp next to my bed and picked up the bonobo book, thinking it would make me drowsy. Instead, I became engrossed in our funny-faced, hairy relatives with long arms and no inhibitions. The story of their discovery and how they were once thought to be chimpanzees made me, for the first time, take an interest in science. Looking forward to seeing them at the zoo, I wondered what I would think when seeing them in person. Would I see them as fellow people, as the author did, or would I view them as wild animals, distinct and beneath us.

I already knew the answer.

I fell asleep with the lamp on, thinking about our drive to San Diego in the morning. It would give us time to talk. Garrett would have nowhere to go and nothing else to distract him. We would make up and see things eye-to-eye.

Tomorrow, our relationship would be solid as the earth we walk upon. All would be better in the morning light.

What a naive and silly girl I was then, living in my little world. Didn't I know that most of the Earth is covered with water?

Chapter 44

I woke to the sound of the gate buzzer. Someone was pushing it repeatedly. I lurched out of bed, immediately imagining Wayne had returned. When I reached the intercom, it was Garrett's voice that spoke to me.

"What are you doing here so early?" I asked him.

"Early? It's after ten. I kept calling and you didn't pick up. Aren't you ready?"

"Yikes, it is? I didn't hear the phone or my alarm."

I pressed the release to open the gate and scurried back to my bedroom. Thinking back to last night, I knew he wouldn't be pleased if I greeted him in my pajamas. I was tempted, but decided that chancing upsetting him might start the day off wrong.

When I came downstairs, fully clothed, he took me in his arms and gave me a kiss.

"There's my beautiful girl."

He lifted me off the ground in a hug and spun me around. All my doubts vanished. Daylight proved he was the one. Despite my not being ready and his reluctance to visit the zoo, he was in good spirits.

"You're in a good mood."

"With statistics class over, it's a weight off my shoulders. No more infernal inferential questions."

"Did you eat? Let me grab something for us, then we can go."

"I had breakfast. It'll be faster if we stop on the way and pick something up for you."

"Okay, but I need to feed Wolfie."

"We need to get going. It won't hurt him to miss a meal."

"It won't take long. How would *you* like to skip a meal? It's bad enough I didn't take him for our run this morning."

"He's just a dog."

"And you're just a guy," I said, and poked him in the stomach.

After mixing some dry kibble with half a can of dog food, I put down his bowl and unlocked the doggie door.

"Be a good boy," I said. "Guard the house."

He looked at me with an expression as if to say, "Do you doubt me?" and then turned his attention to his food.

When we went out the front door, Garrett said, "The Chugger is overdue an oil change. Mind if we take your car?"

"You want me to drive?"

"I'm the guy, I'm supposed to drive. Besides, you'll need to eat on the way."

"No way, you'd be too embarrassed to be seen behind the wheel in Mister Aphid. Remember, you said Beetles are girlie cars."

"Yeah, it would be embarrassing," he said. And then, as if the idea just struck him, he added, "We could take your mom's Cadillac. I wouldn't mind driving *that*."

"My mom's car?" I said, weakly.

"Sure. Why not?"

I didn't have an answer, so I got her car keys and the garage remote. I'd not even opened my parents' double garage since the accident. I always parked in the driveway because the single garage was filled with my mom's sculptures, old furniture, and my surfboards.

I opened the garage. The lights automatically came on as the door lifted to reveal the empty space where my father parked. The golden-pink, champagne-colored paint of the Cadillac was already covered with a fine layer of dust, but it still sparkled quietly under the overhead lights. I stood alternating my gaze between the empty spot and my mother's car. My throat felt like a band was tightening around it.

"I wonder if it'll even start. It's just been sitting in the garage," I managed to say.

"No use in letting it sit and rust."

"I don't know if we should take it."

"Why not? It's good for a car to be driven and not sit for too long. Lubricants start breaking down, parts begin to rust. That kind of thing."

"It just feels weird that it won't be her driving it. Even my dad never drove it."

"I mean, we don't have to," he said, looking disappointed.

"No, you're right. There's no reason not to take it," I said with more certainty than I felt.

Garrett didn't seem to notice my hesitation as he took the keys.

He turned the key in the ignition. It started instantly and he grinned. For the first several miles as we headed south toward San Diego, he fiddled with the controls and was preoccupied with driving.

He broke his silence saying, "This is comfortable. Rides smooth. Nothing like The Chugger. Do you want to stop at Taco Bell or McDonald's?"

"I don't care. Either is fine."

"How about we stop at that Mexican joint in Topanga? I could devour-chug one of their breakfast burritos. We'll go through the drive-through. That will be a hoot in this car."

I was very careful not to spill any food when I ate, because I kept thinking how my mother was as fussy about her car's appearance as her own. When we came to the Los Angeles Airport, Garrett turned inland off PCH. The air smelled like burnt matches and I rolled up my window.

"You're awfully quiet," he said. "I thought you were excited about going to the zoo."

"I am. It's just riding in my mom's car brings back memories."

He reached over and rested a hand on my leg.

"Maybe it wasn't a good idea to take it," he said. "I thought it would be fun."

"No, it's okay."

"What made you want to go to the zoo of all places?"

"Do you know what a bonobo is?"

"What? No. Why? What is it?"

I put my hand on top of his. "They are one of our closest relatives."

"What do you mean, like cavemen?"

"No, like chimps and gorillas,

"Not mine. They might have arms and legs, but they're animals."

"Of course."

So are we, I wanted to say, but didn't.

"So?"

"We're going to see them at the zoo."

"What do you mean they are our relatives? They are not made in the image of God."

"They are, genetically, our close relatives. We share most of our DNA with them. That's what scientists say."

"Scientists say a lot of stupid things. I guess you could say they are clay that God played with before making us. Why do you want to see them?"

"Do remember that weird guy at the funeral? The friend of my father's? Professor Pinsky. He's a biology professor at Cummings. He worked on mixing genes of bonobos, chimpanzees, and humans."

Garrett turned toward me. "That's horrible."

"There was an article in the paper about it. It claims they made a human hybrid."

"I thought that guy was a fruitcake. Disgusting. Why would they even do that?"

"I don't know. They were trying to find ways to cure diseases and do fertility treatments. Stuff like that."

"That is revolting. They shouldn't be messing with God's work. If they did it, they created a freak, something soulless."

"You're not the only one who thinks that. There are protests at the university."

"That's good. We should join them," Garrett said.

We hit traffic by LAX. A jet flew low above us with a deafening rumble that interrupted our conversation.

When its noise lessened, Garrett said, "Why do you care what this professor did, anyway?"

"Because my father was on the research team and worked on the project with him."

Garrett opened his mouth as if to say something, then closed it. He kept his eyes on the freeway. His hand began slipping from my thigh, and I realized I'd removed my hand from his.

I didn't grab it when it slipped away. I looked around at all the cars surrounding us, different shapes and sizes, different colors, all forced to slow down as the traffic increased. People isolated in their metal boxes as they rolled along. It felt for a moment as if Garrett and I were in different cars.

I'd forgotten to bring the basketball pendant—I'd planned to give it to him today. It would have brightened our day.

"Are you mad at me for what my father might have done?"

"No, what makes you think that?"

"You took your hand away."

"I need them both on the steering wheel in this traffic. You never know what these crazy L.A. drivers will do."

With the windows rolled up, the car was beginning to smell like sausage and eggs. Not being used to the heavy food, my stomach felt like there was a lump in it. I rolled the window down a crack, and the exhaust from the traffic mixed with the fast-food smells. I rolled the window back up.

Chapter 45

The zoo was colors, noises and smells that penetrated my being at a primal level. Too, it was an artificial construct with sheets of plastic and metal bars that were incongruous with the life they held. People wandered the grounds, clustering around the cages of popular animals like ants swarming pieces of candy. Thoughts tumbled in my mind through the cacophony of people's voices and the howls, grunts, and growls from the exhibits. I recalled one of Mysti's eco-preaching rants about humans usurping the niches of other species while expanding the landscape for us, rats and cockroaches. I saw no cockroaches on display.

The pink flamingos seemed perfectly content parading about on their stilt legs and dipping their bent beaks in the water. The rhinoceroses looked sad—their ears twitched as they viewed the world foggily through their myopic, little eyes. They were two-ton pessimists. Such weight to carry upon four legs, giant tanks without wheels and treads. As we held hands, I kept tugging Garrett along. It was the bonobos I wanted to see.

I paused longer watching the penguins, old folk in formal attire on unsteady legs, wearing too large shoes, wandering about in a comedic play. When they tipped over into icy water to revive memories that must not be forgotten, they swam with balletic grace that tinged my smile with envy.

We hadn't been there long when Garrett wanted to eat again.

"Nothing for me. I still feel a lump in my stomach."

At the food court, I took a seat and held a table for us while he went to order. He was taller than everyone else in line. I noticed that most of the men were wearing shorts, but not Garrett. He never wore them except when playing basketball, which was too bad because he had nice legs.

After he'd downed two hotdogs, we got up and went directly to the bonobo exhibit. I stood and watched them through the plastic glass in quiet wonder while Garrett sipped his coke.

I don't know what I expected to feel when seeing them in person. Perhaps horror or revulsion, that my father had played with their genes, mixing them with humans. I could understand his curiosity and excitement at attempting such a thing.

Mostly, I didn't feel anything.

In fact, after observing them for a few minutes, I found them boring. Their enclosure had large trees resting on their sides and ropes strung about them, not unlike a playground. They simply sat around sharing food, like a family on a picnic. I tried to think deep thoughts, but my only revelation was that, other than being covered with hair, they weren't all that different than we are.

When the younger ones started playing, running around, and swinging on ropes and branches, I said, "They're athletic. Look how they jump. Somebody ought to put them on a basketball court."

"Ha, ha," Garrett said. "Monkeys playing basketball."

"They're apes, not monkeys."

"Same thing."

I didn't bother to respond.

As we watched, two females who had been grooming and caressing each other heightened their affection to a sexual level and began rubbing genitals. A few people in the audience snickered. One lady led her children away. The bonobos were completely indifferent to our watching. I found it fascinating.

I glanced at Garrett and gave him a poke.

"That's disgusting," he said. "Filthy animals. Come on, let's go."

"So, two females getting it on doesn't interest you?"

"No."

I decided to push his buttons. I couldn't help myself from teasing him. "What if I told you about me and Mysti?"

He made a grimace.

"Next time we're together, we should invite you to watch. It gets hot and steamy."

His mouth opened and his tongue slipped out. He made gagging noise to match his disgusted expression. He turned and started walking away from me.

"Hey," I called after him. "I'm just kidding."

I caught up to him and poked him again.

"Stop it. It's unnatural and shameful. You should know that. I let you surf and hang out with Mysti, who I don't think is a good influence, but I will not tolerate that kind of talk. You shouldn't even joke like that."

I forced myself to ignore his comment. I didn't want us to have another fight.

It was a funny thing. We never talked about God and such things—he was religious, I was not—but it had never posed a problem. Honestly, I'd always avoided the subject with him because of our differences. I figured I could get along pretending, but not committing.

"People that do perverted sex acts are no better than animals."

"Oh, I'm sure the bonobos have hetero sex too, or they wouldn't be here."

He took my hand and led me away from the bonobo exhibit.

I would like to say we wandered around like other people, but following Garrett was more of a march than a meander for the next few hours. He seemed to feel that if we were at the zoo we needed to see everything possible to get our money's worth. When the loudspeakers reminded everyone that closing time was at seven, he picked up the pace.

"We don't need to see every animal here, you know," I told him.

"You're the one who wanted to come to the zoo."

"Yes, mostly to see the bonobos. I want to see them again before we leave."

Reluctantly he agreed. "Let's hope they're finished with their perversion."

I didn't respond.

One of the amorous females was now sitting on a branch, looking through the glass at the people watching her family. One black hand stroked her forearm. Her eyes scanned the crowd as if searching for someone. When she came to me, she stopped and looked at me with eyes not unlike my own.

"They are really a lot like we are," I said.

"Except they're hairier and don't have souls."

When I made a face to show him that I didn't think he was funny, he said, "Animals aren't created in the image of God."

"I know you believe that, but I feel a connection to them. Look how they interact with one another. They care for the little ones like we do."

"Yeah, but they're not human. It's not the same."

In defense of them, I said, "God made them, too."

He pointed at the female sitting on the branch, and said, "The only thing you've got in common with them is that their hair is parted in the middle, just like yours."

It was probably just a coincidence, but when Garrett pointed, the bonobo on the branch became agitated. She began bouncing up and down, shaking the branch. Still staring at me, she let out a howl. Other bonobos began howling too. Then they broke into a cacophony of screams and high-pitched cries. Several of them rushed around the enclosure, as if trying to find a way to escape. An adult male began rolling on the ground, flailing as if he were possessed.

Suddenly, I felt flushed, hot and cold at the same time. My fingers started quivering. I tried to speak, but my words came out as gibberish.

"What's wrong," Garrett asked.

His voice sounded distant as if I were at the bottom of a well and he was far above me. I reached out to steady myself. My hand thumped against the glass of the enclosure. Several of the bonobos turned their heads toward me. The one sitting on the branch lost interest in me. She looked away and jumped down to join the others. My knees felt weak. I clutched Garrett's arm to keep from collapsing.

"They don't belong in there," I said.

"What? They're just monkeys, excuse me, *apes*, not people. You look pale. Are you all right?"

I muttered something about not wanting to be in a cage.

"You're too sensitive. You're not making any sense. You're faint from not eating any lunch, or something was rotten in your breakfast."

He pressed his fist against his stomach and rolled his tongue around his cheeks, as if checking for a bad taste.

I looked at him and couldn't focus. He opened his hand and pressed it against my forehead to check if I had a fever.

"I think you're sick. Let's get you out of here."

* * *

I don't remember leaving the zoo. The next thing I remembered was having my eyes closed. I was sitting in the passenger seat of my mother's car with the window down as we drove up Pacific Coast Highway. I didn't open my eyes or turn my head, but I knew Garrett was driving. I put my hand out the window and felt the air rushing past. If I raised my hand with the palm against the wind, it was pushed back and I had to work to keep my arm from flying back. When I pointed my fingers forward, the air streamed over my hand, and my hand sailed through the air with ease. This simple discovery absorbed my attention. I lifted and dropped my hand over and over again, playing with it in the wind. Eventually, I tired of this amusement and opened my eyes.

We were zooming along at a good clip. I rolled my head against the headrest to look at Garrett. He was focused far ahead on the highway. As always, he was in control, concentrating on the future. His right hand was gripped tightly on the steering wheel. The muscles in his forearm were taut, like cords of steel beneath his skin.

I reached over and placed my hand on his wrist. He was solid, unlike the wind. When I touched him, the muscles in his arm relaxed.

"Hey, you're awake. I was worried about you. You didn't have a fever, so I figured you were just exhausted and needed to rest."

I snuggled as close as I could get to him with the seatbelt on. I would have taken it off, but I knew he would have protested. I rested my head against his shoulder. He put his arm around me and gave a squeeze. His embrace made me feel safe.

As I sat with my head pressed against him, I realized he was what I wanted, not this mad pursuit of whatever my father had been involved with, whatever might have driven him insane. I didn't need to understand what had happened and why. That didn't matter. What was in the past was in the past.

I didn't need to let my imagination run wild. It all seemed so clear at that moment: no doubts, no questions. I knew that, to move forward, I needed to entwine my life with Garrett's. That would be my path to happiness.

I stroked his arm, and said, "You know how important you are to me," I said. "I love you."

He kept his eyes on the road and answered by squeezing my shoulder, drawing me closer. The seatbelt dug into my hip, and the shoulder strap locked against my neck nearly choking me.

I couldn't breathe, but I didn't mind.

When I couldn't hold my breath any longer, I pulled far enough back from the strap to inhale.

"I know I've been difficult lately. I'm sorry. I haven't been myself."

"Don't be," he said. "I understand. You've been through a lot."

"Your mother is right."

"About what?" He took his eyes from the road for a moment and glanced over at me.

"We should get married right away. This summer. As soon as possible."

Garrett nodded.

The rest of the ride home felt as if we were gliding on air, and it wasn't just the smooth suspension of my mom's Cadillac.

The world seemed right again.

Chapter 46

When we turned onto my street, the sun was down, but it was still light. Donny was across the street from his house talking to someone sitting inside a car. If he wasn't moving his hands, I would have missed him because the color of his shirt matched the oleander bushes. It took me a moment to realize the car he was standing next to was Wayne's.

Oh, great, I thought. *Just the two people I don't want Garrett to see.*

"Hey, I just remembered that I need a few things from the market. Would you mind turning around and stopping there before we go home?"

"Sure, one last spin of the Caddy."

Garrett pulled into my driveway apron. When he reversed to make a three-point turn, Donny crossed the street. I was glad Garrett still hadn't paid attention to him. Then, as we started off, he looked in the rearview mirror and took his foot off of the gas.

"Wait," he said. "is that the little pecker who lives next door? He might need a reminder to stay away from you."

"No, it's okay. He's been good. He won't bother me anymore since you talked to him. He even sent flowers."

"I want to make certain his memory doesn't lapse. A little reinforcement never hurts."

I hoped Donny would see Garrett and disappear. Knowing Wayne wouldn't recognize the Cadillac and wouldn't know that I was inside of it, I slumped down in my seat. Garrett backed up, stopped in the middle of the street, and jumped out. I slumped down farther in my seat.

"Hey, you little peeping tom. What are you doing?"

"Nothing, I live here," I heard Donny say.

"Yeah, well, you better be doing nothing. I'm watching you."

I peeked out to see Garrett towering over Donny and shaking his finger at him. Donny looked scared, but he wasn't backing away. I heard another voice—Wayne's.

"What's going on?"

"None of your business," Garrett said. "You a friend of his?"

"Not really, I'm here to see the girl next door."

"I don't think so," Garrett said.

"This is awkward," Donny said. "Schedules get messed up. Boyfriend one meets boyfriend two."

I couldn't hear what Wayne said because, at that moment, a taxi honked as it pulled up. I popped up and saw Donny scuttling to it. He turned back before getting into the taxi and caught me looking. He brushed one finger over the top of the other, giving me the finger of shame.

Garrett said, "She's my fiancée. Who do you think you are?"

There was no longer any point in hiding. I slid all the way up in the seat.

"Oh, there she is," Wayne said, ignoring Garrett and walking over to me. "Hi, Prima."

I rolled down the window and asked him, "What are you doing here?"

Garrett crossed his arms and stood with a scowl on his face. He shifted his weight between his feet, like he did when he was playing ball.

Wayne said to me, "Sorry to bother you again. I came by because one of the files was missing. I hoped we'd just overlooked it, or it slipped out when we moved them. I wouldn't bother you, but the professor said it's important and you weren't answering your phone."

"There wasn't a B9 file, if that's what you're looking for."

"That's the one. It's got to be somewhere. Would you mind checking?"

"I guess, but this is the last thing. You can tell the Professor Pinsky that there's nothing else I can do to help."

When Garrett got back into the car, he shut the door with a bang. He pulled into the driveway, narrowly missing Wayne.

"Who is this guy?"

"He's from Cummings. He came yesterday and picked up some of my father's old research papers. He's a TA for Professor Pinsky."

"How come you didn't tell me about him?"

"I didn't think it was important."

"Why did that twerp next door say this guy was your boyfriend?"

"He's just messing with you. Are you jealous?"

"Hardly, but I don't like some guy just coming over to the house when you're alone."

"He's harmless," I said, feeling defensive. "Besides, I wasn't alone. Wolfie was with me."

As if on cue, Wolfears trotted out from the side of the house. We got out of the car and I saw that Wayne had walked down the driveway. He might have overheard my conversation with Garrett because he had an amused expression on his face.

He crouched down to greet Wolfears. Wolfears ignored him and came over to me and snouted my leg. I tweaked his ear. Then he went around the car and greeted Garrett. Only then did he go over to Wayne, clearly demonstrating his view of the pecking order.

I gave Wayne a glare. The guy sure was forward.

"Wait here," I told him.

He looked disappointed. Then, he perked up and said, "It'll be faster if I help."

I shook my head and disappeared into the house with Garrett and Wolfears, leaving him to wait alone in the driveway.

I went down to the basement, but I knew it wasn't there. I'd been through all the file cabinets already. At least I could honestly say that I'd looked, and to kill a little time, I opened a few file drawers.

Seeing the birth certificate file, I pulled mine out. To my surprise, in line 5A, Place of Birth, was the address of our old home before moving to Concha Pointe. I'd always assumed that I'd been born at Saint Pilar's Hospital. It was signed by my father, and his typed name was in the attendant/certifier box. Stapled on the back of the birth certificate was an "Affidavit of Birth Information for Out-of-Hospital Births" on my father's medical stationery. I thought my mother was quite brave giving birth to me at home.

"What's taking so long?" Garrett called out.

"I'll be right there." I put my birth certificate back and went upstairs. "I'm going back out to tell Wayne the bad news—there is no file. Don't you want to come with me?"

Garrett said, "I better stay in here. I'm afraid I might punch the guy if he makes another smart remark."

"Okay, I'll be right back. Help yourself to something in the kitchen."

Wolfears followed me outside. Wayne had pulled his car into the driveway and was leaning against it, inspecting his fingernails.

I gave him a fake smile and said, "I don't remember inviting you to park in the driveway."

"You didn't want me to get a ticket while I was waiting, did you?"

I was about to give him another glare and tell him I didn't really care if he got a ticket or not, when he said, "That sure is a fine dog you have."

He squatted to Wolfears' eye level and reached out a hand. Wolfears went over to him to have the sides of his head playfully batted back and forth.

Wayne sure knew how to soften me.

"I'm sorry. You have all the files. We didn't miss any. It's not there."

He stood up and shook his head. "That's too bad. B9 is the one for the woman who gave the story to the tabloid."

"Yes, Maria Nogales."

"Pinsky's going to be in a tizzy."

As Wayne drove away, I asked Wolfears, "Are you in cahoots with him? Did he give you a treat when I wasn't looking? You're usually more wary of strangers."

Chapter 47

I found Garrett pacing in the hallway and told him, "Wayne's gone. You can chill now."

"Good. I didn't like him."

"You made that clear to him. You were kind of rude."

"Are you defending him?"

"No, I don't like him either, but he's working for Professor Pinsky, who was my father's friend. So, what could I do?"

Garrett grunted and I followed him into the kitchen.

He said, "I was making sandwiches for us while I waited for you to get rid of him."

"That was sweet."

"You need to eat more. They're only peanut butter and jelly, that's all I could find. Besides, it's all I know how to make. I guess you did need to go to the store. I thought you were creating a diversion so I wouldn't see him."

"I didn't want you to see Donny, I knew it would upset you. He's sorry about what happened. He didn't mean anything, but he's socially awkward and immature. His mom left when he was little, and his father works all the time, so he's not had a particularly good upbringing."

"I'll lay off him as long as he doesn't try to take any more pictures of you, from his window or elsewhere."

"Don't worry about that. With the juniper trees there now, he doesn't have a view of our yard."

Garrett cut the sandwiches in half and handed me one of the plates. I got a glass of milk for him and a glass of water for myself. I needed to get my rice milk at the store.

We sat at the kitchen counter on the barstools. He took the side facing inward, and I sat with a view of the darkening sky through the window behind him.

He said, "Forget Donny. What about that other guy? I thought you saw his car and didn't want me to know about him."

"Did you really think I was seeing another guy? You were jealous."

"No, I wasn't." He stuffed a bite of sandwich in his mouth. He chewed slowly. After he swallowed it, he said, "Yeah, I was, a little. The guy looks like the surfer type you might go for."

I laughed. "*Wayne*? You don't need to worry. Besides, he told me he doesn't know how to surf." I didn't mention that he'd asked me to teach him. "He's not my type. I like them tall, dark and handsome," I said, reaching over and running my fingers lightly down his arm.

"After the way you acted at Atta Patta's the other night, I thought maybe you—"

"You thought what?" I screeched.

"I don't know, maybe you wanted to go bonobo on him after I restrained myself."

I stood, nearly knocking over the barstool. I walked out the back door and left him sitting in the kitchen. At the wall, I stood looking out at the dark sky, which still had a thread of pink on the horizon, separating where the ocean and the night were divided. If there were stars in the sky, I didn't see them.

I sat on the wall and swung my legs around to hang over the edge. I felt dampness under my hands from the light mist that covered the top of the wall. The moisture seeped into my thighs and butt. I ignored it and stared at the pink line, resisting my desire to turn around to see if Garrett was going to follow me, or if he was still munching on his sandwich.

I listened for the sound of the kitchen door or his footsteps, but the only sounds I heard were those of the waves lapping on the rocks below, alternating with the soft swishing sound of the water flowing back out between them.

Finally, I turned around. He wasn't in the kitchen. I knew he hadn't left because I would have heard The Chugger.

Two can play at that game, I thought.

I turned back toward the ocean and waited. Trancelike, I watched the pink line fade until I could only guess where the sky ended and the ocean began. With the pink line inhaled by the falling night, I started to worry. He was better at the waiting game than I was. I gave up and went inside.

The kitchen air tasted stale. My uneaten sandwich was still on the counter and his plate was empty, without crumbs. I resisted calling out his name and went into the living room where I expected to find him sitting on the couch.

He wasn't there.

I checked out the front door. The Cadillac and The Chugger were both still parked in the driveway. Wolfears looked at me expectantly, hoping for another nighttime outing. I closed the front door.

"Where is he?" I whispered to Wolfears.

He trotted to the bottom of the stairs and looked up. When I caught up with him, he scrambled up the stairs. I followed him upstairs and down the hall.

I stopped at the bedroom doorway. Garrett was lying on my bed on his back, with his arms crossed behind head. His shoes were off and his feet dangled over the foot of the bed.

"What are you doing?"

"What you want," he said.

I didn't say anything. He sat up on his elbows. We stared at each other.

"You need to leave," I said in barely more than a whisper.

"I'm getting mixed signals."

I flung my hand from my side and pointed toward the stairs. "Get out! Is that clear enough for you."

He kept his eyes on me as he picked up his shoes. When he stood, his face was set and he avoided looking at me.

He brushed past me, shaking his head, as if I were no more than a piece of furniture. I listened to his feet slapping the stairs as he went down.

He slammed the front door.

When I heard The Chugger start, I went to the gate intercom and opened the gate. The rattle of The Chugger faded as he drove away.

My anger dissipated to be replaced by a hollowness. I wondered why I didn't burst into tears. Only hours ago, he was the center of my world. The future was clear. Now, I felt disconnected from him.

I went and checked the front door was locked. Back down in the kitchen, I took the plate with my sandwich and slid it into the trash. Wolfears looked at me as if asking why I didn't give it to him. I knew I couldn't go to sleep yet.

"It's your lucky night. We're going to go for a late run."

Chapter 48

I ran faster than usual, even though the air felt thick and the iron hand of gravity wanted to press me into the ground. Everything seemed two-dimensional, the scenery surrounding me no more than sketches on cardboard. If I ran fast enough, I could tear through them and return to a three-dimensional world. I sprinted at full speed. The cardboard world remained ahead, unreachable. Before I made it to the nature preserve, I halted, bent over with my hands on my knees and sucked in lungfuls of the syrupy, salt air.

When I returned home, my body was ready to rest even if my mind was still juiced with emotions. I didn't want to sleep in my bed, so I decided to use the guest bedroom downstairs at the front of the house, where I couldn't hear the sound of the ocean. I expected my mind would keep whirring. Instead, once my head hit the pillow, I was out. I slept through the rest of the night.

I spent the morning doing laundry, including my bedspread. After lunch, I did chores around the house. Sometimes I imagined the phone ringing, but Garrett didn't call. Of course we'd had fights before, but it had never taken this long for us to make up. Still, I felt stubborn. He was the one who needed to call me or show up at my door. Even Wayne could do that, and he was a jerk.

Every time I heard a car driving by, I paused what I was doing and listened to see if it stopped. One time a car did, but it turned out to be another taxi for Donny. At this rate, it would have made more sense for him to hire a personal chauffeur.

I needed to get out. I made a shopping list and went to the grocery store. I pushed a shopping cart with a rebellious wheel and admired its independence.

Upon returning home, I checked the answering machine. There were no calls.

I unloaded the groceries with no help from Wolfears. Now there were lots of choices for sandwiches in the kitchen: cheeses, meats, mayonnaise and mustard.

I made a turkey sandwich, took it into the living room and turned on the big-screen TV. I seldom watch television, but I wanted to do something mindless and stop thinking. I flipped through channels and stopped on the local news, startled by the image of a group of protestors. I recognized the front of the biology building at Cummings University.

The protest looked like the same group that I had witnessed, only there were more of them now, and they looked even more agitated and organized. I shuddered at the memory of encountering them. I hate crowds.

The news anchor said, "A group is calling on state legislators to investigate the taxpayer funding of animal research and the unethical use of human embryos."

Before the commercials, I caught the image of one of the protest signs that read, "Medical Research is Blasphemy."

The advertisements were for non-stick frying pans, light bulbs and a shampoo that promised to give more bounce and shine to my hair.

The news returned, but it took several more reports before the segment about the protest came back around. When it came on, a reporter with the face of a porcelain angel and the voice of a screech owl had difficulty speaking over the chanting crowd in front of the biology building. People popped up or ran across the screen behind her to cash in on two or three seconds of fame, often making funny faces. Their antics made the protest seem more festive than the threatening vibes I'd felt when I was there.

The reporter began interviewing one of the protesters, a red-bearded man with a baseball cap. The cap had writing on it that I couldn't read because his head constantly jerked about.

"What are you demonstrating?" the reporter asked.

The man flipped the cap off his head with a flick of his hand. His demeanor abruptly shifted from silly to scary. His head stopped bobbing. He peered into the camera. His jaw muscles tensed and he looked as if he might snarl.

I recognized him.

He was the guy who'd waved at me from the car that followed Pinsky when I was at Maria's rental house. When he opened his mouth, he spoke in a theatrical voice that easily carried over the crowd.

"Here, in this so-called institution of higher learning, atrocities against God have been committed. The apex of God's creation, mankind, has been tainted, combined with genetic material from animals. Creatures that are damned to hell have been born here."

Obviously taken off guard by the man's intensity, the reporter said, "Thank you," and backed away from him.

He shouted, "The image of God has been defiled. Satan is rising." He threw his arms in the air. "Brothers and sisters, behind me you can witness the actual gates of hell." He gestured dramatically at the biology building's front doors.

The report cut away from the protestors to the in-studio newscast. The anchor raised her eyebrows and said, "And in other news—"

I switched off the television and went to check the answering machine, even though I knew there weren't any messages.

It was after five now and Garrett still hadn't called. There was little chance I would hear from him during his shift. Friday nights were always busy. I thought about ordering a pizza from Atta Patta, in hopes that he might be the one to deliver it.

I picked up the phone and dialed from memory. When I heard someone pick up, I started to hang up, but stopped when I heard, "Hello?"

"Mysti?" I said, trying to hide my surprise.

"Yes. Hi, Prima, who else did you expect?"

"Oh, I didn't mean to call you."

"Okay, well, bye, I guess."

"I did want to call you, but I didn't want to bother you when you're leaving so soon and have a lot to do. You've got your last recital coming up and goodbye parties too."

"Are you okay? You sound funny. Do you have a cold?"

When I managed to answer, I said, "My world is falling apart."

"What happened?"

"Everything. I think Garrett and I broke up."

I hadn't cried after our fight, but now I burst into tears. I couldn't catch my breath.

I heard Mysti say, "I'm coming over."

"No, it's okay," I managed between sobs. "You're busy."

The next thing I heard was the dial tone.

Chapter 49

I went out to the backyard while I waited for Mysti, and left the sliding door open so I could hear the gate buzzer when she arrived. In the distance above the ocean were clouds stretched across the sky. They were so straight, they looked like sticks of raw noodles waiting to be dropped into a boiling cauldron. Above the noodle clouds, a single gray elephant resting on her back floated across the sky. At the end of the yard, my mother's sculptures stood, sentries against what, I didn't know. The abstract statues shifted their shapes with the changing light. Butterflies became bats. The woman clawing the sky from the tangled seaweed was, as always, relentless in her quest to free herself. For the first time, I realized that her face was more like mine than my mother's. I wondered if my mother had intentionally chiseled an image of me and that was why she wouldn't part with it. The sculpture was larger than life. I reached up and touched her face. The sun had warmed her bronze skin. Running my fingers over her smooth cheek, she felt almost human.

The ga-ga cry of a seagull startled me. I turned and saw the bird landing on the edge of the fire pit. It spotted me and ga-ga'd again as it reversed course and took flight. The motion of its wings disturbed the ashes and sent up a billow of them that landed on the deck making a mess. I found the broom and dustpan in the shed and swept them up. It gave me something to do.

I noticed the ashes were sloped against one side of the circular pit, having been blown by the wind. Not wanting to tackle the bigger job of cleaning out the pit, I decided to get the hose and dampen the ashes to keep them spreading out from a breeze or the wings of another gull.

As I sprinkled water onto the ash slope, it crumbled, mixing with the water, creating a murky soup at the bottom. When I'd dampened all the dusky slope, I twisted the nozzle to the stream setting and let the water fill the fire pit.

I watched the swirling black soup as its level rose. When it was near the top, I shut the water off. The soup continued spinning, becoming slower and slower. The specks of ash on the surface began sinking. I sat on the edge of the pit and peered into it as the rippling water settled into a black mirror. My dim reflection appeared submerged rather than reflected. I lowered my face to only inches above the water. My breath disturbed the surface and my image shimmered.

The face in the water was no longer my own.

Looking out at me was what Garrett had said was "the unhuman, unholy thing," the "it" of Pinsky's world, the thing Wayne had described as "the freak." My father's laboratory creation was staring at me. I was looking at myself.

I couldn't deny it. All the clues were there: my father paying Maria for her silence, my home birth signed by him as the attending physician, his insistence of my never being seen by other doctors, my hair stubbornly parting in the middle like bonobos, my natural athleticism, my aunt excluded during my mother's "pregnancy," the way I was sheltered, how my parents were overprotective and my mother's body had no signs of childbirth. When I was a toddler, I was even afraid of water like the bonobos.

The missing file was about me.

I was B9.

I must have been born a year earlier than the date on my birth certificate.

How could I have not seen it before? Maria must have demanded more money. My father refused. She went to the press, and Pinsky got wind of her. My father realized that he would no longer be able to keep me hidden from the world. I would be exposed to the cruelty of those who are considered "the other," the "outsiders, not part of the group." He was right. He only wanted to protect me. I knew why he was hiding me. How could I have been so blind as to have not seen it before?

I plunged my face into the water. The feeling, the chill of it, instantly turned my mind to panic. I felt as if I were once again living the moment when our car drove off the pier into the water.

I opened my eyes. They burned in the soot-soaked water, but I couldn't shut them. It felt as if there were a hand on the back of my head pressing me down, holding me under, keeping me from rising. I was being baptized for another world.

My lungs began screaming for me to inhale.

I opened my mouth, tasted the foul, grit-stained water. The back of my throat remained closed. My eyes twitched, seeking. There was no escape from the gray, dimming world. My arms flailed as if trying to strike my imaginary assailant. I was being pushed back into the womb. I never was meant to be born. My body was being turned inside out. Like water inside of a fire pit, I was unnatural, an oxymoron of living.

Involuntarily, my body jerked back and my head was thrown free of the water. The daylight was a knife-stabbing brightness. Choking and sputtering, I collapsed onto my side. I sucked air as if each breath would be my last. My breathing slowed to a pant, and I curled into the fetal position.

I don't know how long I lay on my side, but eventually I rolled onto my back and shielded my eyes with my arm. Though the sun was lowering in the sky, the sky was still a rich, deep blue. The elephant cloud had drifted almost directly overhead, only now it had broken into two, an open-mouthed pelican chasing a rabbit with ears longer than its body.

I heard a horn honking in the distance. The honking sounded insistent. It wasn't far away. I realized it must be Mysti. She was at the gate. I scrambled to my feet and rushed inside the house to the intercom.

"Is that you Mysti?"

"Yes. Where have you been? Are you okay? The gate code didn't work."

"I'm fine. Hold on," I said, and pressed the gate opener. "Meet me out back."

Instead of heading out back, I dashed through the house to the front and to meet her in the driveway.

Wolfears rushed after me, his toenails clicking on the tiles. "Where were you when my head was stuck under water?" I asked him.

In the driveway, Mysti jumped from her car,

"Where were you?" she shouted. "I was about to ram my car through the gate if you didn't answer."

Without waiting for an answer, she ran over, gave me a hug, then stepped back and looked me over from head to foot.

"You look a mess. What are those black streaks on your face? Were you giving yourself a charcoal facial? Your hair is dripping wet. What is going on?

Suddenly feeling like I might start sobbing again, I said, "Garrett and I broke up. I'm an animal. I'm a bonobo."

I might have scrambled my words because Mysti made a slow blink, and said, "Slow down. Garrett's a bonobo? What's a bonobo?"

Chapter 50

After listening to my woes and calming me down, Mysti said, "Are you going to be okay? I want to stay here with you, but I'm already late for my last rehearsal."

I gave her a big hug and sent her on her way. In talking with her, she'd helped me to realize that my fear of being a laboratory experiment might be totally in my imagination. As she'd said, without proof, did I really know? Did it really matter, anyway? Besides, I was who I was. I was still the same person in her eyes, even if part of me was from something else. It was no different than having a prosthetic limb or, if one thought about it, even tooth fillings were not something natural. The most comforting thing she helped me realize was that even if I was part bonobo, what did it matter if no one knew?

We'd hardly talked about Garrett before she left. Now that I'd been able to compartmentalize my fear of being a freak, my will to hold out for Garrett to be the first one to call was weakening. I imagined him being consoled in the arms of Kathy.

I was pacing through the house when I heard a phone ring. My heart skipped a beat. Then, I realized it was only my father's cell phone. I'd left it on the kitchen counter. The caller ID told me it was from Cummings University. Didn't these people ever stop?

I scooped it up and stomped out to the backyard. I wanted to hurl over the wall and watch it crash on the rocks below. Just as I was about to throw it, it stopped ringing.

I paused. The ocean suffered from too many people and too much junk. I didn't want to add to the pollution.

I lowered my arm. Then, it rang again. I spun around and lobbed it in a high arc. I hit my mark. With a splash it landed in the deep end of the pool.

I could barely see it in the dim light as it sunk to the bottom. I switched on the pool light. The pool took on the appearance of a gigantic turquoise jewel. Its glow illuminated the yard and cast shadows, an inversion of sunlight. The bird of paradise arched over the wall as if longing to leap into the ocean. The ripples on the water caused the light to flutter, making my mom's abstract sculptures move like dancers made of elbows and knees. The seaweed tangled woman remained shyly in the corner, a wallflower hiding from her frolicking companions.

Thinking that toxic chemicals might leach from the phone, I took the long pole with the net and fished it out. For all I knew, I might have to turn it in to the phone company when I got around to cancelling the cell service. I left the pool light on so the statues could slowly wind down their spastic dance to the rhythm of the settling water. Feeling alien in my own backyard, I went back inside.

Without something to distract me, I began thinking about Garrett again and my desire to call him. I wanted to cling to my stubbornness.

I remembered my mother's sleeping pills, so I went upstairs. Before I got there, I heard the phone ringing. On my way downstairs, I nearly tripped over Wolfears in my rush to get to it. When I reached it, I intended to let the machine answer. I didn't want Garrett to know how anxiously I was waiting for his call. Then, I thought he might hang up if he got the answering machine. I picked up the phone and said hello. To my shock, I heard Wayne's voice on the line.

"Oh, it's you."

"You don't have to sound so disappointed."

"How did you get this number?" I asked, sounding far calmer than I felt.

Wayne laughed. "You hadn't been answering my calls the last few times. I figured you must have another phone, so when I met your neighbor, I told him I'd lost your number and that's why I'd dropped by. You must admire my cleverness."

"I do?"

"Yeah, your neighbor gave me this number and told me all about you. He doesn't think much of your boyfriend."

"My fiancé."

"Yeah, what's his name Garnet, like the gemstone?"

"Ha, ha, very funny. His name is Garrett."

"Anyway, your neighbor thought I'd make a good replacement because Garnet's got a stick up his ass."

"Goodbye."

"Wait, I'm only kidding."

I didn't hang up. "What do you want? Why are you calling me other than to be annoying? I thought I was perfectly clear that there aren't any more files. I can't be of any help in finding old records."

"You know how it is. We scientists are stubborn. We never give up or we'd never find answers."

"I'm going to hang up now," I said, trying to convince myself more than him.

"No, wait, please. Don't hang up. I have something you'll want to know."

"I doubt it."

"Maria left a message for the professor today. She said, 'Your father once told her that the baby was healthy. So, she thinks he hid it close to home.'"

I felt my hand tightly gripping the phone.

He continued, "I wondered if you have any idea about where it might be? Of course that was years ago. Maybe it's dead now."

I shuddered and was glad that Wayne couldn't see me through the phone.

"Gee, I'll check if there's a mummy in the basement or a body hidden in the freezer."

"It could be alive too."

"You said you didn't think so."

"Yeah, I can be wrong."

"That's a surprise." Talking with him brought out a caustic side of me. My voice also had a hint of flirtation in it, which I didn't like.

At least Wayne paid attention to me, I thought.

"I only meant the viability of hybrid offspring is low, especially considering this one was created in a laboratory. Odds are only odds, not certainties. If we only had the file, we'd know how much DNA was substituted. My guess is it was very little. Anyway, she claims it's alive. It makes sense because why else would your father have kept paying her."

"Pinsky shares a lot with you."

"Yeah, he does. Star pupil, don't ya know. She wants money from him *now*. She's blackmailing him. If he can't come up with it in time, she's going to the press.

"So?" Another shudder ran up my spine.

"I just thought you might have come up with something."

"Maybe you could find it in a zoo," I said with as much bravado as I could muster, hoping to sound flippant to cover my unease.

"The thing is, if Pinsky can show evidence of success, he'll be able to get support and funding to restart the program and pay her for her silence. Some creepy government types came around and met with him a few days ago. He seemed more upbeat than usual when they left. I don't trust the government. They looked more CIA or military than NIH?

"NIH?"

"The National Institutes of Health, the government people who do biomedical and public health research. I mean, if they're military, they will want to create a super soldier or something."

"Again, why should this matter to me?"

"Doesn't it matter to you if your father's work gets used for violence? You're a peace-loving surfer."

"You don't know surfing. Most surfers aren't peace-loving."

"Yeah, but I get the impression you are. I suspect you know more than you're letting on."

"I hardly know what DNA is," I said. "So, no, you're wrong. I don't know anything."

"I didn't say you were stupid. Ignorance isn't the same thing, except sometimes when it's intentional."

I remembered why I didn't like him. Still, he struck a nerve. I knew my father and mother would never approve of any discoveries my dad made being used to harm people. But then again, my father killed himself and my mother. He'd tried to kill me, so I didn't really know what I believed anymore.

"I'm sure my father didn't work with the military."

"He might not have, but Pinsky would. He'd work with anyone who would fund his research and help put him in the history books."

"And you work for him," I said. "You just convinced me even more that I don't want anything to do with all of this."

His voice sounded flatter when he said, "I'll be working tomorrow. Call me if you think of anything."

Chapter 51

The next morning, I felt older, much older. True, if my speculation were correct, I might be a year older than I'd always thought, but I felt as if I'd aged a decade in the last few weeks. I thought of all the troubles in the world, compared to my little sliver of the universe, who and what I was, like when I was surfing and realized how tiny I was within the power of the ocean, yet still connected. Things were bigger than I was, and yet I was focused on my own life through a microscope. Why was I playing this stupid game with Garrett, waiting to see who would be the first to call? It felt childish. If we were soulmates, what did it matter? I picked up the phone and called his house. His mother answered.

"Garrett isn't home, but I'm so glad you called because I've been thinking about your wedding. I think the color scheme should be blue, the bridesmaids in light blue dresses and the groomsmen in darker blue suits. I took the liberty of researching designers and I've found one you'll love, Ida Villanueva. I hope she's available. We'll need to get on her schedule soon. There's so little time. What are your thoughts about cornflowers for the floral arrangements? Of course, blue thistles are quite popular now."

She paused, and I managed to say, "Blue?" Obviously, Garrett hadn't told her about our fight. That was a good sign.

"Yes, but a pastel or summer sky blue for the dresses and darker suits and the blue-violet flowers for accents around the edges of the bouquets. Garrett said you like the ocean, so that led me to decide on the blue theme. Your dress, of course, will be white with blue highlights. We'll see what the designer recommends. Isn't this exciting?"

"It all sounds very good, I guess."

"Yes, yes it does. After all you've been through, you deserve a dream wedding."

"Do you happen to know when Garrett will be back or where he went?"

"I never can remember if Saturday morning is the prayer meeting or Bible study. Either one, he'll be at the church."

"Where we had the memorial?"

"Yes, of course. I'm so happy you decided to have the wedding there. You really couldn't find a more desirable location than our church grounds."

"I need to take some time to think about the colors. I've been so busy."

"Don't take too long. Reservations must be made. I noticed a family portrait in your living room. Does that photographer do weddings? A good photographer is important to capture the memories."

"I don't remember. It was several years ago."

"There's usually an imprint in the lower corner. Be a dear and check."

It took several more minutes of Mrs. Deacon's wedding planning before I could get off the phone. When I finally did, I couldn't help wondering if Kathy would be there studying with Garrett.

I found myself unusually courageous and drove Mister Aphid to the church.

In addition to the church, there were other buildings on the property, and I had no idea which ones were used for Bible study and prayer meetings. There weren't many cars in the parking lot, but I spotted The Chugger parked next to a red Audi convertible. I parked several rows over, under the shade of a carob tree, whose green seed pods had not yet turned brown when they hung like rippled tongues. They were the same shade of green as Mister Aphid. I took one and put it on my dashboard for luck.

Since the visitor parking lot was on the other side of the lawn from the buildings, I took the upper path across the expanse of lawn that stretched down the slope. Walking across it now, the grounds felt entirely different than at the memorial. I checked inside the church first. When I attempted to open one of the large oak doors, it only moved a few inches before a chain through the inside panic bars stopped it. I peered through the crack.

I couldn't see or hear anyone.

One of the other buildings appeared to be the clergy house, so I skipped it and went to the one that looked like a brick schoolhouse with a border of yellow flowers. One end housed a gymnasium. Two young girls were on the court facing each other, sitting hunched on top of basketballs. I asked them if they knew where the prayer meeting was. Without a word, one of them flipped her hair and pointed down the hall. She gave me a look to indicate she thought I wasn't very bright.

In the hallway, I found a black letterboard listing the dates, times and room numbers for various events. The block white letters pressed into the black lined background informed me there was a prayer meeting in room three.

The door was open, so I peeked inside and saw a group of people with their heads bowed, sitting in a circle of chairs. Garrett wasn't there, but Kathy was. She looked up as if she were expecting someone. Garrett, I imagined.

When she recognized me, she got up from the group and stepped outside with me. I noticed her glance down the hallway.

"Hi, Prima," she said as if we were best friends.

"Hi, I didn't mean to bother your group. I'm looking for Garrett."

"Oh, he's not with you?"

I shook my head. *Wasn't that obvious?*

"He didn't show up," she said. "So, I figured he went somewhere with you."

"No, again, sorry to bother you."

"No bother at all. Would you like to join us, since you're already here?"

"No, thanks."

"When Garrett is here, we always say a prayer for you."

That caught me off guard. "Really?"

"Yes, of course, he's so devoted to you. You're incredibly lucky. He's such a gentleman. I really blew that one. I won't lie, if I had a do over, I wouldn't let him get away. At least we're still friends."

She pushed out her lower lip into a pout. I couldn't help but trust her sincerity, and felt my suspicions about her melting into sympathy.

"Sometimes just being friends is a lot easier," I said.

She laughed and her expression returned to her perky demeanor. "I hope you invite me to your wedding. I *love* weddings. Are you planning to have it here? I can't wait for my wedding, but, of course, I'll need to find someone first."

"Garrett's mom seems to be in charge of planning."

She gave a knowing nod and laughed.

"I better get back inside," she said. "If you ever need a friend or feel the spirit to join us in prayer, you're always welcome here."

I checked the other rooms, which were empty, except for one by the back door where a group of older ladies was sorting pamphlets. I rechecked the church itself.

The only place I hadn't looked was the clergy house. I hesitated, but he had to be somewhere on the grounds.

To the side of the house, there were two parking spots, one with a car and the other empty with grease stains on the concrete. I went to the front door. There was a doorbell and a knocker in the center, like at Maria's place on La Tuna Canyon. On the stillness of the church grounds, it seemed intrusive to use them. I knocked with my knuckles and listened for any movement inside the house.

It was quiet.

Then, I tried the knocker and the doorbell, but no one answered.

I was about to leave, completely bewildered by the presence of Garrett's car and no Garrett. I started back to my car and stopped. The only other place I hadn't checked was the backyard of the clergy house. The day was pleasant and they could be there. Even if Garrett wasn't there, I wanted to thank Pastor Andrew for the service.

A narrow path ran along the side of the house that backed up against the hillside. As I followed it, I noticed a bitter, somewhat fruity scent in the air. The bushes needed trimming and, in places, arched over the path. I was easily able to pass beneath several, but a large branch of a laurel sumac blocked my path at one point so that I had to pull it back to get beyond it. As I held it so it wouldn't whack me, I heard what sounded like a groan from inside the house.

I glanced into a window. Garrett and the minister were inside the room.

At that moment, I understood the real reason that Garrett's lust fell far short of mine, at least his lust for *me*.

Chapter 52

I slowly released the branch and backed away from the window, hoping they hadn't seen me. Busy as they were, I was fairly sure they hadn't. I wanted to run to my car, but didn't want to attract attention, so I forced myself to walk across the church grounds. The next thing I was aware of was finding myself turning into the Concha Pointe community. On automatic pilot, I took the familiar turns and wove around to my house.

When I arrived there, I didn't stop and continued driving, looping back the other way to the north side highway exit. Instead of turning onto it, I sat there watching the cars zooming by, going up and down. Finally, when a car pulled up behind me and honked, I turned south onto the highway and drove without knowing where I was going.

Driving more slowly than the traffic, cars whizzed by me. To show their offense at my slower speed, several drivers nearly clipped me when cutting back into the slow lane. I pulled over into a dirt apron and stared at the ocean until I'd calmed down.

When I pulled back onto PCH, I forced myself to drive at the fifty-five miles per hour speed limit. Many cars still flew by me.

Of all the places, I found myself ending up at Cummings University.

The campus was peaceful. There were no protesters outside of the biology building and I went inside. The quiet and the lights reflecting on the polished floor made the building seem sterile and devoid of life. Again, I smelled the pickle odor from the basement by the stairs, but I walked past them, deciding to take the elevator this time. As if it had been waiting for me, the elevator doors parted immediately when I pressed the call button.

I rode up to the second floor and went to Pinsky's office. The outer door wasn't locked and I went inside. No one was at the reception desk. A few of the professors' doors were open. Pinsky's and another office door were closed.

I went to his door and listened. It was quiet inside.

I gave a gentle knock. No answer.

I turned the knob and opened the door just a crack. No one was inside, so I shut it. I walked quietly, feeling like a thief sneaking around. As I was about to exit through the reception door, I heard approaching footsteps in the hallway. Feeling like I didn't belong there, I panicked and backed up. I thought of hiding in Pinsky's office, rationalizing I could say I was waiting for him if discovered, then realized how suspicious it would look. And if it were Pinsky himself in the hall, why would I say I was there? I didn't even know myself. Just before the door opened, I slipped into the chair at the reception desk.

The door opened and Wayne entered carrying several books and a stack of papers. I suddenly realized why I was there, and I didn't want to be.

Garrett had betrayed me, and I wanted to hurt him back. Wayne was the obvious choice. The phrase 'cold feet' came to mind. My feet didn't feel cold, but my brain did.

When Wayne saw me, he looked startled for a moment before recovering and saying, "I guess you couldn't stay away from me."

"Don't flatter yourself."

"What are you doing in my chair then?"

"I got tired of sitting in the guest chairs. This one swivels and the back reclines. You sure start work late."

"It's Saturday, and I've already put in seventy or eighty hours this week. Besides, I have been working. I was down in the basement," he said defensively. "Did you think of something important? Is that why you came?"

Stalling for time to think of something, I said, "Maybe Maria was right."

"About what?" he asked as he placed the books and papers on the desk.

Winging it, I suddenly felt brilliant. "Maybe the hybrid is alive. How would you know it was the right person?"

"What do you mean, how would I know? Test it."

"Yes, I mean would it be hard to prove?"

"Not at all. Simple. Typically, a blood test or a cheek swab. Heck, you could even test saliva or hair for that matter. There's lots of choices. Why?"

My feeling of brilliance was abruptly replaced by a feeling of idiocy. I was setting myself up to be a laboratory rat. And the lives of lab rats weren't known for their pleasant experiences. The last thing in the world I would want was to be found out and become a specimen to be studied. If I were truly a hybrid, my father had been right about one thing: being discovered would be a disaster. Yet, I desperately wanted to know if it was simply my imagination running away with me or not.

"What would a hybrid look like? Couldn't you tell by looking at her?"

"Not necessarily. Sure, she might be hairy and have bonobo features, but depending on which genes were replaced and which ones expressed, she could look like anybody walking down the street. The B9 file would have helped to make an educated guess."

I had another inspiration, and said, "I have a cousin, well, she's supposed to be my cousin. She's, well, let's just say she's a bit different."

"This is incredible news! This is big. *Huge*. Where is she? Let's go see her. I can drop everything for this," he said and plopped the books and papers onto the desk.

Scrambling, grasping for an out, I said, "I haven't seen her in a long time."

"All you have to do is get a sample. We can test it and we'll have proof." In his excitement, he slapped the top of his head with both hands and flung them up in the air. I thought he might start pulling his hair out. "This is incredible."

"You sound as fanatical as the professor."

"No, not contamination by association." He glanced at Pinsky's door.

"He's not in," I said.

"It would be a major breakthrough. Pinsky said you thought she might be your sister, which sounded silly at the time, but who knows what went on. If you gave a sample too, we could see if there's a match or not."

"I don't know," I said. "What will happen to her? There must have been a reason my father and Maria kept her hidden."

He dropped his hands to his sides, then raised one of them to his chin. "What's she like? Is she, you know, special? Would she even know what's going on?"

"Do you mean is she stupid?"

"You said it, I didn't."

"That's irrelevant. What I mean is, will she be turned into some kind of experiment, poked and prodded, abused like a laboratory animal? Pinsky said she was property of the university."

"Well, she is part animal," he said, and a grin broke onto his face.

It was a nice grin, I have to admit that. He was cute, smart and witty, but completely lacking in empathy. How could I have imagined having an affair with him? Besides, I wasn't an affair type of person. I just wanted to hurt Garrett like I'd been hurt.

I zoned out thinking about Garrett. I felt betrayed. I didn't care that he was gay. On most levels, that was irrelevant. What hurt was that I was supposed to be the person he was closest to in the world, and he couldn't share who he was with me. I felt my head dropping. Too many things at once.

And I felt relief when I heard Wayne say, "Earth to Prima?"

"What I'll do," I said. "is get you a sample. If it turns out that she is the hybrid, you'll have proof of that. Whether she wants to come forward, or not, will be her decision. Besides, you said the military might be getting involved. I want to know more about that so I can help her with the decision."

"Sure, sure, I'll let you know more as soon as I do. I got carried away with everything. You're right, we've got to think it through."

I started to get up.

"You looked like you were in another world for a moment. Also, your face is blotchy. Are you okay?"

I didn't want to say anything, but I blurted it anyway. "It's my fiancé. We had a fight."

I expected him to gloat. Instead, he looked genuinely concerned. He walked around the desk and stood next to me.

"I'm sorry," he said. "Relationships can be a bitch."

Chapter 53

Wayne placed a hand on my shoulder and let it slowly slide down my arm. When he reached my elbow, he gave a gentle squeeze. I didn't move. Then, he started caressing my upper arm. I bolted from my chair and ran past him without another word, leaving him standing with a surprised expression on his face.

Rather than walking quietly to avoid breaking the silence, this time I rushed down the hallway, my feet smacking the floor. I didn't want to wait for the elevator and ran past it to the stairs. Taking them three at a time, I vaulted over the turn. I reached the ground floor and rushed out of the building. I ran all the way to my car, not caring what anyone would think.

When I sat inside Mister Aphid, I felt less vulnerable being encased in a metal shell. I started feeling claustrophobic and rolled down the window. It didn't help and I didn't want to drive until I'd calmed down. I checked my face in the rearview mirror. It was blotchy. I wondered if I was breaking out in hives. Just in case, I took the bottle of antihistamines from the glove box. Not wanting to take a pill dry, I recalled a snack bar I'd seen on my way through campus. I went there and bought a pink lemonade drink. If the girl at the order counter noticed my blotches, her expression didn't acknowledge it.

I found a seat at the end row of tables. A row of pine trees bordered the tables. They blocked the sunlight, making table umbrellas redundant at that hour. The scent from the pines mixed with the food smells. The dark green of the pines helped me to calm down. I took out the pill bottle from my pocket and tapped out two into my palm and swallowed them with the lemonade. It was sweeter than what I made at home. I was in no hurry to go anywhere, so I sat and nursed the soft drink.

Two girls were sitting a few tables over. Watching them laughing and talking, seemingly without a care in the world, reminded me of

Mysti and myself. How my problems of yesterday seemed so trivial now. Now I didn't know who or what I was; things whereas I'd never questioned before.

My cautious self told me to just let the hybrid question go, move on and forget what I couldn't change, but my curiosity wouldn't let it. I tried not to think about genetics or Garrett, but both kept swirling in my mind. What did anything mean anymore? My future felt like a step into a dark pit whichever way I turned.

One of the two girls left their table. The remaining one opened a book. Where she sat, the sunlight through a gap in the branches reflected off of a window and bounced back across the patio. The reflection had been striking her umbrella, but as the sun rose, it was creeping down. When it reached her head, she got up. I thought she was going to leave too, but instead she shifted to the other side of the table out of the light. Where she sat now, I could see her face. She looked enough like me to be related, which gave me an idea. When she left, I could fish her cup out of the trash and give it to Wayne, telling him it was mine, and give my sample to him, saying it was "my cousin's". All I had to do was wait until she left.

That was easier said than done. She was engrossed in her book. I wondered if she'd ever finish her drink and leave. While I waited, I toyed with my empty cup and punched a hole in the bottom with my thumb. When she finished her drink, she took off the lid and straw and emptied the remaining ice in her mouth. Then she recapped it, moved it to the side and returned to her reading. Every so often, her hand would reach over and shake the cup, as if to check if it were still empty. After several more pages, she picked up the cup and noisily sucked air through the straw. She looked up and caught me staring. She gave an embarrassed smile, evidently assuming I was looking at her because of her slurping. I took her eye contact as my opportunity. I got up and went to her table.

"What are you studying?" I asked.

"Nothing for school. Thank goodness the quarter is over."

She lifted up the book to show me the title, *Half Past Human*. At that moment the universe seemed to be telling me something, as if it had led me to her. I caught myself as my mouth dropped open and my eyes widened to saucers.

"What's it about?" I asked to cover my amazement at the coincidence.

"It's New Wave, an old science fiction novel set way in the future. Earth is mostly populated by hive humanoids. The few actual humans that are left are being hunted."

"Sounds interesting."

"You don't sound convincing. I bet you don't read SF."

"I think I had to read one in high school," I said.

"You're missing out."

"Real life is crazy enough."

"Sure is. SF is better."

I shrugged, and said, "What are you drinking?"

"Just a coke."

"I'm going to get a refill. Would you like me to get you one too?"

"They don't give free refills, you know."

I knew that. I'd seen the sign at the order window.

"Oh, they don't?" I asked innocently. "Okay, I can throw that away for you if you want."

"Gee, thanks," she said, and handed me the prize.

Her eyes dropped toward the book again, so I probably didn't need to pretend to dump the cups in the trash can when I walked by it.

I returned to Pinsky's office. Wayne wasn't there. One of the interior office doors opened and a professor stuck her head out. When she learned I wasn't there to see her, she closed her door. The books and papers Wayne had been carrying were still on the desk. I thumbed the papers and saw they were exams. I guessed he hadn't left. Since he'd mentioned having been in the basement, I headed there.

Going down the basement stairs, I smelled the pickle odor, but it didn't become stronger as I descended and disappeared altogether when I reached the basement, as if it had been only trapped in the stairwell.

The basement laboratory was filled with long tables and equipment. Most of the tables had beakers, burners, and ovens on them, looking to me more like they were used for chemistry than biology. Covering the bench against the far wall were various kinds of sophisticated looking equipment. I had no idea as to their functions. The only person in the room was Wayne. He was seated in one of the stools at the far bench with his back toward me.

"So, this is where you mad scientists perform your evil experiments? I expected cages with captive animals."

He turned and saw me. "Nah, we play with the small stuff, microbiology. We don't get our hands dirty here."

"I have something for you," I said.

"You are a curious one," he said as I went over to him. "Running off without a word and returning with a smile." He looked at the cups. "You brought a peace offering. How'd you know I'm thirsty?"

"They're empty. I misled you before. I know a little bit about DNA testing. I saw my cousin this morning and already had saved the cup she used, and mine too."

His grin returned. "I think I love you."

He reached for them. I pulled them back. He looked like a dog that had a treat pulled out of reach. I wondered if he'd start drooling.

"You have to promise me that if she tests positive for bonobo genes, you won't go searching for her if she wants to be anonymous. I'm very emotional because I feel I'm being dishonest with her. I don't want her being pulled into something that could turn her life upside down.

"Okay, I promise. Which one is hers?"

"The one with the hole punched in the bottom."

Chapter 54

Driving home, I looked at everything with the view of an outsider. Feeling lost, not knowing who—or *what*—I was, where I belonged, seemed to be becoming my new normal. Being human is something I'd never questioned. Now maybe that was only part of my story.

If I did indeed test positive, how would I view myself? What would be my place in the world? Would I even *have* a place?

The test results from the little paper cup would either help me feel better, or push me into insanity, further over the edge of reality. Either way, I had to know.

Thinking about those things made it easier not to think about Garrett. But again, my connection to him was something I was once so sure of, an immutable path to the future that had now been washed away like a road in a flood. Was there anything in which I could believe? Was there anything I believed that would not suddenly, like an earthquake, surprise me and crumble beneath me?

It is not advisable to drive while thinking such thoughts. Somehow, the autopilot in my mind made it up the highway without incident, until I was crossing from Malibu into Yitha where the road curves. The red BMW convertible in front of me stopped suddenly. With my conscious mind far away, it took me a fraction of a second longer to react. I hit the brakes hard. My tires squealed in protest, screeching as they skidded. I began fishtailing, heading broadside into the rear of the BMW. My eyes opened wide in terror. Just before I collided, the BMW moved forward half a car length. I stopped inches from its bumper. Miraculously, I'd not smashed into it, or one of the parked cars beside me. I sat there panting as if I'd run up a hill. There was no room to pull over to the side. When the BMW moved forward again, I had to back up in order to straighten out and stay in my lane. In the next block, I pulled into the service station to get gas and collect myself.

When I arrived home, I paused in the driveway, looking up at my home, its timeless presence, and questioned whether it was a solid as I always assumed. Was it even real? A place where I belonged? Afterall, it was on the edge of a cliff. Would it suddenly rise into the clouds and no longer be there? Would the earth collapse and tumble it into the sea while I slept in its embrace? Would I find myself in the ocean, unstable, ever moving? Maybe the ocean, a place of constant motion, was where I belonged.

As I stepped onto the driveway, Wolfears bounded from the side of the house and greeted me, banging against my side with joy as I went to the front door. He felt solid in my liquid world.

The game I'd played with Garrett, of who would call first, now felt more senseless than ever. It was no longer a game. It had become a fear of confronting the reality of him—of us.

I spent much of the day on the couch, not even bothering to turn on the TV. He called several times. I didn't answer the phone. It felt as if by speaking with him, an emptiness would open between us, and I might fall endlessly. Yet, I wanted to get it over with, whatever *it* was. And who was I, anyway? *What* was I?

I couldn't see a path forward for us. The betrayal was too great. But how something ends matters. As the hours passed, I began feeling more sorrow for him, trapped in a world of deceitfulness with his nature and the desire to please his mother. Yet, my sympathy vacillated with anger and could abruptly shift. One moment I wanted to console him. The next, I wanted to scream and flail at him.

I sank into depression and forced myself to go outside and sit in my half-moon sanctuary. The ocean stretched endlessly. Its relentless heartbeat smashed itself upon the rocks. Life didn't crawl from the sea. It was hurled from it, slapped naked and vulnerable into a new world. The sinking sun had been witness to the emergence of life. I was a momentary grain of sand. Thinking of things beyond myself helped me to relax a bit.

When the phone rang again, I went inside and picked it up. It was Garrett.

"There you are. Where have you been?"

"I've been here, thinking."

"Thank goodness, are you okay?"

"Why wouldn't I be?" I said, my voice flat, not my voice, someone else's.

"I don't know. We never fight. I thought you were still upset. When I saw Kathy, she said you were looking for me at the prayer group."

"I was."

"I wasn't there."

"I know."

"I got there late. I must have just missed you."

"Late, huh? I saw your car in the parking lot."

"Oh, we must have just missed each other."

"Un huh."

"Anyway, I'm sorry. I hate admitting it, but I was insensitive. Can I come over?"

I didn't answer.

"Please? We need to go over plans for the wedding."

Sounding surprisingly calm, I said, "There's not going to be a wedding." I added with a needless barb, "I'm sure your mother will be disappointed."

"So, we had a fight. Couples fight. It's normal. Everything will be okay. We just need to talk about it."

"No, we don't."

"Are you jealous about Kathy again? We're just friends. You're welcome to come to the prayer meeting, you know that. There's nothing going on between us. How many times do I have to tell you that?"

"I believe you. I'm not jealous of her. I've just realized we're not right for each other."

"What do you mean? Of course we are."

Again, I didn't answer.

"What are you so upset about?"

"You lied to me."

"What? When?"

"It's over between us. Let's just leave it at that. I need to move on."

After a long pause, in a quiet voice, he said, "Are you breaking up with me over the phone?"

"Yes, I am," I said.

I hung up, feeling I was a horrible person, but I couldn't face him.

Chapter 55

I stood there feeling guilty, expecting him to call back. When he didn't, I wandered around the house in a daze. I ended up in my parent's bedroom, where I'd not been since the accident. The room was dominated by my mother's belongings. Looking at her things made it feel as if she wasn't really gone and might appear at any moment. There was scant evidence that my father shared the bedroom with her. I opened his closet—his row of suits, shirts and pants were nearly all identical. In his quest for efficiency, he'd eliminated the daily decision of what to wear.

I drifted into the en suite bathroom where there was more evidence of my father. In the corner of the counter were his hair tonics and other personal items. The rest of the sink counter was taken up with my mother's stuff. In the medicine cabinet, she had enough pill bottles to open a pharmacy. I turned them all so the labels faced outwards. None of them offered a solution to my problems. I sat at her makeup vanity and looked at myself in the three-paneled mirror. My hair clung to my cheeks. My face wore a sad expression. Since my parents' death, I looked ten years older.

I opened the vanity drawers. One of them was filled with bottles of nail polish, shades of every color. Resisting the temptation to organize them, I scooped up a group of bottles and took them over to the bed. I sat on it and sunk in. The mattress was softer than mine.

I started painting my toenails, each with a different color. I had just finished painting my left foot's baby toe a dark blue color, named *Midnight Love*, when the phone next to the bed rang.

It rang only once.

I resumed painting my toes. When I reached the fourth toe on my other foot, I choose a shade of polish called *Popcorn Lemon*. The phone rang again, six rings before the answering machine picked up downstairs. I knew it had to be Garrett. As much as I didn't want to talk to him, I couldn't help but be curious as to his message, my guilt gnawing at me. Maybe I would break down and call him back.

I forced myself to finish applying the yellow polish before capping the bottle. I got up and walked duck-like on my heels. Wolfears watched my odd stepping down the stairs with his head tilted, no doubt wondering what was wrong with me.

The light on the answering machine wasn't blinking. He'd not left a message. I wished I'd painted my last toenail.

I turned around to head back upstairs when the phone rang again. When the answering machine began recording, it wasn't Garrett's voice on the line.

My hand shook and I almost dropped the phone when I picked it up. I pressed it against my ear and forced myself to take in a breath before interrupting Wayne's message.

"I didn't expect you to have the tests results this soon."

"No, of course not. I'm a scientist, not a sorcerer. I wanted to give you an update."

"Oh, okay."

"When I called Pinsky and told him about the samples, he was so excited that he rushed right over to school."

"On a Saturday? Wow, he is obsessed."

"Yeah, obsessed or maybe crazy. I won't argue with you on either of those. When he got here, he wanted to get to work right away. He let me help with the preparation and extraction. Then, he told me he was going to run the tests alone, undisturbed. He kicked me out and locked himself in the laboratory. See? Crazy."

"So, what happens now? When will you know anything?"

"I'm going to go to my place and get some sleep. I'll head back over in the morning. If he works all night, he should have some CE tests done by morning."

"The what?"

"CE. Capillary electrophoresis."

"I'm supposed to know what that is?"

"Oh, sorry, I forget you're not one of us. It detects genetic variation. Do you want to be at the lab with me when I learn the results?"

"Can you call me as soon as you know anything?"

"That's why I called you now. If he gets positive results, he'll probably have lots for me to do, so I don't know when I'll get a chance to call you. He might even hold a press conference."

"I'm sure you can sneak a phone call to me."

"I can't promise. It could be history in the making. You're part of it because of your father. Are you sure you don't want to be there?"

"Not really."

"Okay," he said, sounding disappointed.

"Besides, I don't feel like driving, and I don't feel comfortable with the protestors."

"I can pick you up. If you come with me and they're around, I can sneak us in through a back door. You won't even see them."

"There's a secret entrance to the building?"

"There actually is. It goes directly to the basement."

"Oh," I said,

"Just think," he said, almost pleading. "It wouldn't have been possible without your help getting the sample for us."

I thought about it. The alternative was moping around the house. I was tired of waiting for phone calls. At least it would get me out.

"Okay, I guess I could come," I said.

"That's great. I'll pick you up in the morning."

"No, I'll drive myself," I told him.

"Okay, meet me by the Chartres Labyrinth. Do you know where that is?

"I'm sure I can find it," I said.

The conversation felt normal. Weird, huh?

When I hung up, I went back upstairs. I couldn't decide on a color for my baby toe, so I put the polish bottles back in the drawer and left it unpainted. I sat on the bed staring into space until Wolfears joined me. He rested his chin across my knee to remind me that I'd forgotten his evening meal.

I went to the kitchen to feed him and unenthusiastically had a little food for myself too. The phone rang again, and I jumped. It turned out to be Mysti. She planned to drop by on Monday morning for us to get together one last time before she flew to Europe.

The rhythm of the waves nuzzling the rocks were whispers of my conscience.

Breaking up with Garrett over the phone was wrong. He deserved more than that. Yet, I couldn't bear the thought of seeing him. I got up and closed the glass door to muffle the sound of the ocean.

I couldn't sleep. I looked at the clock—it was eleven-thirty.

Wolfears raised his head, stretched his legs and stood. He knew we were going out before I did. I threw on some clothes and my flip-flops. Before I reached the door, I went back to get the basketball pendant. I started to put it in my pocket, but instead hung the chain around my neck. I needed to hurry to get there before Garrett's shift ended.

Chapter 56

I reached Atta Patta's Pizza a few minutes before midnight. The Chugger wasn't in the parking lot. The first "A" in "Atta" was flickering as if it would die soon, the sign's green light casting a sickly pallor on the parking lot, not helping my trepidation.

I saw two employees inside. One pushed a broom, the other was behind the counter looking bored. I went inside.

"Has Garrett left for the night?" I asked the broom pusher.

The guy gave me a blank stare. Maybe he didn't speak English. He tilted his chin toward the guy at the counter.

"Yeah, you missed him," the counter guy told me.

I decided to see if he was home. In all the time we'd been together, I'd only been there once, and had never gone inside. We'd driven back to get a forgotten pair of shoes for a game once, and I'd waited in the car while he retrieved them.

Garrett lived with his mother near Windmere Cliffs, an unstable section of the coast. Unlike most of the khaki cliffs, with occasional landslides from rain saturation, the deep red slabs of Windmere fell without warning in sheets of lethal rock . The mobile home park beneath them had been condemned and only a vineyard was nestled there now. Garrett's house was in a tract of older homes to the north. His house was in the cul-de-sac at the far end. The only egress was a narrow road that ran through the vineyard. More than once, rockfalls had blocked the road. As I drove through the vineyard, part of me wished the cliff would crash upon me so I wouldn't have to face Garrett and all my other troubles.

The Chugger was parked in his driveway. Television light danced on the living room curtains of his house. I parked across the street and left Wolfears in the car. The neighborhood was still, with most of the houses dark. It would have been quiet if not for the traffic hum from the highway, but the sound was dampened by the strips of fog rolling in. Headlights illuminating the bands of fog made them look like fingers reaching out above me. As I hurried across the street, moist, salty air filled my lungs. I tried not to hyperventilate. Somehow, my legs carried me to his front door.

I'd hoped his mother was asleep, but when I knocked she shouted over the voices from the television, "Garebear, somebody's at the door."

The television sound muted. Moments later, the door pulled open with a whoosh. Garrett had a scowl on his face, the kind he had after his team lost a game. When he realized it was me, his face sprang into an unsteady smile.

His eyes quivered.

For a moment, my heart started to flutter. He bent to kiss me and I turned so that his kiss landed on my cheek. He wrapped his arms around me and lifted me off the ground. My heart beat faster. It learns more slowly than my brain. I steeled myself.

"Put me down," I said in a toneless voice.

As he lowered me, his mother called out, "Garebear, who is it?"

"It's Prima."

"Oh, my," his mother said. "I wasn't expecting her. The house is a mess."

His brow knitted when he looked into my eyes.

To avoid them, I called out, "Hello, Mrs. Deacon."

"How many times do I have to tell you to call me Mom, or at least Betty? she chided.

"Please come outside," I whispered to Garrett.

Before he answered, his mother said, "Why didn't you tell me she was coming? If I'd known, we could have picked her up."

"I'm going to step out for a few minutes with Prima," he called to her.

"I won't hear of it. I'll survive if she sees the house a bit untidy. Come inside or you'll likely both catch a chill. I'm sure she's seen a mess before."

Garrett shrugged and told me, "We can go in my room."

The idea felt claustrophobic, but I followed him.

His mother had not exaggerated. The living room looked like a rummage sale. She sat sunken in the corner of a gray and black striped couch across from the television. The rest of the couch was covered with newspapers and magazines. A smile was plastered on her face. Her head swiveled with her eyes as she watched us weave through the clutter to his room.

The volume of the TV went back up. Over it, his mother yelled, "Keep the door open. No hanky-panky until you're wed."

Garrett rolled his eyes and closed the bedroom door behind us.

In contrast to the living room, his room was sparse and neat. A mattress rested on the floor in the corner, covered with a plum-colored sheet. A small desk was beneath the window and the desk lamp was the only illumination in the room. Two posters were neatly taped to the wall, one of a basketball player, the other a chart of the stock market. Its tidiness shouldn't have surprised me.

Garrett glanced around his room as if searching for something. His eyes came to rest on the desk chair. He motioned for me to sit there and sat on the mattress. Sitting below me, he was still almost at my eye level. I still couldn't look at him. He cleared his throat.

"Thank you for coming."

"You left work early. Are you sick?"

He thumped his hand on his chest over his heart. He wasn't making this any easier. I didn't know what to say or how to begin. All the words I'd rehearsed on the way over were now forgotten. He spoke first.

"Why? Why are you breaking up with me?"

I looked at the floor.

"Is it Wayne?"

I shook my head.

"Is it Mysti? Did she tell you? I admit I hit on her. It was just for show. The guys were egging me on, you know? I didn't want to look like I wasn't one of the gang. Nothing happened. It wouldn't have. She's not my type."

"I believe you, I don't doubt that," I said, and briefly lifted my eyes to his face, and saw he was staring at his hands.

"I know," he said. "You must have cold feet about the wedding. I know how you hate being the center of attention. You should have said something. I didn't realize how much it must have upset you. It's not that important. It was for my mother. She didn't get to have a big wedding. In fact, they got married at city hall because she was pregnant with my brother. We can scale it down. I'll talk to her. She'll understand." When I didn't say anything, he added, "We can elope to Vegas. We can leave tonight and be there in five or six hours."

"We're not getting married," I said.

My eyes drifted to my feet and I stared at my multi-colored toenails.

Chapter 57

"Why did you come over if you're not going to say anything?"

I could tell he was getting frustrated, because his speech was becoming choppy. I knew him so well, and I didn't know him at all. I needed to say something. The truth was too hard. His secret was sacred to him, or he'd have shared it. I wanted to take the easy path. I looked into his eyes.

"I've been thinking a lot lately. We're just too different for it to work. I'm introverted, you love being around people. It just won't work. It was great, but we both need to move on."

"Lots of married people are different. It makes a team. We complement each other."

"No, we're too different."

"What do you mean? We aren't. In what way?"

"You love sports. I don't."

"What do you mean? You surf."

"That's not a sport for me. It's not competitive. It's the joy being in the water. There is no winning and losing. I'm soul surfer."

"You were on the swim and dive teams in high school."

"Yeah, only because I'm naturally athletic. The coach was always after me, saying I was lazy. He wanted me to train harder to break the school record in the one hundred free. I just didn't care."

"You come to my games. You enjoy basketball."

"I only go because you're there. You're ambitious." *Like my father*, I wanted to add, but didn't. "I can barely figure out what I want to do from day to day."

"Those things are minor. They don't matter."

He looked up and gave me a closed-lipped smile. He knew me as well as I knew him. I couldn't circumvent the truth.

"You're not being true to yourself," I said slowly.

"What do you mean? Of course I am."

"The other day when you mother told me you were at Bible study
... I went looking for you. You weren't there."

He paused, looking thoughtful, maybe a bit perplexed.

"Right, I went to see Pastor Andrew, for guidance on our
marriage, actually, because I know you've been having a tough time.
And about our fight at the zoo."

He sounded so self-righteous. It made me want to hurt him.

"The Chugger was in the parking lot. I looked everywhere. I
rang the pastor's doorbell. Nobody answered, but a car was in the
driveway. The only place left that I could think of was in Pastor
Andrew's backyard. I went around the side of the house, and . . ."

It took a moment. In a falsetto voice, he said, "Oh my God, you
know." He sucked in deep breaths, then said, "I was so upset about
our fight. I don't know what happened. It was a one-time thing."

I didn't believe him. My anger bubbled to the surface. I looked at
him incredulously.

I spit my words at him. "Don't lie to me. I've heard enough lies
for a lifetime. Each one rips out a piece of my soul."

I didn't need to say any more. His expression looked horrified
and wretched. My anger left me as I watched his control disappear.
My pity must have shone because he put his face in his hands. He
broke down and gasped air in choked breaths.

"Yes, it's happened before," he said, almost too softly to be heard.

His confession had tones of relief in it. I reached out to touch
him. He recoiled, threw his arms over his head and flung himself
backwards onto the bed. He twisted over and buried his face in
the sheets, his big, long body shaking like a child whose world had
shattered.

I was afraid to touch him. I didn't want to leave him like that;
I *couldn't* leave him like that. Eventually, his body stilled. He rolled
back over and sat up. He started talking—to me or himself, I
couldn't tell.

"I wanted to tell you, but for my mother. As you know, she has her beliefs. It would be too much for her to bear. My dad left, my brothers left—we don't know where they are. I know she can be hard to live with, but I can't disappoint her too. I just can't."

We talked, or should I say *he* talked and I listened, for maybe an hour. I felt his pain, but I couldn't take on any more. I didn't know if I could manage all that I had already. When he was calm, and I knew he would be okay, I stood.

"Your secret is safe with me."

"I know it is," he said. "I didn't mean to hurt you."

We hugged and I felt the basketball pendant pressing against my breast bone. When we released, I lifted the necklace over my head and held it out to him.

"I'm sorry I can't give you the engagement ring back. Though I do have something for you. I meant to give it to you days ago."

"I can't accept that."

I didn't ask him why. Maybe he thought it was charity.

When I left, the television was turned off, but the lamp was still on beside the couch. The back of his mother's head was resting on the top of the cushion, and I thought she was staring at the ceiling. I was about to say goodbye when I realized she was asleep.

Outside, the fog had become a heavy mist. Wolfears let out a yip when he saw me. When I opened the door, he jumped out. He found a bush, lifted his leg, and let out a long stream. When he was finished, we sat in my car.

I felt drained.

Turning on the engine seemed like it would take more energy than I possessed. I didn't know anything about breakups, but it seemed like a weird one to me. Maybe all breakups were weird. I was tired of losing things, but sometimes there is no turning back.

As the mist swirled around us, it felt like a dream. I wanted the past month to have been a dream. I wanted to wake up from it.

Wolfears spotted a cat creeping along the edge of Garrett's driveway and became restless. I turned the key and started home.

No red rocks fell on us from the Windmere cliffs when I drove beneath them. I took it as a sign of a better future.

Chapter 58

On Sunday morning, the Cummings campus was nearly deserted. No one was at the labyrinth. I followed the pink concrete path to the labyrinth's center. As I was making my way back out, Wayne arrived and called out hello, startling me and breaking my meditative state. I quickened my pace, but still followed the path back to the beginning. Somehow it felt disrespectful not to take the designated trail and cut across.

As we were walking to the biology building, Wayne asked, "I don't mean to pry, but is everything okay now with your fiancé?"

"Yes, it's been resolved," I said, and faked a smile.

He led me to a row a cypresses at the back of the biology building. We slipped through them, over the dirt, which had a set of footprints leading out. We came to an unmarked door—the secret entrance. Wayne had a key that unlocked it. I expected the hinges to squeak, but it must have been well oiled because the door glided open easily.

Wayne reached inside and brought out an old broom, which he used to erase our footprints. He switched on a light that illuminated stairs leading down. We stepped inside. It was narrow with rough, concrete steps, certainly not constructed to smuggle anything large in or out of the building. We followed the steps down through the stale air until we reached a door at the bottom. Wayne flipped another light switch. For a moment, we were encased in darkness. The cool air seemed colder. Then, he opened the door and we stepped out beside the double doors of the laboratory. Taped on one of them was a piece of paper. In large, black ink, it read: *Closed until Monday*.

Wayne rapped on the doors three times. It echoed. He knocked again.

From inside, a voice called out. "Go away. Can't you read?" I recognized Pinsky's voice.

"It's me, Wayne."

"I don't need you right now. Come back in an hour."

Wayne looked at me and shrugged. "I guess we'll need to hang. I'm thirsty. Want to go grab something while we wait?"

We went up the inside stairs to the first floor. I was glad to avoid using the creepy secret passage. Wayne stopped at the vending machine and couldn't decide what to get. Then, he suggested that, rather than hanging around and waiting in the biology building, we could go to the snack bar. I liked the idea of getting outdoors. Since he was unconcerned about being seen leaving the building, we went out the front doors.

There were no protestors milling about, only a lone security guard looking bored. The only evidence of the protestors was a discarded sign on the lawn that read, '*Stop abominations. Only humans are made in the image of God.*'

Wayne kicked it when we went by. Then stopped, went back and picked it up, and stuffed it into a trash can. We cut across the grass to the main walkway. It felt good not being closed within the walls of the building and having the sky, glorious and endless, above me.

"As a thank you for your help, I'll buy you whatever you want," Wayne said.

I gave him a suspicious look. "I'm not telling you where my cousin is, or anything about her, if that's what you're after."

"No, I gave you my word, I'll not reveal her without her consent."

I nodded. "That's good."

"So, you'll let me buy? You realize that on my TA's salary, letting go of pennies is a big deal. You should be flattered."

I didn't answer him.

The campus was quiet as we walked. Our footsteps on the concrete sounded intrusive. I edged over and walked on the grass.

He followed beside me and our feet brushed through the grass that was due for a mowing. He obviously liked me. I had to admit his attention was validating, but I didn't want to lead him on.

I broke the silence between us saying, "You can buy my drink to make up for being obnoxious when we met. Just friends, right?"

"Yes, of course, no need for your boyfriend, I mean your fiancé, to get jealous."

"You don't need to worry about that," I said.

He gave me a curious look with his eyebrows raised, but didn't pursue it.

The snack bar was open, but it wasn't doing much business. I stepped up to the counter first.

"What would you like?" the woman asked.

I was about to order a lemonade, then caught myself and ordered a coke. Wayne ordered a coke and a grilled cheese. We sat at the same table at the end as I had when I was there the last time.

The shadows stretched as before. I had a hard time not grimacing when I sipped the coke. I couldn't understand why they were so popular—not only did I find the taste unpleasant, but the prickly feeling the bubbles made in my mouth was annoying.

We didn't seem to have anything to say, so I asked, "Did you ever find out about who those military or CIA guys were that visited the office?"

"Yes, boy was I way off base. It turns out they were auditors. Pinsky had gone over budget on one of his grants."

"Oh." I took another sip of my coke, pretending I enjoyed it.

At that moment, someone behind me called out, "Hi, Wayne."

I turned around and saw the girl who'd worn the white shorts when I'd first gone to Pinsky's office. Now, she was wearing tight jeans and a pink crop top. She tossed her hair. There was a big smile on her face.

Chapter 59

"Hi, Candy," Wayne said. "What are you doing here on a Sunday?"

"I'm taking a break from the library. I've still got one paper to turn in for my anthropology class. What are you doing here? Hanging out with your girlfriend?"

"We're just friends," I protested.

She gave me a quick glance and returned her eyes and smile to Wayne. "Do you think you could tutor me? I'm taking another of Professor Pinsky's classes this summer."

"Yeah, maybe, I don't know. He keeps me pretty busy. I have to clear any extracurricular activities with him."

She laughed as if Wayne had said something funny. "That must cramp your style."

"Yeah, well, in some things, but not everything."

Candy tossed her hair again. "That's good."

Wayne introduced me to her and she asked if I was a biology major. Wayne answered for me.

"Not yet. I'm trying to recruit her. Her dad went to school here. She's been a big help with some research that her father did."

"Oh," Candy said. "What research?"

For the first time, she did more than glance at me. Her look was intense, so much so that the full gaze of her attention made me feel uncomfortable.

I said, "He was a doctor in reproductive medicine. He collaborated with Professor Pinsky on some experiments."

"Yeah," Wayne added. "He coauthored papers with Pinsky. He gave a guest lecture last semester, too."

"Was he the one who worked on the chimera experiments? Was it those?"

I shrugged. Wayne nodded yes.

"How fascinating," she said, and gave another smile to Wayne.

She turned back to me and her smile faded a few degrees. "So, what's your major?" she asked.

"Earth and Environmental," I said. "For now, anyway."

"Wow, science is hard for me," Candy said. "Just one more bio class and I'm done with them."

I was about to ask her what her major was when Wayne asked her to join us.

"Okay, but I'm meeting a friend. I'll grab something and hang with you guys until he gets here. Do you want anything?"

We shook our heads and she left us. Wayne had a confused expression on his face.

He lowered his voice and said, "Do you think she likes me?"

"Duh."

"Yeah, it's weird. It's like she's chasing me. I'm not used to that. It feels backwards."

"It must be flattering," I said.

"I'm not complaining, it's just surprising, that's all. The way she looks, she doesn't have to work that hard."

"Why are you surprised? You seem to think pretty highly of yourself."

"It's mostly an act," he said. "Besides, she's not my type."

"Oh, really? What about when she's wearing white shorts? I saw you checking out her legs the other day."

"Yeah, I have to admit she has nice legs." He shrugged his shoulders. He smiled and leaned slightly toward me. "So, you said that you and I are friends. That's better than just someone who annoys you. I'm making progress."

"I was being polite. We're on friendly terms. Besides there's many levels of friendship."

"Yeah, it's one of those ambiguous words. No scientific rigor to it."

"Some words are intentionally ambiguous," I said. "They're like song lyrics that allow everyone to fill in their own experiences."

He glanced in the direction Candy had gone and I imagined he wished she were wearing her white shorts again.

When he looked back at me, I asked him, "So, what *is* your type?"

I felt stupid the minute I asked it because it sounded as if I were flirting. *Was* I flirting, or simply making conversation? It was only a day after my breakup with Garrett. I felt guilty. Was I becoming like Mysti, who was like a hummingbird going flower to flower. No, I didn't have any feelings for Wayne, but it was nice to have his attention.

"Yeah, she's cute, but she doesn't compare to you. Too bad you're engaged."

My guilty feelings were washed away with embarrassment. I looked away from him, up at the pine trees, which had suddenly become very interesting. I thought about Garrett and wondered if he was in church right now.

I must have stared at the trees for a long time because Wayne said, "Did I say something to upset you? I didn't mean anything."

As I took my eyes from the pine trees, Candy reappeared holding a plate with brownies. She set it down in front of us.

Wayne looked from her to me as if waiting for my approval.

"Wow, thanks, what are these for?" I asked.

"They just baked them. I thought you might like some while they're hot and fresh."

"That's really nice of you," I said.

"Now you definitely have to join us," Wayne said.

"My friend just got here. Maybe another time. Enjoy."

She skipped away. Her smile hovered in the air. I shouldn't be so judgmental, I told myself.

Wayne stuffed half his brownie in his mouth. When he swallowed it, he took a sip of his coke.

I made a face and said, "How can you drink a coke with a brownie? Sugar overload." Wanting to get the taste of the coke out of my mouth, I said, "I'm going to get a water. Do you want one?"

"No, thanks," he said.

When I got up, I saw Candy hugging a bearded man wearing a gray beanie. He looked familiar, but I couldn't place him. Maybe he was one of the protestors. Their hug looked more friendly than amorous. When I went back to the table, the rest of Wayne's brownie had disappeared, and I caught him eyeing mine. I pushed the plate in front of him.

"You don't want it?"

"Not really. It's too early for me. I had a late breakfast."

"Are you sure. Didn't you get your water to have with the brownie?"

"Yeah, but I don't really want it now."

He snatched the brownie. We sat without speaking while he ate it. Fortunately, when he resumed our conversation, he dropped the discussion of his type.

"I meant what I said about you being a tremendous help. If you hadn't brought your cousin's sample, we wouldn't have a chance at the proof we need."

"That was simple enough," I said.

"Just think, your cousin could become part of history. How incredible is that?"

"It's not like she had any choice in the matter."

"That's true. Still, fate may have landed upon her. The sister goddesses of the Greeks still live on."

I didn't know what he meant, but tried to look as if I did. I took a sip of water to avoid commenting.

He sucked on the straw of his empty cup. It reminded me of the girl whose cup I'd taken.

Wayne stood and said, "I better get back to the lab before Pinsky misses me. I'm going to grab another coke first. Do you want anything?"

I shook my head. "I'm not that thirsty. You can have the rest of mine if you want."

"Oh, thanks. Like I said, a penny saved is a good thing on a TA salary."

I pushed my coke across to him. When he took it, he lifted my cup up and down, as if weighing its contents. I assumed he'd replace my straw with his. Instead, he threw his cup in the trash. I watched for him to take a sip from my straw. He didn't.

"You sure you don't want something? You hardly drank any of your coke."

My mouth suddenly felt dry. "No, I'm not thirsty."

"Maybe a lemonade?"

He was playing with me. He knew my DNA was on the straw. I didn't like being the mouse.

Chapter 60

On our walk back to the biology building, I kept watching the cup out of my peripheral vision. He never took a drink.

Put your lips on the straw. Take a drink, I wanted to scream.

I considered asking for a sip, spilling the cup, and throwing it in the trash. Knowing his dogged determination, he would have fished it out or come to my house to rummage through my trash to find a sample of my DNA. So, I walked beside him like a dog on a leash being taken to the vet.

There were a few students hanging out in front of the biology building. As we approached the front steps, they glanced at us with mild curiosity and then ignored us. If they were gathering to protest, they were the leaderless first arrivals.

"We can sneak you out the back when we leave if more of them show up," Wayne said.

A pigeon was flying back and forth in the hallway. I paused at the entrance and held a door open for it.

Wayne asked, "What are you doing?"

"I'm giving the bird an escape route. Try and scare it this way."

The bird avoided his waving arms. Instead of flying to the door, the bird flew to the vending machine and landed on top of it. I tried to prop open one of the doors, but they were self-closing, no doubt for energy efficiency in the newer building.

When we walked by the pigeon, I smiled at it. It was just a common gray pigeon with a splash of iridescent green on its neck ruff. There was nothing remarkable in its appearance. From its perch, it appraised me with one black eye, an eye that could have been nothing more than a fruit seed or a shiny drop of licorice.

"Stupid bird," Wayne said.

"It's scared."

"That's evolution in action. If it can't adapt to the changing environment, poof, extinction. Come on, let's find the professor."

We descended the stairs and found the laboratory doors were open. The laboratory counter tops stretched uniformly across the room, unlike the sea where nothing is a straight line, except the horizon whose straight line is an illusion.

Professor Pinsky was sitting on a stool at the benches where Wayne had been. When he heard us, he spun around and stood. He crossed to us. The grin on his face told me the answer before he spoke.

"We did it. B9 was a success," he said. "We created a hybrid, or, according to the protestors, something unhuman, a freak. The luddites."

I thought I'd prepared myself for the news that confirmed my fear, but I was wrong. I felt a sense of other worldliness, as if what was happening was somewhere else or it wasn't real. Before us stretched long tables with beakers and machines that might have been in another universe. I felt claustrophobic and my breathing became staccato and shallow.

As if far away, I heard Wayne exclaim, "You did it! You opened the door into the future."

"Yes, I did," Pinsky said, his voice loud as if speaking to an audience of hundreds. He handed at steel binder to Wayne, who took it with his free hand. "Lock my notes in my office and clean up this mess. Then, take the day off. I'm going home to sleep. I hope those damn protestors aren't out front."

Wayne said, "There are a few milling about. Maybe they're taking the day off too. You could use the back exit so they won't see you leaving."

"I'm not changing my routine to suit them," Pinsky said. "Filthy gnats." He reached out a hand, extending a key to Wayne. Then, he drew it back. "I've locked up the sample, so no need to lock up the lab."

He ripped down the closed sign, wadded the paper into a ball and handed it to Wayne. Wayne slipped the binder under his arm to free his hand for the paper.

I heard footsteps, soft almost dainty, coming down the stairs behind us. I wanted to turn around to see who it was, but just then, Professor Pinsky turned his glowing, tired eyes to me.

"I'm sorry your father isn't here to share in our success. Don't you worry, I'll make sure he gets the recognition he deserves."

"So, what does this all mean?" I asked. "Is the hybrid half human, half bonobo?"

Professor Pinsky gave a condescending chuckle.

"No, the results show that only her mitochondria is genetically a bonobo's. It is mtDNA, genetic material passed only from the mother to children. We can trace all homo sapiens mtDNA back to a woman who lived two hundred thousand years back. We have replaced it with one from our relative, the bonobo, and created a hybrid that is in essence a new species."

I opened my mouth to ask a question, but I didn't know what to ask.

The professor said, "If I'd not been working all night, I'd explain how the bonobos and chimps have greater mitochondrial diversity than humans."

"It sounds like you've done something exciting," said a voice behind me.

I turned and saw Candy.

"Yes, we created something the world has never seen. We have created a woman with no maternal human lineage," said the professor. "You can read all about it when I publish my paper."

I couldn't take anymore and started toward the stairs, but Candy didn't move aside.

"Gosh," she said. "Is that your cousin? The one you and Wayne were talking about?"

She wasn't as slow as she pretended to be, and she evidently had big ears beneath her freshly combed hair.

Pinsky ignored her. For a moment, all the fatigue on his face disappeared as his eyes bored into mine.

"I need more samples for testing," he said to me. "Also, I want to see her. I imagine her appearance and facilities are human. Of course, she'll need to come forward at some point."

"That's her decision," I said.

"I'm sure she'll be well compensated," Pinsky said. "Wayne, I'm sure you can convince Prima of the necessity of revealing her cousin. See to it."

He headed up the stairs with Candy following.

I heard her asking him, "Professor, I'm fascinated by your work. Would it be okay if Wayne tutored me for a couple of hours each week?"

I didn't hear his answer.

I turned my attention to Wayne, and said, "You must have told Pinsky that I'm just putty in your hands."

"No, it's not like that," he said, avoiding my eyes.

I glared at him. "What did you tell him?"

"I might have said something about being able to get you to help us."

"I'm just another stupid girl to you, aren't I?"

I reached for the cup in his hand, and he drew it back.

Chapter 61

I left Wayne standing at the laboratory doors and ran up the stairs. Candy was standing at the top of the stairs. I ignored her. The corridor stretched before me, lifeless, gray floor and walls, all horizontal and vertical lines, straight edges, a mathematical dream in a universe of curves.

Professor Pinsky appeared at the far end of the hallway, returning in our direction. He must have forgotten something. Backlit by the light through the glass doors behind him, he appeared featureless. As he approached, he grew larger, as if he would expand until he became wedged between the walls. I stood staring in macabre fascination at his lumbering shape, out of place in the aseptic stillness and symmetry of the corridor. When he reached the center of the hallway, he transformed into his recognizable form when side-lit through the main entrance doors.

He spotted me and his coat tails flared as he marched toward me. I couldn't see his expression clearly, but he looked to be smiling. He didn't walk with the fatigue of a man who'd spent a sleepless night working.

He startled the pigeon, which took flight. As if the pigeon were attacking him, Pinsky raised and flailed his arms, which panicked the bird who flew erratically, bouncing off of the ceiling and banging into walls in a mad flutter of wings.

When Pinsky stopped in front of me, I saw that indeed there was a smile on his face, a grin. Candy stood a couple of steps behind me. She wasn't talking for once. Pinsky paid her no attention.

"Prima Otomo," he said and paused. I waited for him to continue. His eyes twitched as if watching a tennis match on fast forward as he scanned my face. "Tell me about your cousin?"

"What about her?"

"Is she normal? Can she walk? Can she talk?"

"Of course."

"Good, good. What color are her eyes?"

"Brown," I said.

"Light or dark?"

"Medium."

"Of course, like yours."

His eyes crawled over me. The smile frozen on his face. I noticed one of his eye teeth was crooked. There was a draft coming from the stairwell and I felt cold. His chest puffed out like a bird's feathers in cold weather when he said my name again.

"Prima, I would like to get a cheek swab from you to compare to your cousin's hybrid DNA. We can show you that you're not related all." When I shook my head, he said, "Oh, its painless and simple. You merely run a cotton swab over the inside of your cheek. It'll only take a moment."

"You already have my DNA on the second cup that Wayne gave you."

"Indulge me with a fresh sample. I'd like to run some additional tests."

"You can have *my* DNA," Candy said from behind me, startling me.

Pinsky ignored her and kept his eyes on me.

"Do you know what your name means?"

"It means the first," I said. "As it turns out, I was my parents first and only."

"It also means cousin in Spanish," Candy said.

Pinsky shifted his eyes to her, and his smile disappeared.

"Young lady, this conversation does not concern you."

With a huff, Candy moved past me and went down the hall with her hips swinging. She stopped in front of the vending machine, shifting back and forth as if trying to decide what to buy. The pigeon eyed her. Pinsky stared at her until she left through the front doors.

The pigeon remained on top of the vending machine and didn't take the opportunity to escape. Maybe it was an indoor pigeon.

"Prima," Pinsky said again.

I didn't like the sound of my name when he said it. He pursed his lips and looked thoughtful.

"Did you know your father had an admiration for bonobos? He said they were our noble cousins because they are less warlike than chimps and people. That doesn't serve them well in the reality of life on this planet. I prefer chimpanzees. Violent, standing their ground. I imagine bonobos would be extinct if they had not been isolated by the natural boundary of the Congo River. Your father, he could be sentimental. I never imagined how much. Have you ever seen a bonobo?"

"Yes, in the zoo."

"And your cousin, what is her name?"

I said, "Vickie." It was the first name that popped into my head.

"Appropriate." He smiled again. "I imagine your father named her."

I must have had a puzzled expression because, by way of explanation, he added, "Victory, for our achievement. Yes, he could be sentimental." His smile faded and his eyebrows knitted as he focused on my face. "Your parents named you Prima, the first. It also forms the first letters of primate."

He was playing with me. He was enjoying this. I felt like a net was closing slowly around me. With Wayne already having the new cup with my DNA, he didn't need my consent to prove that I was the match to the hybrid DNA, but Professor Pinsky didn't know that.

Yet.

I looked directly into his eyes. "Why don't you just come out and say what you're thinking?"

"Your father had amazing skills," he said, his tone shifting down. "We made a good team until your mother came along. Now I see it.

Even someone as meticulous as your father leaves clues. It was such an obvious clue, and I missed it until now."

His lips pursed, briefly. He looked angry with himself. I heard footsteps on the stairs behind me. I felt like everyone was sneaking up on me one way or another. It was Wayne with my coke cup still in his hand.

Pinsky said to him, "I was just telling Prima how nice it would be to get a sample of her DNA to run more tests and compare to her cousin's. Could you run back down to the lab and bring up a sample kit for her?"

Wayne gave me a fleeting look. I couldn't read his expression. Was he gloating? Perhaps looking at me with pity or detached amusement, as if looking at a laboratory monkey in a cage and wondering how the experiment would turn out.

"Oh, you brought my drink," I said and reached for it, expecting him to draw it away from me.

To my surprise he extended it toward me. I bumped against it, nearly knocking it from his hand. I closed my fingers around it and took it from him.

"I'll go get a kit," Wayne said.

"Maybe another time," I said, and slipped past Pinsky toward the front doors.

I expected one of them to say something, or to feel a hand upon my shoulder. I tried to retain a shred of dignity and forced myself to not break into a run.

When I opened the doors, the bird flew out with me.

Chapter 62

Outside, I could breathe again.

I couldn't wait to get home, and quickly stepped down the stairs. In my hurry to leave, I saw more protestors were milling outside now. At least I assumed they were protestors, because they weren't protesting, chanting or singing songs, not yet, anyway. I only noticed one person with a sign, but she was dragging it upside down with the blank back of the poster facing my direction.

Maybe they were waiting for their leader.

The security guard was walking the building's perimeter, so it looked as if the university was aware that something might be happening soon. Candy was chatting with two girls that looked like sisters or maybe twins. They were tall and very striking. The three of them could have been models on the cover of a fashion magazine.

When Candy saw me, she detached herself from the pair to cut across the lawn and intercept me. I didn't want to talk to her. I kept my head down and started walking faster. She didn't take the hint and nearly had to run to catch me.

When she caught up, she lowered her voice and spoke in a gossipy, conspiratorial fashion. It reminded me of the babble of students in high school between classes.

"The professor was sure badgering you. He even attacked your name. What happened after I left?"

I shook my head, rolled my eyes and kept walking. It didn't dissuade her from tagging along at my side.

"Are you sure there isn't something between you and Wayne? I'll back off if there is."

"Not a thing," I said.

"He kinda has that look guys get when he looks at you. Of course, you probably get that a lot."

When I didn't respond, she said, "Do you think he likes me?"

"I don't know. Sure, why not? Why are you so interested in him?"

"Well, you know, he's dreamy," she said, which told me nothing. She changed the subject. "How horrible you must feel about your cousin. I don't blame you for not wanting to reveal her to the professor. She's just a laboratory experiment to him."

I slowed my walking. "Why are you so concerned?"

"I don't think it's right to experiment on people."

I stopped walking and stood facing her with the biology building behind her. The twins were striding toward us. One of them yelled, "Hey, Candy."

Candy gave her a dismissive wave. They weren't dissuaded and continued toward us, moving like graceful equines on their long legs.

Seeing my opportunity to break away from her, I said, "I think your friends want to talk to you."

Candy kept her attention on me and looked uncomfortable. "They want to meet you."

"I really need to get going."

Suddenly, it dawned on me why the girl who didn't like science was hanging around Pinsky and giving so much attention to Wayne. "You're part of the protestors," I said.

"Yes," she said. "Of course. You should join us. We know you could be an asset."

I was tired of being pushed into doing things I didn't want to do. I didn't want to disagree with her and start a long conversation. I just wanted to go home. Even so, I couldn't not respond.

"I don't even understand what you're protesting."

"Professor Pinsky is a Frankenstein."

I stopped walking, something between a smile and a grimace on my face. "Do you think he created a monster? Do you think my cousin is a monster?"

"Well, she's not human."

"Then what is she?"

"I don't know. Something corrupted. Professor Pinsky and his kind need to be stopped. If we don't stop them, God will. It won't be pretty. So, we better take care of it ourselves. I'm sorry, but something like your cousin isn't made in God's image. It's an affront to God."

"*It?*" I shrieked, my voice loud enough that several people nearby turned their heads. "You're saying she's an *it.*"

Candy looked at me with grave sincerity in her eyes. "I'm sorry, I didn't mean to offend you, but I can't change the truth. She doesn't have a soul. She's not human."

I started laughing. I couldn't help myself.

I doubled over, laughing so hard that it hurt my ribs. I couldn't catch my breath. I pounded my fist on my knee. When I finally was able to stop, I looked up. Candy was standing over me giving me a look of pity, as if I'd gone mad. Perhaps I had.

I straightened up and brushed my hair from my face.

"Are you all right?" she asked.

"I'm okay. It's just been a really tough few days."

The twins and several other people had joined us. Up close, I could see that they probably weren't actual twins.

The one with the sharper features said to me, "Are you the one hiding the monkey chimera?"

I must have given her a blank look because she repeated chimera enunciating each syllable slowly and added, "Half monkey."

She was deadly serious. All the remnants of laughter disappeared from me.

"She's not a monkey," I said.

"Are you on our side or theirs?" she asked.

"I'm on nobody's side," I said. "I just want to be left alone."

The probably-not-twins gave each other a look.

One of the other girls who'd gathered around us pointed and exclaimed, "Look, there she is. The news reporter is here."

"Finally," someone else said.

A woman smartly dressed in a pantsuit was walking purposefully toward the biology building. A man carrying a tripod with a camera was a few steps behind her. Behind them was a large gaggle of people following.

Whatever was happening was attracting a large crowd. Pinsky had mentioned a press conference—was it happening now, already? I felt a sinking feeling at the thought. Everyone around me but Candy had taken off in the direction of the reporter.

"What is going on?" I asked her.

"It's the news conference. Didn't you know?"

"No. Are they going to interview Professor Pinsky? I've had enough of him for one day."

She gave me a puzzled look. "Why would they interview him? I don't think he'll show his face. We better hurry if we want to get a good view."

"That's okay. I'm leaving."

"Don't leave now. You'll miss out on the big news," Candy said, looking pleased with herself.

Chapter 63

"What is it about?" I asked.

Candy was already heading to the biology building. She didn't answer me, other than to motion for me to follow her.

The reporter and her entourage had stopped near the main entrance. I noticed that many in the group following her had red in their clothing. They talked in hushed tones, in contrast to the reporter who spoke loudly, giving directions to her camera crew. She went over to several people wearing suits and lowered her voice while speaking with them. Surrounded by the suits, as if they were protecting her, was a woman dressed in white, except for a red scarf. Her head was turned toward the reporter. Dark hair covered the side of her face, so I couldn't get a good look at her.

A golf cart arrived with two more campus security personnel. One of the arrivals jumped out and fingered the baton at his belt while scanning the crowd. The other one remained in the golf cart, talking on a two-way radio. The lone guard who'd been walking the perimeter looked relieved. Since it looked like they were expecting trouble, I didn't follow Candy and went left to where the grass sloped up. My view wouldn't be blocked by tall people in front of me. Also, if things turned ugly, I'd have a better chance of staying out of the way.

I saw the woman circled by the suits was facing in my direction. When she noticed me looking, she looked away.

She looked familiar, but I couldn't place her.

The crowd's attention turned to a woman making her way through the crowd. The camera followed her as she ascending the steps. With hair like coiled ribbons, she was easily memorable as the one who had led the protestors the other day. The camera followed her. She faced the crowd and raised a red scarf above her head. A man holding a sign ran in front of the camera. His sign read: *Christians,*

Jews and Muslims, United Against the Unholy. The crowd quieted and the coil-haired woman began addressing them.

"As promised, we are joined today by a victim of the atrocities committed in this so-called institution of higher learning."

She gestured toward the woman in white, who gave a quick wave and an uncomfortable smile at the crowd.

Her demeanor, makeup and clothing were so changed from the time that I met her, that I'd not recognized her.

The woman in white was Maria Nogales.

To my surprise, the crowd did not erupt with claps and shouts, but soft chatter. Nonetheless, their energy became palpable, like a low-pitched hum of electricity. I found it more unsettling than a raucous response.

Maria didn't step forward, but one of the suits did. He introduced himself as an attorney with a law firm bringing litigation against Cummings for the travesty committed under the guise of medical research. He spoke for several minutes, painting the unnamed Maria as an innocent person maliciously harmed by the university. Before the team of attorneys whisked her away, she gave another wave to the crowd, which finally broke the tension.

They let out a roar. People waved red scarves, red rags, red ribbons, anything red, above their heads, shouting as if cheering at a football game. Several guys had removed their shirts and were swinging them vigorously over their heads. One woman perched on the shoulders of a man had a red sweatshirt that she'd wrapped around her fist. She thrust it in the air repeatedly, as if punching the sky.

I'd not seen Pinsky venturing out. I wondered if he had escaped through the secret back door or slipped unnoticed from one of the side ones. Perhaps he was still in the building listening to the event.

The ribbon-haired woman took the stage again and announced that today they would be marching their demonstration to the administration building and then to the campus entrance.

As the crowd swept in my direction toward the administration, the reporter began interviewing individuals. I spotted Candy moving in my direction at the same moment I noticed my hand was wet. I'd unconsciously been squeezing the cup and coke had leaked out. Rather than heading to my car and getting lost in the crowd, I made the mistake of cutting over toward a trash can, intending to toss the cup. Before I could reach it or melt into the crowd, Candy was upon me with several others in tow.

Flanked by her friends, she said, "I figured out what the professor was talking about. I know what your name means. I know *who* you are, I know *what* you are. I'm not stupid. Your name doesn't mean cousin. It means monkey."

Candy had transformed into an entirely different person, or maybe had simply revealed herself.

Her companions laughed, not in a humorous or amusing way, but menacing. She jabbed her finger at me. I backed up and bumped into someone.

As I turned around to apologize, the girl shoved me. The lid popped off. The cup slipped from my hand. Coke splashed on her. The front of her light-blue top was covered with coke. The dark brown liquid ran down her top onto her pants, making stripes down the center of each leg as if by design.

She looked down with an expression of disgust and brushed the back of her hands over her clothing, flicking drops of coke on me. Her eyes rose from her clothing to my face. Her thin lips retracted from her teeth and her grin looked like the grimace of a chimpanzee that was about to go berserk.

"Look what you did, you freak. You've ruined my clothes."

"I'm sorry. It was an accident."

"You gotta pay, bitch."

I glanced around and saw no sympathy in the faces surrounding us, only amused expressions, animal intrigue, raw curiosity as to what would happen next. I imagined their expressions would not have been out of place at a guillotine during the French Revolution.

Candy avoided my eyes. The crowd widened into a circle around the two of us, like kids in an school playground about to watch a fight.

This can't be happening, I thought.

She was taller than I was, but her skinny arms didn't look toned. Surfing and running kept me in good shape, but I'd never been in a fight. I didn't want to fight, even if I could win.

Her angry little face squeezed into a ball. She doubled her fists and began to bob back and forth. I backed up until I was pressed against people behind me. She stepped closer and unleashed a raking swing, trying to grab my hair. I slipped to the side, and she missed.

I didn't see any point in fighting. Maybe it was the bonobo in me—make love not war. I knew it was her fault not mine, but I only wanted to escape. I tried another option in the hope it would get me out of trouble.

"Wait," I said. "I'll pay for your clothes."

She gave a cunning smirk. "Three hundred dollars," she said.

She thrust out a greedy little hand. It was obviously much more than what her clothes cost. Someone behind me hooted and pushed me. I stumbled into my attacker. She sidestepped and tripped me. I staggered, starting to fall face first. The spectators in front of me parted to avoid my crashing into them. I managed to regain my footing and darted through the gap.

I started running, cutting across the lawn, knowing they'd have little chance of catching me.

When I reached the main walkway, I glanced back. No one was following me. Only their laughter pursued me.

I slowed my sprinting. The trees arched above me, their branches a web of fingers ready to trap me if I didn't keep moving. I ran all the way to the parking lot.

Chapter 64

My mind had been so shaken by what had happened that I'd not been my usual vigilant self about being followed. Not until I'd reached Yitha and was getting close to home on Pacific Coast Highway did I become suspicious about a car behind me. The only reason I happened to notice it was that the driver had stayed behind me at a greater distance than usual. Cars kept filling in between us until each driver became impatient with my speed and went around me. Then, I'd spot the same car lagging back in the gap.

It was an older, dark-colored car with a boxy grill. Something about it seemed familiar.

I was fairly sure it wasn't a car from the neighborhood because, like Garrett's Chugger, being an older model it stood out.

I moved over from the right lane and sped up as to not annoy traffic. The car shifted into the left lane too and hung back. Maybe I was being paranoid. It was probably just a coincidence, I told myself.

I moved into the left turn lane to turn into Concha Pointe at the Clover Street entrance. If it were following me, it would have no choice but to get into the turn lane or lose me.

It pulled in behind me.

As I made my turn, I looked in the rearview mirror and saw that the car was a dark blue sedan. That made me nervous. I knew where I'd seen it—it was the car that had been at Maria's place and had followed Professor Pinsky. I told myself it might just be a coincidence, but I didn't believe it. Last time there'd been two people in the car. I could only see a driver this time—maybe he was the guy who'd been in the passenger seat and had smiled at me.

I came to the stop sign just beyond the Concha Pointe realty office where I turn right to my house. Turning left leads to the nature preserve.

I flipped on my left turn signal. The car stopped behind me and signaled left too.

The man had a beard. I couldn't be positive, but he looked like the same guy.

Then, instead of turning left, I went right. He followed me and didn't bother turning off his left turn signal. I couldn't wait to get home, but I didn't want him to find out where I lived. Being away from the highway, there were no other cars around which spooked me even more.

I was surprised when a scattering of plump raindrops hit my windshield. The other thing I'd not paid attention to since morning was the weather. Most of the sky was blue, but for a few clouds above me. As I wove around the streets, past homes like fortresses behind their gates and lush foliage, I peeked at the sky and saw heavier clouds to the south. The storm front was moving in early.

I sped up. He didn't stay right on my tail but kept me in sight. The only thing I could think of to do was take the loop to the far exit of Concha Pointe and head back down PCH to the highway patrol station. I forced myself not to even look at my house when I drove by it. I made a turn onto the next street. The sedan followed. As I came to the last curve before reaching the highway, a Concha Pointe private security patrol car rounded it from the other direction. I'd never been so glad to see one. I stopped my car, pounded on my horn, and waved at the guard. He pulled his car to the side of the street, leaving enough room for the blue sedan to go around me, whose left turn signal was still blinking. It pulled around me. The rear end was covered with bumper stickers. I was certain then that it was the same car I'd seen at Maria's.

The guard got out of his car. He was tall and thin with bent shoulders. He didn't look fit or inspire much confidence, but luckily the sedan continued driving away. When he came over to me, I saw his oily hair was parted on the side. His most striking feature was his skin—it looked pore-less, so smooth that I wondered if he even shaved. He avoided making eye contact with me while I gave my address and reported the blue sedan.

"Oh, I know the house. The one with the towers," he said. His voice was as smooth as his skin. "You live right next door to Donny. I'll put out an APB, an all-points bulletin, for the vehicle. We'll do extra patrols by your house," he assured me. "I'll follow you to make sure you get home safely."

When I reached my house, I turned into the driveway and looked up at the towers on either side. Normally, I wasn't conscious of them unless someone mentioned them. Now, looking at them, I thought of my home as a castle, a place that protected me from the outside world. As I waited for the gate to open, I felt glad the property was fenced.

A breeze was picking up because the tops of the junipers on Donny's side of the property were swaying. The gate opened and I drove inside. Wolfears rushed out to greet me.

After kissing him on the snout, I opened the double garage. I didn't want to leave my car out in case the blue car was still prowling the neighborhood looking for me. I hoped he thought I'd turned into Concha Pointe only to evade him, and had driven away on PCH.

I sat staring at the empty space in the garage, unable to put the car in gear. I thought how matter-of-factly my uncle had uttered the phrase "*ikka shinju.*"

I took the carob pod from the dashboard and unconsciously begun breaking it into pieces. The fragments fell onto my lap like the dust of sorrow, anger, and emotions I couldn't name. When there was nothing left to break, I put the car in gear and pulled into the garage.

When I came out of the garage, I saw the red glow of taillights on the hedges across the street. I hoped it wasn't the blue car that had just driven by.

Chapter 65

The next morning, an hour after I usually rose, I finally psyched myself up to get out of bed. My internal clock told me it was time for breakfast, but I ignored my hunger as I'd planned to keep up my discipline of running.

As usual, I'd slept with the glass door open. There were more clouds than the day before, but most of the sky was a summer blue. I heard voices and wondered if Donny's father had come home from his shoot in Asia—sometimes he drank and fell asleep with the television turned up.

As I slipped on my running shoes, the jangle of voices continued, which made me doubt it was a television blaring.

"Come on, let's go," I told Wolfears.

He didn't make his usual rush out the door, but looked at me with a questioning expression. When I stepped outside on the balcony, he followed. Still in shade, the balcony was damp with morning dew. Outside, the voices were louder.

It sounded like a crowd of people working themselves up.

We went downstairs, where the voices became muffled. Going along the side of the house, the volume increased. Something about the din made me cautious. Keeping Wolfears behind me, I crept on the walkway between the juniper trees and the house until I reached the front and stopped.

Gathered on the street in front of my house was a group of fifteen or twenty people. Their voices were a disorganized cacophony, like chattering rainforest birds. Their volume rose and lowered. Their attention turned facing down the street. Some waved their hands, others pumped fists. Their voices began coalescing in unison into a rah, rah, rah. They could well have been the protestors from the school, but I wasn't sure until I saw who they were looking at come into view.

It was the woman with the lion's mane hair and her entourage marching up the street to join them.

I ducked back before they could spot me and hid behind a juniper. A couple of her people were carrying signs, which they began distributing to those already gathered. I'd seen most of them before. One new one that struck me read: *God is not a monkey.*

There was a chance I could go around the other side of the house and sneak out of the lower gate, but being that there were so many of them, someone might see me. Then, I thought, why should I adjust my schedule and let them affect me? I've done nothing wrong.

I walked out onto the driveway. No sooner than they spotted me did they started shouting.

There is a deep, primal fear of being jeered at by a crowd. Rather than go forward with my run, I retreated back to the side of the house. Wolfears remained on the driveway with his front feet squared, facing the crowd. A low growl emanated from his chest. I had to call him back three times before he responded. I couldn't chastise him for his delay.

By the time I was in my backyard, I was breathing as hard as if I'd run. Once I was out of sight, they'd quieted down.

I went upstairs and peeked out the front window. They were milling around as if at a social event. Only when the occasional car drove by did their energy pick up, and they would hold up their signs, gesture and shout. Other than keeping me captive in my own home, they weren't accomplishing anything.

I wasn't really a hostage—they couldn't stop me from leaving—but the thought of passing by them caused a wave of overwhelming panic to ripple through my chest.

Maybe I'm not brave, I told myself.

I decided to call the Concha Pointe security, who, in turn, called the sheriff. Even without sidewalks, people have the right to walk on the street as long as they stay close to the left side of the road facing traffic. Loitering is prohibited, so they couldn't congregate in front of my home and had to keep moving.

Unfortunately, that didn't stop them.

They marched up and down either side, going one way and then the other as they made a big circle.

I'd lost my appetite after I'd seen the protestors and barely managed any breakfast. However, by lunchtime, my hunger had returned.

Back at the window, I watched them while I waited for Mysti. I wanted to open the gate as soon as she arrived, so she'd not have to interact with the protestors. While sitting there, the phone rang.

"I have bad news," Mysti said. "I know we were supposed to get together, but my uncle showed up unexpectedly. I've got to spend time with him. My flight to Europe is at seven tomorrow morning."

"I guess that means there won't be time to see you before you leave."

"No, I guess not. I'm sorry. I'm already crazy busy getting ready."

"Oh," I said, trying to hide my disappointment.

I didn't want to worry her about the protestors, so I didn't mention them. I also badly wanted to talk to her about my breakup with Garrett and spill everything else to her.

"Are you okay?" she asked.

"Yes, I'm just disappointed about not seeing you."

"You'll be the first person I see when I come home," she promised.

I returned to the window and my useless watching of the people on the street.

Throughout the day, individuals came and went. I assumed that, by evening, they would give up. Their numbers dwindled, but they remained moving back and forth. When it turned dark, a few remained, usually walking two or three abreast, except shifting to single file when a security patrol or a sheriff came by.

"Time for us to venture out," I told Wolfears.

When I pulled Mister Aphid out of the driveway, the protestors didn't do anything other than look at me. Some of them waved.

I waited until the gate was shut before driving off.

To my surprise, there were a couple of them on the sidewalk outside the local market, so I decided to go elsewhere to avoid them.

At the exit to Concha Pointe, I saw, to my dismay, the old blue sedan parked near the entrance in the realty office lot. When I pulled onto the highway, it followed me.

Chapter 66

Even though it was late on a Monday night and the traffic was light, he didn't bother to keep his distance like before. If I'd have had to stopped quickly, he would have rear-ended me. At the stoplights, he aggressively crept within inches of my bumper. From the oncoming headlights, his pale forehead shone as white as a bleached skull. His teeth glinted as the cars whooshed past us, making his frozen smile looked like the grimace of a rabid canine. I was afraid he might get out of his car holding a tire iron and smash my windows, but he stayed hunched over the steering wheel.

I wondered if he ever blinked.

I kept driving down the coast, dreading stoplights. My gas tank was nearly full. I hoped his wasn't. Nevertheless, I couldn't count on his gas guzzler sputtering to a stop. I considered pulling into a public place with lots of people, where I could call the police. That was the best I could come up with until I neared the Getty Villa.

When I saw a gap in oncoming traffic, I slowed and whipped my VW in an illegal U-turn across the double yellow line. I turned so quickly that Wolfears' paws scrabbled on the seat as he lost his footing. I cast a glance at him as his legs fell into the footwell, and he slammed into the passenger door. He let out a yelp.

If I've hurt you, I'll never forgive myself.

I slowed to check that he was okay.

Behind me, I heard the brakes of the blue car squeal. He was unable to slow his old Detroit Iron enough to make the U-turn before the traffic thickened. I knew he'd be able to turn around and head back north at the next light. I sped up and made a right on Topanga Canyon, drove a few hundred yards, made another U-turn and parked behind another car. I killed my lights and watched the cross traffic on PCH.

As I waited, I smelled sage through the crack in my window. A few fat raindrops landed on my windshield. It didn't take long before the blue sedan zoomed through the intersection, speeding past the other cars. We'd escaped.

I threw my arms around Wolfears and told him how happy I was that he was okay. He snuck a wet kiss on my cheek.

After waiting a few long minutes, I started home. The rain picked up, so I switched on my windshield wipers. Headlights approached rapidly behind me. Fearing my tormentor had guessed my trick and looped back, I held my breath until I saw it wasn't Skull Head.

I hit a patch of heavy rain up the coast. Taillights in front of me reflected off of the glossy pavement like streaks of smeared blood. I decided to stop at the corner market to get groceries. There was no telling how long I'd be under siege at my home. It made me nervous leaving Wolfears in the car.

I surveyed my surroundings before getting out. With the rain, few people were out.

From the short jog across the parking lot, my shoulders and hair were already wet. The shopping cart I took had a sticky wheel. It pulled to the left, as if to direct me to what to buy.

I didn't bother to get another one. I tossed groceries into it without checking expirations. I scooped up bananas and apples without inspecting them. Each time I went down an aisle, I checked out the front windows in fear that I'd been found. I got cans of dog food and a sack of kibble. My cart was a jumbled mess. The checker raised his eyebrows when he saw the bread and bananas crushed beneath the kibble.

At the entrance to the Pointe, there was a white car parked at the realty. It was in the shadows. Someone was inside. I expected it to follow me, but it didn't. The wind was whipping at the Pointe. The rain was little more than a drizzle. My neighbors were ensconced behind their walls. When I reached my house, I saw the protestors were still there. Several were huddling under a neighbor's trellised archway. They followed me with their eyes. My window was rolled up, and I couldn't hear their shouts. The lights were on at Donny's house. I wondered what he thought of them.

As I turned into my driveway, my headlights caught another person standing at the edge of the driveway. He was rake thin and soaking wet, making no attempt to shelter from the rain. His frizzy locks drooped. His head was bent, making his eye sockets look like empty pits in his blue-gray face. He gripped a soggy cardboard sign that read, '*Stop the pollution of the human race.*' His motionless form was more chilling than the taunts they'd hurled at me during the day. The set of his face, like that of the skull man, made me believe that these people were capable of anything under the banner of their zealotry. They were fanatics driven by ideology, making them resistant to logic.

My house was a prison not a fortress. I drove in and parked by the front door, facing out. When the gate clanged shut, I reached across and let Wolfears out first. He hated rain, but did a patrol of the front yard.

It took two trips to take in the groceries—I had enough food for a week.

I locked my car, something I never did. I facetiously wished my jailers a good night, closed the front door and tossed my keys onto the entry credenza.

The aberration was locked away. The world was safe.

In the kitchen, I put away the refrigerated items and left the others on the counter. I sat and forced myself to eat. I gave Wolfears a chicken strip dog treat.

"Wouldn't it be wonderful to fly away and start a new life?" I asked him.

He gulped his chicken and didn't answer my question.

Before going to bed, I went to the upstairs window. I could only see a couple of the protestors out front from my vantage point. With the burned-out gate light, I couldn't see if the thin man was still there, clutching his sign. The rain had stopped as if my wish for them to have a good night had been granted.

I never thought I cared much about what other people thought, but there is something about being ostracized, shunned. I felt an emptiness inside. I wished I were more like Mysti and didn't care about other people's opinions.

My father must have known that my world would fall apart once my secret was revealed. Lying in bed, I thought about how he had been right all along—I wasn't meant to live. I was a mistake that needed correcting.

I laid on my bed with my clothes on and drifted off to sleep, despite my unease about the people gathered outside.

Around midnight, I woke with a start from the sounds of loud laughter.

I'd been dreaming that I was inside the bonobo exhibit at the zoo. Protestors were mobbed outside the enclosure, staring through the plexiglass sheeting, watching my every move. It was their laughter that had woken me.

Chapter 67

The rain had started again. Its soft brushing on the deck accompanied the imperfect rhythm of the waves on the rocks. I stayed in bed, lying perfectly still, listening. Maybe the waves were laughing.

I couldn't hear the protestors from my bedroom and wondered if they were still outside demonstrating against the contamination of humanity. I got out of bed and went to the front window to check. They were still there. In fact, more of them had gathered. They all appeared to have umbrellas at the ready now. They no longer chanted in the late hours, knowing they could be cited for disturbing the peace.

Watching them, I didn't feel the sharp jab of anxiety like before. Instead, I felt a peculiar detachment, not only about them, but myself. It was as if I had become both the observer and the observed.

I returned to my bedroom and realized that, despite the little rest I'd had, I wasn't sleepy at all. A gust of wind rattled the screen door. In bare feet, I stepped out on the balcony to the railing. There was an electrical tingle in the air. The moon and stars were hidden behind the clouds. The clouds shone only faintly down the coast where the lights reflected off them. Over the ocean, the clouds were as black as the ocean. My backyard was dark too.

I didn't need any light to make my way down the wet stairs. Wolfears had remained beneath the eaves out of the rain, but I heard him follow as I went down. I walked around the pool and out to the wall.

I stared into the darkness.

In the distance above the ocean, the clouds illuminated briefly from a flash of lightning. It was too far off for me to hear the thunder. With the wind tossing the rain, it didn't take long until my clothing was soaked.

I went to the kitchen door where Wolfears was huddled beneath the balcony. It wasn't raining directly on him, but the wind still blew it his way. I'd mistakenly left the kitchen door unlocked. I opened it for him, but he didn't go inside.

I flicked on the switch for the pool light.

I was momentarily blinded as the center of the yard filled with turquoise light. When my eyes adjusted, I saw the liquid blue topaz was divoted by rain drops and undulated when the wind rippled over it. I was mesmerized by its beauty.

At the end of the yard, my mother's statues danced in the shifting light. I went over to the rising mermaid and looked up at her. I reached up and ran my fingers down her arm.

Her face turned into my mother's. She smiled at me—it made me happy.

As I walked back from it, I nearly stumbled on the fire pit. Its center was filling with water that looked like black ink. I went around it and crossed to the deep end of the pool, where I suddenly felt a desire to dive in and swim.

With difficulty, I managed to peel off my soggy jeans. As I lifted my drenched top over my head, it caught on my chin and clung to my face. I struggled against it, panicking until I wrestled it off. I felt the chain of the basketball pendant snap in the process. Once I was free of my top, I easily removed my bra and panties. Standing naked on the deck with the feel of wind and rain against my skin, I began breathing more easily. As the storm was coming from the south, the wind and rain were only cool, not cold. My detached, surreal state of mind returned.

I felt vibrantly alive, more than I had in many days. I stretched my arms out to the side and twirled twice, nearly falling into the pool. I stood on the edge and curled my toes around the coping. Then, I dove into the silky wet world and became a different living thing, an aquatic creature, swimming back and forth, lap after lap, without counting. The sensual feel of the water flowing over my body became my entire universe.

Eventually, my desire to swim became sated. I took the corner steps in the shallow end out of the pool and at once had that sixth sense of being watched. From the light of the pool, I saw the junipers pressed down like a line of old men with bent backs trudging up a hill. Between the gaps in the junipers, I saw the side of Donny's house. The wind shifted direction and released the junipers. As they whipped upright, I caught a glimpse of the dim outline of Donny at the window.

The harsh reality of being a prisoner in my home fell back upon me. Before the wind pressed them down again, I looked away so that he'd not know that I'd seen him.

I stood on the pool deck, undecided. Now that I was no longer moving, I was beginning to feel chilly.

The storm was moving quickly.

I wrapped my arms around myself. The pendant had fallen on the deck next to my wadded-up clothes. I stooped and picked it up. I decided it was gaudy and ugly. I thought about throwing it in the pool and watching it sink to the bottom. Instead, I threw it. As it arced above the pool, the diamonds glittered. When it sailed over the wall to the waiting ocean, like a shooting star, it disappeared into the darkness as if it had never existed.

Slowly, with my head hung down, I made my way across the yard to the half-moon. The wind kept changing direction, but I knew that Donny would be able to see me through the junipers when the wind pressed them down. The part of me that was outside myself gave an encouraging laugh.

I climbed onto the step and then up to the top of the wall. Below me, the sound of the laughing waves rose up, along with an updraft of air that kept me from falling.

The updraft suddenly disappeared, and the wind buffeted me, nearly knocking me over the edge.

I caught my balance.

Below, the storm surge had covered the rocks. Knowing their pattern beneath the water, I wondered, if I landed in the spot between the two largest ones, whether I would survive the fall. Even if I did land there, the stormy water would be unforgiving. I would be hurled against the cliff or sucked under.

I was meant to die with my parents. I knew that now.

I had to escape.

Taking in a deep breath of salty air, I raised my arms above my head, arched my back, and pressed my palms together. Diving seemed more terrifying than jumping.

I changed my mind and dropped my arms to my sides. I crouched and swung my arms back and forth in preparation for the jump.

The bird of paradise next to me batted its leaves against my leg as if saying, "What are you waiting for? Get on with it. Jump. Jump. Jump."

Chapter 68

Behind me, Wolfears whimpered. I kept swinging my arms back and forth as the wind blew fiercely, pushing me in one direction and then another. Wolfears whimpered again. I forced myself not to look back at him. The wind lessened its assault and shifted onshore. I nearly stumbled backward off the wall, but held my balance.

I glanced back at Donny's window. The junipers had swung back upright, his line of sight blocked once more. I stopped swinging my arms and jumped back onto the patio.

"Come here, you big, beautiful dog," I said, and pulled Wolfears to me.

I buried my face into his fur and inhaled the wet, earthy, doggy smell of him and tried to keep from sobbing.

I couldn't waste any time. This was no time to be emotional.

I crept along the edge of Donny's property, where he couldn't see me even if the wind pressed the junipers down again. I kept Wolfears close because I couldn't let Donny see him either.

Once we were beneath the balcony, we were out of sight. I had to think fast and not make mistakes.

The first thing I needed was clothes.

I sprinted up the wet balcony stairs and stopped outside my bedroom's glass door. I couldn't move forward. My hands clasped together as if they were magnets. My fingers twisted around one another like writhing snakes. I forced my hands to break apart. They were shaking, not only from the cold. I knew what I was about to do was wrong, yet, I didn't see any other way out.

I shook myself like a dog to get some of the water off. I told Wolfears, "Sit. Stay," and slipped inside. Trying to drip as little water as possible, I made my way to the bathroom and grabbed a towel.

After a quick dry off, I returned to my room and dressed quickly. There was so much I needed to take, but there wasn't time. I grabbed an old surf bag from the back of my closet and stuffed in another set of clothes. I took a pair of running shoes, but didn't put them on. I didn't trust Wolfears' patience and didn't want him wandering away and being spotted by Donny. So, rather than head downstairs through the house, I went back outside through the bedroom. I closed the screen and left the door open so that any water I'd tracked in would look like it had blown in from outside.

Once we were downstairs, I dried off my feet and tossed the towel on the deck by my wet pile of clothing. Again, I told Wolfears to stay, this time by the kitchen door.

I went inside and called Wayne, remembering how he said he owed me.

I wished I had time to think it through.

He was the weak part of my plan—if he didn't answer or betrayed me, it would fall apart. He picked up.

"Can I trust you?" I asked him.

"You know I didn't tell the professor."

"Yes, I know. If you do something for me, will you promise never to tell anyone?"

He paused. A few seconds seemed like infinity. "Okay," he said.

"I need you to give me a ride."

He didn't ask where to and said, "I'll be right over."

"Don't come to my house. I'll meet you at the bus stop on Pacific Coast Highway by Concha Pointe."

"Huh?"

"I don't have time for questions."

"Okay," he said, as I hung up.

Then, I went to my father's office. I pulled open the drawer with the envelope of cash and stuffed it into my bag. I rushed back up the stairs, past all my father's awards and certificates. I left my house and car keys on the entry table. I also left my wallet with my credit cards and driver's license behind too. On my way out, I shut the kitchen door. It sounded like the lid of a casket closing.

When I put on my shoes, Wolfears assumed we were going for a run. He started to yip. I shushed and leashed him. Instead of taking the path through the driveway to the lower gate, we went around the other side of the house. We made our way along the fence at the property line. It was overgrown and kept us hidden, but a plant with spines had grown through the fence. The spines scratched me when I squeezed by them.

When we reached the wicket gate, I peeked out. A few protestors were in view of the gate, including the one who'd chased me. He didn't look so frightening now that he wasn't behind the wheel of the car. I couldn't risk being seen, and waited.

I considered climbing over the fence into the neighbor's yard, but I couldn't get Wolfears over. Besides, their security motion detectors would trigger lights. Wolfears didn't understand the delay. I kept a hand on him.

I was trapped. Time ticked. If I was delayed too long, I'd miss Wayne. If he called and left a message, it would wreck everything.

I heard a siren on Pacific Coast Highway. It grew louder as it approached. When it ceased, I assumed it had stopped for an accident on the highway. Then, I heard a rumble and realized it had turned off its siren when it had entered Concha Pointe. I felt the ground vibrate and caught a glimpse of the headlights before the fire truck came into view. I felt a stab of guilt when it stopped at my driveway.

Donny had called 911.

Now bathed in the flashing red light, the protestors attention was drawn to the truck.

It was the opportunity we needed.

We slipped out. I didn't need to worry about the gate clanging behind me, but I closed it gently anyway. We ran down the street, keeping close to the side. I needed to get away before my neighbors came out to investigate. We hadn't gone far when another set of headlights appeared. I ducked into a driveway and crouched behind a hedge. It was awkward running with the bag hanging from my shoulder. While I waited, I shifted the strap diagonally across my chest.

An ambulance drove by. I wondered if it was the same one that had taken me to the hospital.

I started off again. With the wet pavement splashing beneath my feet, it felt like one of my regular morning jogs in the rain, except for the strap digging into my breast and the fear that we might be seen.

On Clover Street, I turned toward the highway. The white car was gone. The blue car was back, parked next to an SUV. They were facing the street. I couldn't see anyone sitting in either of them. Out of caution, I planned to run behind them. Then, I spotted an orange speck in the shadows—it was the glowing ember of a cigarette.

Someone was sheltering from the rain on the realty office walkway, another sentry.

I retreated to the intersection. I'd already been delayed once. The way to the nature preserve was a dead end and getting to the north end of Concha Pointe was blocked by the fire truck and protestors. Going past the realty office was the only way I could get to PCH.

I stood in the wind and rain trying to decide what to do. At least I couldn't get any more wet.

Then, lightning lit the sky like daylight. In the flash, I saw the man with the cigarette. He was facing in my direction.

He couldn't have missed seeing me.

Chapter 69

Darkness returned. I watched the orange glow of the cigarette somersault to the ground. There was no point in trying to hide now. I continued toward the realty office. If I could get to the highway, and Wayne was there, part of my plan still had a chance.

I'd not run far when the boom of thunder sounded. The man hurried down the steps and ran hunched over with a jacket pulled over his head. He got into the SUV. He started the engine as we ran past.

Having Wolfears with me, I didn't think he'd try to stop me. I expected him to go to my house and alert the others. Instead, he made a right turn behind us. Our bodies cast long shadows from his headlights. To my surprise, he accelerated and drove past us, then turned south on PCH at the light. He must have only been a motorist stopping for a smoke and not a lookout.

I hoped Wayne would be parked by the bus stop waiting, but he wasn't there.

We huddled under the awning to get out of the rain. The awning didn't help much because the wind blew sideways. Wolfears tugged at the leash. PCH always made him nervous, likely because he'd been abandoned there before I'd found him.

Headlights of the cars whizzing by shone like the glowing eyes of mechanical cheetahs. A car slowed. Its tires sprayed water on me when it pulled up beside me.

It wasn't Wayne.

There were two guys in the car. I didn't like the look of them.

I pulled the bag's strap over my shoulder. The passenger stepped out and motioned me to take his seat.

"No, thanks," I said.

"Hurry up, I'm getting wet out here."

The driver got out of the car and said, "Hey baby."

I wondered if I was heading into a worse fate than jumping off of the cliff. He came around the side of the car and stood in front of me. He stepped close enough to me that I could smell alcohol on his breath. I wished I'd stood up before.

"I'm waiting for a friend," I told them.

"We'll be good friends. We won't leave you in the rain."

Wolfears growled. The man took a step back. The passenger pulled out a baseball bat from behind his seat.

"Be a pity to hurt your dog."

Just then, a box truck pulled up behind the car. The passenger's bloodshot eyes were blinded by the high headlights. He shielded his face with a hand. The truck's horn sounded.

"There's my ride," I said.

I scooted off the bench and dashed toward the truck, tugging Wolfears after me.

"We saw you first. You don't get away from us that easy," the guy with the bat said.

His friend reached out to grab me. Being drunk, he lost his balance and missed. The truck's window opened. I couldn't see up in the cab, but heard a voice.

"What's going on here? You having trouble with your friends?"

"I don't know them."

"Then what are you doing out here?"

"I was waiting for someone."

I looked back and saw the guy with the bat helping his friend up. He shrugged his shoulders and gave a dismissive wave. They got back in the car, but they didn't drive away. The truck sat there idling. I knew they were watching to see if I got in.

"Good thing you have your dog with you," the truck driver said. "Looked like it was gonna get ugly anyway."

"Thanks for stopping," I said.

"Hop on up."

"Are you sure? We're wet. My dog has to come too."

"Yup, it's unlocked. Get out of the rain, at least until they leave."

I opened the door. The man looked just like his voice suggested: long face with a scraggily beard, a pot belly and a cowboy hat on his head. He seemed okay.

Wolfears jumped in without being prompted. I followed.

The cab was warm and dry with a lived-in smell that overrode the wet dog tang of Wolfears. Being a box truck, there was no center mirror from which to hang an air freshener. The car didn't move.

The man inhaled. "Smells like my dog," he said. "Normally, I've got my dog with me, but this was a long trip. What's your dog's name?"

"Condor," I said. The name just popped into my head.

"That's a first. Never heard of a dog with that name."

"There's never been a dog quite like him," I said, and wrapped my arms around him. I thought I'd need to come up with a name for myself too, but he didn't ask.

A helicopter came up the coast, flying low beneath the storm clouds. The trucker leaned forward and peered out the top of the windshield.

"Now that's something you don't see every day, a Sikorsky Jayhawk doing search and rescue in weather like this. Must be a serious call." He laughed and said, "In this neighborhood, probably somebody got kicked out of their country club or lost some jewelry."

He didn't know how close to the truth he was.

Reality hit me. I was about to leave behind everything I ever knew. I closed my eyes and tried to ignore my guilt and trepidation. The truck shook as the helicopter passed above us. With a squeal of tires, the car left and pulled onto the highway. Wolfears shook and sent water drops flying around the cab, spraying the man and the windshield.

"Sorry," I said.

"I've got to get moving. Are you sure you don't want to ride along?"

Wayne should have been there by now. Maybe he'd come and gone. I was about to take the trucker up on his offer when Wayne pulled up in front of the bus stop.

"Thank you so much for your help," I told him.

As we got out, he chuckled and said, "I didn't think I'd have a drenched angel riding all the way to Santa Fe with me."

Wayne's car wasn't as warm as the truck. I sat in the back seat with Wolfears to keep him from getting anxious.

"Where do you need to go? Why aren't you driving? What's going on?"

"Too many questions. Please take me downtown."

"Which downtown?"

"Los Angeles."

To my surprise, he nodded and started driving. He took the same route that Detective Yates had driven. He seemed to sense that I didn't want to talk.

I had him drop me off a few blocks from the railroad station. It was pointless, really, because he could easily have figured out where I was going.

"When will you be back?"

"I don't know when or if. Please keep your promise."

The streets were gray. People moved like shadows and spots of ink in the night. I was scared, but made it to Union Station without any trouble. As it turned out, I wasn't allowed to board the train with Wolfears.

I had better luck with the bus. It departed at 12:30 am and there were few passengers so the driver pretended he didn't see Wolfears.

When we reached Phoenix at 11:30 the next morning, I gave him a generous tip, even though I needed to start watching my limited money. I took a cab from Phoenix to Yarnell. The only address I had for my aunt was the P.O. Box. Luckily, being a small town, I only had to ask a few people before someone knew where she lived.

Her home was in a trailer nestled against the hillside. When she opened the door, I don't think she recognized me.

"Hello, Aunt Pearl."

Epilogue

The wood that was replaced at the end of the pier has aged in the last twenty years. It now matches the surrounding wood. It is just after dawn on an overcast morning in January. I grasp the railing with my chilled hands and shake it. It is solid. There are now barrier posts at the edge of the parking lot to keep vehicles from driving onto the pier. The restaurant is no longer named The Pelican's Roost. Having a changed name is something I have in common with it.

This is the first time I've returned to Concha Pointe.

On my way to the pier, I drove by my old home, but the new owners have a new gate that blocks the view from the street, so I will remember it as it was.

Though the odds of my being recognized are slim, I've come at this early hour, when there are only a few people about. I hear footsteps behind me on the wooden planks, but it's just a couple holding hands. Their other hands hold rods and buckets. Like seabirds, they are only interested in fish and will take no notice of a woman in an oversized coat staring at the ocean.

Time has softened the splinters of horror, yet I felt a need to come here, perhaps if only to prove that I am stronger than my memories and that I can give priority to joy and let the tragedy be submerged like an old shipwreck, with its anchor chain rusting and its hull disappearing as worms gnaw upon the planks.

The ocean rolls beneath me and slaps the pylons. As I rest my elbows on the railing, I feel my eyes filling with tears. They slide over my cheeks.

Maybe it was a mistake to come.

The wind pushes the tears back against my ears. The sun has almost crested the mountains behind me. Remembering my ignorance and the beauty it possessed is almost too much.

A line a brown pelicans flies northward over the ocean, as their ancestors have done for millions of years, their long beaks and flexible pouches perfectly adapted for scooping fish from the sea. They have found the pinnacle of evolution for their niche, unlike humanity; unlike I, who stumbles awkwardly forward. What can one do but go forward in life?

I take a tissue from my purse, dry my eyes and tuck loose strands of hair back.

I gave myself a new name after I arrived at my aunt's. We concocted a story that I was her child from an affair, and I'd been left behind overseas. It worked and my new identity became official. Because I was presumed dead, my aunt, along with my father's family, received my parents' inheritance.

Some years later, I got married. My husband's eyes are the color of the Caribbean Sea. When I first met him, his eyes reminded me of someone else's.

Wayne never told the secret of driving me away that night. We never saw each other or even spoke again. I hope he achieved his dreams.

A discarded fishing line catches on my ankle. I pick it up and stuff it into the trash bin. Then, I return to the end of the pier.

One more time, I test the strength of the railing as my father did so long ago. In my pocket is a journal with my story. As I stand here, I'm debating whether to toss it into the ocean or let it be found one day by my children.

I lift my eyes to the ocean and speak to it.

"My name is Prima Otomo. I am human."

The End

About the Author

John Pulver is a Southern California-based writer whose fiction has appeared in various publications. The Hollywood Bodies and Killswitch novels, under the J.R. Waterbear pseudonym, are coauthored by him. He is a member of The Natural Muse, a group that connects authors with the joy and inspiration of writing in nature. When not reading or writing, he's often swimming, hiking or playing chess.

A note from JP:

Thank you for reading Prima.

Please consider posting a review, something as simple as "I liked the book" or even a star rating without comments. They help bring readers to the story and are appreciated.

J.R. Waterbear books:

Hollywood Bodies

A rock 'n' roll mystery set in the Hollywood scene of sleaze, delusion, and bad-hair bands of 1987. A Halloween of tricks, treats and a killer clown.

Glenda Birdsong, onetime rock star brought low by drugs and bad dieting advice, is working on her comeback album — until, that is, her sleazy manager steals her best song and winds up dead.

Suddenly, bodies are piling up, and all the evidence points to Glenda. She'll need all her wits and legendary stubbornness to survive and find the killer.

Welcome to the jungle, Glenda.

Killswitch

On post-apocalyptic Earth, Mavo is an Outsider whose dream is simply to join Unity, the computer-guided society that saved humanity after devastating wars and environmental destruction. Instead, he and fierce rebel Rin are framed for a massacre. Now the couple must flee from Unity troops and vicious terrorists as they prepare to battle a hidden monster that wants to rule and warp humanity.